I0682213

The Last Dragon War

The Dragon Wars: Book 2

by

Glenn T Ryan

Arin House Publications

National Library of Australia Cataloguing-in-Publication entry

Author: Ryan, Glenn T., author.

Title: The Last Dragon War/Glenn T Ryan

ISBN: 978-0-9874619-4-0 (paperback)

Series: The Dragon Wars; Book 2

Copyright © 2018 Arin House Publications

First Published by Arin House Publications 2018

All rights reserved.

As always: To Milly and Mighty

Visit
www.facebook.com/TheLastDragonHome

1

PIP

'Shadowclaw is coming! Shadowclaw is coming!' one of the sultan's guards yelled, pointing frantically to the eastern horizon. 'We have to get out of here now, now, NOW!'

Pip snatched up his bow and bolted for his horse. He had been trained for this sort of emergency.

'Hurry, young Prince,' urged the other guard. 'It will be our heads if Shadowclaw gets within a league of you.'

Pip didn't need to be told to make haste. He leapt on his steed with one graceful movement and shifted his weight forward, ready to ride fast.

'Yah, Jasper. Take us home. Yah, yah!'

The royal Arabian stallion responded to the Prince's urgency and galloped hard west, towards the palace and away from the green forest in which Pip had been hunting. Sweat gathered on his pure white coat as his hooves ate away at the ground beneath him; he was trained never to hesitate at his master's command.

Jasper had been Pip's horse of choice for a few years now, and he had never seen his master so panicked. It wasn't often that Pip dug spurs into his side either, and all the delicious looking game his master had caught lay abandoned at the edge of the forest. Usually after these outings the Prince would pluck any fowl and skin any hare he had shot, repack the saddlebags, have a black tea, and then the party would amble back home. The guards would compliment Pip on his marksmanship and recount the best shot of the day on the way. They never had to embellish the truth because Pip was perfect with the bow. If the young Prince aimed at it, it was as good as dead.

None of those things had happened today. Something was definitely wrong and Jasper didn't like it.

Sorry, my friend, Pip thought as he dug his heels in harder. *But the Scourge of Aldallah is not something we ever want to see as long as we live. If you get us to the palace alive, I'll give you nothing but the finest grain for the rest of your days. I promise.*

As they left the forest behind them and the ground beneath turned from dirt to sand, the Prince risked a quick look back to see if they were being chased.

The sky appeared empty.

He relaxed his shoulders a little, but kept up the pace—his curly, sunlit hair flailing about his face.

His two royal guards, Jumba and Balad, caught up and rode their horses hard on each side of the Prince, ready to protect him from danger. Both guards wore white robes tied with a yellow sash. The older one, Jumba, was tall and thick with well-trained muscles.

Balad was shorter and softer, but still strong in his own way. Both were very proud of Pip and had been in charge of his safety since his birth.

'I don't see anything in the heavens, Jumba,' said Pip. 'Are you sure it was him?'

The dark-skinned man on his left gave a severe frown and answered in his slow, measured voice, 'Sure enough, my ward. Don't forget, I saw him in the battle of Aldallah. I know his shape when I see it.'

'Sorry, Jumba. It was a foolish question. Perhaps I was hoping you were mistaken. I just can't believe he could be this close to the palace. Why is he so far west?'

'Let's hope we never find out,' Jumba called back over the rushing of hooves.

The two guards unsheathed their curved swords and cast worried glances upwards, looking over their shoulders, over their heads. Shadowclaw could show up anywhere. It was said that he could become invisible and appear when least expected.

After a tense while of riding, the majestic round tops of the Sultan's palace slowly came into view. Balad gave a relieved sigh that could be heard over the thunder of the racing horses.

'It seems we will make it home this day, young Prince,' Balad said. 'I can already taste those delicious cinnamon buns that Cook makes after our expeditions.' He patted his little pot-belly with one hand.

Pip gave a smile in return. 'I don't think I've ever been so happy to see the—'

FWOOOSH!

'What was that?' Pip's head snapped up to look above him, expecting to see the thing of nightmares descend upon them. All he saw was the peaceful blue sky.

FWOOOSH!

It came again, louder this time.

The three horses heard it too, for they began to buck and rear.

'Yah, Jasper. Not now, boy. Not now!'

Jumba and Balad fought their reins and tried to control their animals. The three of them pulled to a halt. Jumba stopped so quickly that he was flung forward. He would have sailed over the horse's head had his feet not been caught in the stirrups. The brown turban he was wearing flew off his balding scalp and landed on the sandy earth in front of them.

Pip worked hard to calm his mount who pranced and snorted beneath him.

'Woooooooh,' he soothed and patted Jasper's neck. 'It's alright. Shh, shhh, steady boy.'

'I don't like this,' Balad said when he got his horse back under control. 'My steed is listening but he won't move an inch forward.'

'Nor will mine,' Jumba added.

'They're scared, that's all,' Pip reminded them.

'They aren't the only ones,' Balad said. 'Maybe we should run the rest of the way?'

Jumba agreed. 'We are so close to the palace and I can't see Shadowclaw. I feel we should leave the horses too.'

Pip decided not to argue, though he didn't like the idea of leaving Jasper. He gave one final nudge with his heels, but the horse refused to take another step.

'Hurry down, Honoured One. We can't stand here idle.'

Pip dismounted and joined the guards on the ground. As soon as they began to run towards the palace, the horses fled back to the shelter of the forest.

Balad turned his head to watch them go. 'That is *not* a good sign.'

Pip said nothing. He focused on his home and ran forward, pumping his arms at his sides.

That's it, Prince,' Jumba called after they had covered some distance. 'Keep up that pace and we will be there in no time.'

But Pip's blue eyes narrowed and he slowed to a cautious walk. He motioned for the others to do the same.

'What are you doing, Honoured One? This is no time to get a stitch. We're so close.'

Pip stopped walking. 'It's a trap!' he answered, pulling an arrow from the quiver on his back. 'Look, look at the ground.' He pointed to a scrap of dirt a short distance from them.

'A dark patch, Prince?'

'A shadow, Jumba.' Pip's voice came out tight.

'Oh no,' said Balad. 'It has made itself invisible. The rumours are true. We're food!'

5

At those words, the Prince drew back his bow and let his arrow fly. It gave a soft whistle as it soared forward. The three watched it intently.

All of a sudden, it stopped mid-air and made a thunking sound. It had hit something.

A second later there came an angry howl of an animal in pain. The air above the shadow shimmered, grew dark, and took on a terrifying form.

Balad took a step backwards and raised his sword. Jumba's face became stony and the Prince drew another arrow from the quiver, ready to shoot again.

There before them, with Pip's arrow sticking out of its raised paw, was the wrecker of cities, the Scourge of Aldallah, the most feared beast in all the lands.

It was Shadowclaw, the silver dragon.

It was hovering inches above the ground and it looked very angry.

2

YUNAS

The Sultan's palace was made of pure white stone and was the largest structure in the massive city of Nalib. The floors were a cool, green marble, and the walls were adorned with delicately woven rugs and tapestries. It smelled of sand and spice and contained a hundred rooms, each expensively furnished. But there was no gold anywhere to be seen. Even the Sultan's throne, bejewelled and crafted of a solid and rare wood, was bare of the precious metal.

The law decreed that no one, bar Yunas the Sultan, could keep gold, and even then it had to be hidden, sealed in the massive vault in the centre of the palace, never to see the light of day. Breaking that law meant death, which was unfortunate for Robert Dugasi, who was facing the ruler's wrath.

'You imbecile! You fool! You absolute TOOKER!' shouted the Sultan, spittle flying from his lips. 'You know the law. No one, NOT ONE LIVING SOUL EXCEPT FOR ME, is allowed to open the vault. Do you *know* what you have done?'

7

Robert was on his knees in front of Yunas. He didn't dare make eye-contact with the Sultan. He kept his forehead pressed to the ground, as he'd been advised to do back home.

'You are a guest here, Robert. Your Queen sent you here as a diplomat, not a spy! Stand up and speak for yourself.'

Robert did as he was told. He suddenly felt very self-conscious in his fancy clothes. The frills and velvet trimmings, the brass buttons and leather boots—all of it looked out of place. He was always too hot. He was probably the only one in the country not wearing a cool desert robe, except for the Sultan himself, who wore loose silk trousers and a vest.

'I'm s-s-sorry, your Majesty,' he stammered. 'I-I-I j-just wanted to see. I'm not a spy!'

Yunas breathed deeply through his teeth.

'You have put me in a difficult position, Robert,' Yunas said slowly, trying to pronounce the foreign name correctly. 'The law says you must die. But you are a royal visitor from the foreign Queen. To kill you would strain the friendship.' Yunas massaged his temples. He was not as handsome as his son, Pip. His hair was dark brown whereas Pip's was blond, though he had the same honey-coloured skin that the ladies simply adored.

The Sultan's servants made themselves busy by cleaning around him. To be truthful, the throne room was spotless, but none of them wanted to miss the action. They dusted and re-dusted, polished and re-polished, watching from the corners of their eyes.

'What should I do, Pukami?' Yunas asked, turning to a leathery old man who stood like a post next to the throne. 'You are my Vizier; I pay *you* to solve these riddles.'

Pukami closed his eyes and hummed. 'It is a puzzle, Sultan. But I do have an answer. I think we should inform his Queen and let *her* punish him as she sees fit. That way it's all out in the open, and if Mr Dugasi is killed, the blood is not on our hands, so to speak.'

Yunas nodded. 'Once again you've earned your keep, Pukami. So be it. Send a message to the Queen at once!' Here he turned to Robert, whose face was the colour of a cooked tomato. 'You are free to roam the palace, Robert, until I hear back from your Queen. Please do not abuse the privilege this time. On second thought, maybe you should just stay in your room. I'll have meals sent up.'

Robert Dugasi was deeply ashamed. Not only had he made a fool of himself in front of these strange people he had come to respect, he had let down his Queen as well. His actions would reflect badly on her and this hurt him worse than anything.

'If you please, wise Sultan,' Robert said quietly. 'I beg you not to send that message.'

The servants, who thought the incident was over and were leaving to find work elsewhere, suddenly retraced their steps and found more invisible grime in the throne room that needed seeing to, their ears ever open.

'I have to, Robert,' Yunas answered sternly. 'You must face your actions. Do not be so cowardly.'

'It's not that, Majesty of the Sands. I don't want to be spared punishment. I want the death sentence. Please, do not tell my Queen. Kill me instead, as your law dictates.'

Dugasi took off his spectacles and polished them with his shirt. Then he got to his knees and shut his eyes tight. 'Anything would be better than sullying the name of the Monarch.'

Yunas looked to Pukami, who nodded sagely.

Yunas stood, hesitantly unsheathed his curved sword and held it to Dugasi's neck.

'I'm ready,' Robert said.

The servants dropped their cleaning act and stared openly at the scene, ready for the ultimate punishment to be handed down. But the Sultan didn't move. Dugasi didn't move. Pukami... well he never moved anyway.

Everyone in the room stayed frozen for what seemed like an hour.

Suddenly, several guards broke into the room shouting urgently.

'Majesty, Majesty, come! We have an emergency!'

Yunas dropped his sword with a clatter and wiped his eyes with his palm. His hands shook.

'What is it?' His voice came out choked, so he cleared his throat and tried again. 'What is it?'

'It's Shadowclaw!' one of the guards yelled. 'One of the lookouts saw his shape not far from here. He must have smelled the gold!'

Every eye in the room turned to glare at Robert.

'This is why we don't open the vault, Mister Dugasi. Everyone knows that dragons don't touch the ground.' The Sultan's voice was icy.

Dugasi looked back at them, wiping tears from his eyes. 'I don't understand. What are you talking about? What have I done?'

This time Pukami spoke.

'A dragon considers it a dishonour to even scrape the dirt with its tail, Dugasi. If it can avoid the ground and find a mountain cave, it will. If the mountain isn't high enough, it will make a bed of gold and sleep on it. Anything but touch the ground.'

Robert nodded and hid his face with his hands and cried loudly.

Pukami continued, 'You opened the vault; the Scourge of Aldallah smelled the gold. Now he has come.'

'Oh no!' gasped the Sultan as he suddenly remembered. 'Pip is out there! My son!'

3

SHADOWCLAW

While the Sultan was bellowing orders to his royal army, his son was staring into a terrible eyeless face, bow drawn and forearms trembling.

'Gold,' Shadowclaw said, his voice sounded like rocks scraping together. 'Where is it? Where is the gold?'

'Ahhh,' gasped the Prince in fright, almost setting an arrow free. 'It talks!'

'Nonsense, said Balad, not taking his eyes off the dreaded dragon. 'Dragons do not talk.'

Pip tried to look at Jumba without turning his head. 'Did you hear it, Jumba?'

The older man spoke through his teeth. 'No, Honoured One.'

'He asked for gold! I heard him!'

'You're just scared and imagining things,' said Balad. 'Like I'm imagining being back at the palace in the hot tub.' For once Balad did not laugh at his own joke.

Shadowclaw began to glide towards the three shaking men, his massive paws walking on air.

Pip couldn't help but feel disgusted as he got a better look. The dragon was the colour of silver oil, shiny and slick. Its face looked all squashed out of shape and skin grew over the place where its eyes should have been.

'Does it know we're here?' Pip whispered. 'Its eyes—'

'Of course it does,' Jumba hissed. 'It has a nose that can smell and ears that can hear. It doesn't need eyes to know of our presence.'

The three backed away instinctively, but ten of their steps was only one flap of the dragon's wings. It was only a matter of seconds before he was upon them.

'Why hasn't he killed us yet?' Jumba wondered aloud. 'Is he playing with us?'

Balad's nerves got the better of him.

'Curse you, Silver Scourge!' he screamed as he rushed towards the oncoming beast.

'No!' Pip said, stretching out his arm. It was too late.

Balad raised his sword and brought it down with all his might on Shadowclaw's leg. But before the metal could hit the rough skin, it was stopped by an invisible force.

Balad's mouth fell open in surprise and shock as something unseen grabbed him and hurled his round little body like a toy across the sand.

'Balad!'

Pip swore in rage. He aimed his arrow at the dragon's face and shot. It sang through the air and hit right where the dragon's left eye should have been. Again, Shadowclaw's howls filled Pip's ears. The dragon clutched at the arrow and pulled it free. It motioned with its front legs and suddenly a huge fireball appeared out of nowhere. It zoomed towards Pip and Jumba.

The two men dived out of the way as the ball of flames burst on the ground between them.

Pip heard Jumba cry out in pain as he rolled to his feet. The young Prince pulled another arrow from his quiver, nocked it and let it fly, all within the blink of an eye.

This time the arrow was aimed at Shadowclaw's heart. It hit the chest of the beast and bounced off the tough skin without leaving a scratch. Pip guessed that Shadowclaw didn't even feel it. He saw the dragon summon another fireball and doubted he would miss a second time.

Before he could launch it, however, Shadowclaw was struck from behind. Balad had rejoined the battle and was hacking away at the dragon's tail. With a simple flick, Balad was once again thrown through the air, shouting curses as he flew.

The distraction gave Jumba an opportunity. He bolted for the silver beast and got underneath him. Now he too smacked the dragon's hide with his sword, hoping to do some damage.

It didn't appear to faze Shadowclaw at all; his skin was like armour.

The Scourge merely picked the guard up between his claws and dangled him above his open jaws. Pip gave a cry and waited for the horrible sound of crunching bones, but instead of eating him, Shadowclaw tossed the guard over his shoulder and turned to face the palace.

Something has caught his attention, thought Pip. *But what?*

And then Pip felt the ground vibrating beneath him. He followed the dragon's gaze and saw his father riding towards them with fifty horsemen on either side, kicking the sand into heavy clouds as they thundered closer.

The Prince gave an inward cheer.

The cavalry had arrived.

4

THE MELEE

Shadowclaw rose higher in the air and sped at the oncoming army without a moment of hesitation. The way the fearsome dragon flicked its tail before it pounced made Pip think of a hungry cat about to catch an easy meal.

The Prince looked on as the Silver Scourge ploughed right into the first line of horsemen, knocking them over like skittles, missing Yunas by only a few paces.

The dragon landed in the middle of the throng, causing absolute chaos among the ranks. Some men dismounted and charged at the dragon, while others forced their horses in so they could reach up to the terror that hovered above. Pip saw that even in the heat of battle, Shadowclaw did not let any part of his massive frame touch the sand. He also noticed a few men running in the other direction.

Cowards, he thought angrily.

Shadowclaw was ripping the soldiers off his body, crunching some in his mouth and others under his massive paws. Pip saw

Yunas take a beating from Shadowclaw's tail, so he ran into the fray with an arrow in one hand and his bow in the other.

No one hurts my father and gets away with it!

Pip could hardly hear himself think above Shadowclaw's roars and the screaming, moaning men, but he pressed himself through the crowd and closer to the mighty monster, shooting arrows as he went. *Twang, twang, twang.*

Just when it looked like the army was gaining the upper hand, Shadowclaw would let loose a few more spells. Sometimes he called forth magic fire and other times summoned fearsome wind gusts that threw the men off their feet. Each time, the army would regroup and hurl themselves at the Scourge, only to be cast off with invisible hands.

Pip was tossed back on one occasion and hit his head on something sharp. He looked down and saw he'd landed on a soldier, only this one would never fight again — his armour was broken and lay in jagged pieces on the ground.

Tears blurred Pip's eyes as he glared at the dragon, who still seemed to be having fun.

'You think this is a game?' he yelled. 'You think killing is *fun*? I'll show you!'

Pip bent down and picked up some of the shards he'd landed on. He fished out some twine from his pocket and tied the broken pieces of armour tightly to an arrowhead, making it look like a cruel spear. Pip also made sure that some of the metal spikes faced backwards, so that once the arrow went in, it would be hard to pull out. He touched the tips with his fingers and gave a satisfied nod when he saw he'd drawn his own blood.

He drew this ugly arrow and aimed at Shadowclaw.

I've found two weak spots on you already. The first was your paw, the other was...

The Prince let his shot fly, raising his bow higher than usual because of the added weight of the arrow.

The arrow wobbled madly through the air, its tail making circles as it went. It completed its arc and began to come down as gravity took hold.

Pip gave a shrill whistle to catch Shadowclaw's attention. It worked! The dragon turned its head into the oncoming missile.

SMACK!

The arrow struck the dragon's face in the exact same spot Pip had hit earlier—the empty eye.

This time Shadowclaw yelped like an injured dog. His front legs went up to his face to try and pull the arrow free, but the barbs of armour stuck fast and the dragon kept yelping.

The army gave a ragged cheer for their Prince and redoubled their attack.

Shadowclaw ignored them, worked some more on the arrow in his face, then ignored that too.

His head swung in Pip's direction and sniffed the air, oblivious to the soldiers banging their swords against his skin. With one mighty mid-air jump, the dragon pounced on Pip, pinning him to the ground with his front legs and bringing his snout to Pip's nose.

'YOU!'

Again, Pip heard the rasping voice of the terrible monster.

The Prince was dimly aware of a tremendous heat burning up his forearms where the dragon held him. It was as if the Scourge was using Pip's arms as a barrier against the ground, the same way he used gold.

Why won't he touch the land?

His vision was filled with the monster's magnificent teeth. He could smell Shadowclaw's terrible breath and feel its horrible saliva dripping on his face.

This is it, he thought. *Father, I love you. Please take care of mother.* Pip closed his eyes and waited for the end.

The dragon opened his jaws wide and brought them down with tremendous speed.

CLANG!

Shadowclaw's mouth bit down hard on metal. A man had come running at them and wedged a straight sword between the dragon's gaping jaws as it bit down, causing the beast to pierce the roof of his own mouth with the sword's point.

Shadowclaw gave a fearsome roar and jerked his head from side to side.

Pip opened his eyes and saw Robert Dugasi standing over him, helping him to his feet.

Robert was something of a joke around the palace; with his odd clothes and weird manners, he was the last person Pip expected to see on the battlefield. He didn't know that it was Robert's curiosity that had brought this terrible nightmare on them, or that Robert was willing to give his own life to atone for the mistake.

'Come on, Prince,' he said in his foreign accent. 'Let's get out of here.'

Pip gladly accepted the offered hand.

Shadowclaw opened his wings and beat them hard, causing the troops below to sway and trip under the heavy wind. The dragon hovered high above the ground, away from the men below.

From a safe height he cast another fireball at Pip.

The Prince of the Sands had no time to react. He'd only just got to his feet when he saw the burning orange sphere coming right at him.

He was doomed.

But Robert, to everyone's amazement, was not finished being a hero. He knocked Pip aside and threw himself in front of the Prince, arms thrust out to make his body a shield. Pip saw his shape, black against the blinding fire.

'Robert! Nooooooo!'

But it was too late.

In a flash of flame, Mr Dugasi was gone.

'Nooooo, no, no, NO!' Pip fell to his knees in disbelief.

The men that were left stood silently and watched the Scourge of Aldallah fly away, shaking its head as it tried to dislodge the sword from its mouth.

They relaxed a little when the dragon disappeared over the mountains in the distance. Nobody cheered the victory though. It had cost them too much. They quietly went about tending to the injured and transporting them back to the city where they would get the best care, eyes always scanning the sky.

Pip stayed where he was in a daze for a while and tried to come to terms with the horrible events of the day. It was too much to deal with.

He wandered the smoking battlefield and began to look for his father. Instead he found Jumba and a very sore looking Balad.

'Prince,' Balad breathed as he limped forward to embrace Pip. 'Thank the heavens you're safe. Your father would have roasted me on a spit if that dragon had harmed a hair on your golden head.'

'He has been harmed, Balad,' Jumba said sharply. 'Look at his arms.'

'Goodness me!' Balad said as he let Pip go. 'You're right. Prince, you need to get to the palace immediately. How much does it hurt?'

'Hmmmmm?' Pip said as he fainted on the spot.

The two loyal guards caught him before he fell.

'Quick, Jumba. Let's get him home.'

5

THE AFTERMATH

Pip tentatively opened his eyes—afraid he might see Shadowclaw's gaping mouth, teeth shining and ready to chomp. Instead he saw the pale white walls of the palace and felt cool bed sheets beneath his skin.

I'm safe, he thought. *It was all a bad dream. I'm home in my room and I'm alive.*

At that moment, Pukami, Jumba, Balad, and his mother and father strode into the room talking in hushed voices.

'No need to whisper,' Pukami said. 'The Prince is awake.'

Pip looked to his mother. Her face was as pale as the walls around him. Her mouth was a straight line of concern, not the smiling, happy mouth he was used to. And her long, curly blonde hair, almost a mirror of his, looked unkept. She leaned over and kissed him gently on the forehead.

'Thank the heavens you are still with us,' she sobbed.

Pip scanned the others in the room and stopped to take in Balad's bruised face and bloodstained clothes. The memories of the battle flooded back to him. He looked down to see what the pain was in his arms, only to find them heavily bandaged.

'It wasn't a dream at all, was it?' he asked.

Yunas slowly shook his head.

Suddenly, Pip remembered something.

'Mr Dugasi?' he said urgently. 'Is he really—'

'Yes, my son.' The sultan moved to the side of the bed and stroked Pip's head. 'I have sent a letter to his Queen detailing Robert's brave deed. I have told her that because of him, our country will be forever in her debt. He would have liked it that way.'

'What do you mean, father?'

Yunas told him about Robert's actions with the palace vault.

'But he certainly redeemed himself,' said Pip's mother.

'Yes, Zilofa, that he did. So there is no need for us to speak of his blunder ever again. Let's remember him for the good.'

'Yes, father.'

Pip took a deep breath and let it all sink in. He tried to remember every second of the fight. It seemed all muddled—a blur.

'You really distinguished yourself on the battlefield today, young Prince,' Jumba said after a while. 'That shot with the arrow, best I've seen. You really have an uncanny knack of hitting a target every time, don't you?'

Pip blushed. 'Well I *do* practice every day.'

'Even so...'

There was an awkward moment where nobody spoke. Pip's skill with the bow earned him a reputation throughout the lands.

Some said that he was such a good shot that magic must be involved. Sometimes Pip secretly thought the same. He never missed. Never! Sometimes it even unnerved *him*.

'Well I must get back to it,' Balad said to break the silence. 'I think I need to soak these sore muscles in the hot-tub, with your Majesty's permission.'

'Of course, Balad. You did well today, you've earned it.'

Zilofa gave Balad an appreciative smile and nodded for him to leave. When the squat warrior had left, Yunas turned back to Pip.

'How are you feeling, my boy?'

'I'm fine. I think. My arms hurt where the Scourge held me.'

'Let's see them,' Pukami said. He unrolled the bandages carefully, but even the slightest bump made Pip wince and shut his eyes. Zilofa jolted every time her son did.

'Hmmmmm,' the old man said as he inspected the wounds. 'This is bad. Look, Sultan.'

Yunas looked and made a face. Zilofa gasped and put a hand to her mouth.

'What does it mean, Vizier?'

Pip peeked at his injuries and instantly closed his eyes again, wishing he hadn't been curious. The skin was black and burnt. It smelled bad too.

Pukami made a clicking sound with his tongue. 'It's not life threatening. The pain will go, but these wounds will never completely heal. I'm sorry, Honoured One, but you can never take these bandages off. The slightest bump will split the skin and open the wounds again. There is nothing we can do. Curse that foul dragon!'

'Never take them *off*?' Pip said, alarmed. 'I have to keep them on *forever*? Latos!'

'It could have been worse,' his mother said. 'What is a bandage when you have a life?'

Pip grumbled, 'I guess.'

Yunas cleared his throat and looked to Pukami, who gave him a slow nod.

'There is something I need to tell you, son. After our battle today... We lost many men.' Yunas rubbed his temples and breathed out in a rush. 'Ahhhh, I don't know how to put this.'

'Just say it plain, father.'

'Well,' the Sultan continued. 'The army. It has disbanded. It will never fight again. The troops are too scared, too spooked. They came very close to death, you see?'

'They're cowards,' Pip insisted. 'Today I saw some running away before the fight had even begun!'

Yunas made a wave with his hand. 'They're not cowards, son. They're smart. Everyone who didn't run away from Aldallah was lost. Give them some other army from some other land and they would fight, I bet. But Shadowclaw is the stuff of nightmares. Just laying eyes on him is a death-sentence.'

'*We* didn't die!' Pip said defiantly.

'We had a miracle. And your marksmanship.' Yunas shook his head. 'We're getting off track. What I want to tell you is... The Scourge will be back.'

Pip gave an involuntary gasp. 'No!'

Now Pukami took a turn to speak. 'Young Prince, the gold that Shadowclaw smelled is enough to satisfy even *his* desires. Think about it. Shadowclaw lives beyond the mountains and he *still* got the scent. He knows how much we have! He will be back.'

'And with no army, son, we will be at his mercy.'

Pip dropped his head on his pillow and said nothing. He knew they were right. Shadowclaw had a record of killing more men for less gold at Aldallah. He ruined the whole city—left just a smoking mess.

'What do we do, father?'

Now Jumba spoke. 'It's more like what do *you* and *Balad* do, Prince. Your father wants someone to escort you on a mission, and Balad was the first to volunteer.'

'What mission?'

'You need to sail to Robert's country, to the land of fields and forests. We must find another army. Tough men. Fighters. And new weapons. It is said that the foreign lands did battle with dragons well over a hundred years ago. They may have something that will help us defeat the Silver Scourge once and for all.'

Pip looked up at the Sultan, who nodded in agreement.

'I have booked you a passage on a ship. A sleek vessel that I suspect is used for smuggling. The man who owns it has promised to give you a safe journey, for a price. He may even know where you can recruit some mercenaries. He *is* a shady sort of character after all.'

'Who is he, father? Can we trust him?'

Yunas gave a soft chuckle. 'His name is Blackbeard, son. He is the captain of the ship and is well-known in many countries. And no, son, we can't trust him at all. But we don't have a choice.' He hugged his son tight and then let Zilofa have her turn. Zilofa's embrace was tighter, and Pip nearly had to ask his mother to loosen him and let him breathe.

'Your mother and I have to go now, son. Shadowclaw made a mess of our lives, yes, but also the lives of our people. I have arranged a speech on the city square. We have families to comfort, men to speak to. You understand how it is.'

Pip nodded. He did understand. Being a Sultan was like being a father to everyone *all* the time. It was a lot of work and worry. One day it would be Pip's turn.

'Balad will fill you in on the trip there and Pukami will take care of the provisions. You just get some rest for now.' Here he leaned closer to his son, his face tight with concern. 'Your mother and I hate to send you on this task, son. But without help, the city of Nalib will be just another burnt-out ruin. We can't let that happen. We *won't*. I will return tomorrow to see you off.'

With that, the Sultan and his wife left with Pukami.

Jumba clasped Pip's shoulder and smiled. 'Better get your head together, Prince. You've never travelled with Balad before. He makes even a trip to the kitchen seem like an epic adventure. And something tells me this adventure is going to be very, very big! The stuff of legends.'

6

OLD FRIENDS

Hundreds of leagues away from the city of Nalib, on another continent, two figures lay beside a gurgling stream. One figure was a small white dragon, the other was Mollie the sorceress. Both were lying on their backs making shapes from the clouds overhead.

'What does that one look like?' she asked Whitestaff, pointing to the sky.

'Ummm, a horse?'

'Wait, let me fix it.' Mollie moved her hands smoothly in front of her. 'Now what?'

The dragon wheezed a laugh. 'It looks like Wendy when she was a unicorn. You added a horn to her head.'

'What's so funny?'

'I'm sorry, Mollie. But I have a suspicion that when most people make shapes from clouds, they don't actually *make* the clouds into things. They just look at the clouds as they are, and use their imagination. You see that one over there?' Whitestaff raised his front leg a little.

'Yes.'

'Well, don't you think it kind of looks like a tree?'

'I suppose. A bit.'

'Well that's all there is to it. That's the game.'

Mollie groaned. 'But that's boring. I can make it look exactly like a tree. All I have to do is get the wind to push the cloud into the right shape, see?'

Whitestaff watched as the formless cloud became an exact replica of the giant fig tree that stood about twenty paces from them. Mollie had included every detail. She even made a large scar on its trunk to match the real one Esmae had made when she first taught Mollie how to make a Magic Missile.

'It's good,' Whitestaff admitted. 'But I think that you are the only one who plays it that way. I'm a bit of an expert at this game, right enough.'

'Of course you are! You had years of just looking at the sky.'

Whitestaff nodded slowly, like an old tortoise about to fall asleep.

'What a pair we are,' Mollie said. 'Talk about misfits. A sorceress and a dragon. Friendless. Outcasts. At least you get to go home and be around your own kind though.'

'Mollie, don't make me feel bad.'

The sorceress rolled over to face the dragon. 'I didn't mean it like that, Whitestaff. I meant it as a good thing. I'm happy you can go back. I'd hate for you to be stuck here, as much as I'll miss you.'

The dragon smiled. 'Well, you don't have to miss me for a few more weeks yet. I have to wait until my essence builds up.'

'I still don't understand that,' Mollie said, shaking her head.

'I don't either. But I know the sooner I go back, the sooner my dragon spirit will fade. It will fade very quickly this time too.'

Mollie frowned. 'Why is that?'

'Because I'm going to use a lot of energy fighting in the Championship. I'm big compared to those Nazoor I've told you about. But the Nazoor Champion is an Alpos, and I've been told he's big also.'

'It's strange to think of you as big and strong. Maybe one day you can be mighty here on Earth?'

'Maybe. Or maybe one day we can find a way to take you to Sorteya.'

Mollie didn't say anything for a while. So much had happened since she had first met Whitestaff in Cudgel's cage that it was nice to just relax and listen to the stream and watch the clouds float by overhead. She let her mind wander to Terry and her mother, and how happy they looked at their wedding the week before. Terry looked so strange in his fancy clothes. He was constantly scratching the fabric and adjusting his shirt and pants. It was as though he was wearing ants instead of clothes. Despite this, nothing could take the smile off his face, as Esmae looked absolutely stunning. She wore an ivory dress that had white flowers embroidered in little chains down the front. She carried a gorgeous bouquet at her chest and her ink-black hair was loose about her shoulders. But Terry didn't take his eyes off her eyes. Mollie could tell they were both in love, and this made her happy and sad at the same time.

She gave a sigh and laid back down. Esmae was honeymooning with Terry at his house, and she was due to return any day now. Although Mollie liked having the cottage to herself, she missed her mother's presence and worried about her even though Terry's house was not far away. A few times she thought about visiting them both, but stopped herself—reasoning that all newlyweds deserved a certain period of absolute togetherness.

Maybe I should make figures of mother and Terry out of some clouds, Mollie thought. She was just about to do so when the dragon shattered her concentration.

'Someone's coming!' Whitestaff whispered as he sniffed the air.

Mollie leapt to her feet and covered the dragon with the picnic blanket, leaving his tail still sticking out from one end.

'What are you doing?' asked Whitestaff from the blackness. 'You're a sorceress. Use a spell!'

Mollie cursed herself inwardly and bent the light around her friend.

'Sorry,' she said. 'I tend to forget.'

No sooner had she spoken these words than a girl broke into the clearing. The first thing Mollie noticed was that the girl's eyes were wet and red and her chin was quivering. She was much younger than Mollie, and much dirtier. Shoeless and dressed in a brown sack, she resembled a recently dug up potato—with none of the roundness.

The girl froze instantly when she saw Mollie, who gave her a smile. Mollie walked over to her calmly, as though the girl was a cat that she didn't want to spook.

'Hello, Sprout,' Mollie soothed. 'What's the matter?' She squatted so that her face was level with the girl's.

'Mama is sick. She needs the potions! She's dying! You have to come!'

'Are you sure, Sprout? Maybe she's just...'

But the girl wasn't listening. With her message delivered, she ran back the way she had come, hastened by fear of Mollie or desperation to be back at her mother's side, Mollie couldn't tell.

The sorceress let her invisibility spell vanish and pulled the rug from over Whitestaff.

'I'm sorry, I have to go. Will you be all right here?'

Whitestaff rolled onto his stomach and met Mollie's eyes with his own.

'Of course *I* will be all right. Will *you*?'

Mollie gave him a withered look and dashed into the cottage. She emerged a few seconds later with two small bottles and a spoon.

'It's cheating,' said Whitestaff.

'It's helping,' Mollie insisted. 'Besides, it must be bad for Sprout to come here and find me. She usually hides under her bed when I visit.' She gave him a quick pat on the head before she went to the front of the cottage to find Wendy.

It had been almost a year and a half since Mollie had rescued Wendy the horse from Cudgel's wagon, and Mollie had almost forgotten what Wendy had looked like at the time of their first encounter. The pink paint Cudgel had dressed her up in, and the paper cone which he had stuck to her forehead to pass for a unicorn's horn, was only a dim and ghastly memory for them both. But still, Mollie had instinctively kept Wendy clean and brushed so that the shining honey-coloured coat became a source of pride for them. Wendy's chocolate mane also provided entertainment for them both too, as Mollie plaited it in all sorts of intricate patterns and designs.

'Isn't it a lovely day?' asked Wendy as she saw Mollie coming towards her. She then saw the bottles in her mistress's hands. 'Oh. We have a patient?'

'I'm afraid so. The Leeches. Sprout says her mother is very ill. Would you mind?'

'Of course not,' said Wendy as she allowed Mollie to fit her bridle. 'Should I hurry?'

'We'd better,' Mollie replied as she tucked the potions into her pockets and climbed onto Wendy's bare back. 'Sprout seemed agitated.'

'She spoke to you?'

'Yes. A couple of words.'

'It must be serious! Hold on, I'm in the mood for speed.'

Wendy wasn't lying. Mollie had only touched the reins with the tips of her fingers when the horse shot forward. She accelerated so fast that Mollie slid an arm's length down Wendy's back and had to struggle for the next few moments to get back into a proper riding position, which was difficult due to the lack of a saddle.

'I'm not really sure this has been your best idea, Mollie,' Wendy said as she galloped.

'What idea?'

'This whole potions scheme.'

'Not you too, Wendy. I thought you'd be on my side.'

'Side? What do you mean?'

'Whitestaff thinks it's cheating.'

Wendy tossed her head. 'He would say something like that. It's not the cheating that worries me though.'

'Then what?'

'I'm worried that this will make it worse.'

'What do you mean?'

'Well, you've always been against the whole of Danmurk Shire calling you a witch. And now it looks like you're trying to prove them right. Don't you want to be seen as normal? Or am I missing something?'

'No. I mean, yes. It's more complicated than that. I'm demystifying the whole thing. I'll show you when we get there. If Margaret leaves her shutters open, stick your head close and listen.'

Wendy told her she would and they rode in silence until they reached the residence of Margaret and Tim Leech.

As soon as Mollie eased Wendy into the front yard of the Leech's ramshackle hut, she dismounted and whispered into the horse's ear.

'I'm glad you galloped so fast, Wendy. Something here is very wrong.'

7

THE LEECHS

Tim and Margaret Leech had five children, all of whom appeared to be smaller and skinner versions of either Tim or his wife. Sprout, whose real name was Prudence, was the middle child. She had two elder brothers (Clark and Arthur) and two smaller sisters (Minnie and Lottie), and she was constantly at war with all of them. Sprout was too old for escaping chores yet too young to do any meaningful work around the house, and so it fell to her to be the Leech messenger. She filled this role very nicely too, as she was quick on her feet and knew every shortcut to every house in Danmurk Shire. She also had an excellent memory and could repeat messages verbatim.

The Leech hut was far away from neighbours, which was just as well because the Leech family was very loud. The hut overfilled with their booming voices, their crying children, their shrill arguments and their raucous laughter.

It was strange then for Mollie to find the hut utterly quiet.

'Stay close to that window over there,' Mollie said to Wendy. 'Perhaps you'll be able to hear what I meant before.'

Wendy nodded and trotted to the window while Mollie made her way inside.

'Hello?' she called. 'It's me, Mollie Adkins. Spro— I mean, Prudence came for me. Is everything all right?'

'In here, Mollie!' called Tim. 'The bedroom.'

The Leech hut had only three rooms: a common area which contained a table and a bench on either side, a room for the children (all of them), and the bedroom of Mr and Mrs Leech. It was here that Mollie found the Leech children, minus Sprout, gathered around a bed. When Mollie entered the room, the Leech children drew back to let her closer to the bed. None of them looked at Mollie or took their eyes off their mother. For in the bed, tucked in tight with a dry and crumpled cloth on her forehead, lay Margaret Leech. Mollie's eyes went wide when she saw her.

Margaret Leech had always been a large woman—her body as big as her voice—but not anymore. The woman laying in Mrs Leech's bed and wearing Mrs Leech's clothes was half the size of the original Mrs Leech! Her skin was grey and flaky, her lips crackled and white. Her eyes were closed and her breath was a shallow whisper.

'How long has she been like this?' Mollie asked, trying to hide her astonishment.

'A week or so,' answered Tim. 'She *was* getting better, but this morning she wasn't even answering me when I asked...' Tim's mind wandered off as he took his wife by the hand and knelt next to the bed. 'Can you help her? Make her well again?'

Mollie looked away from Mr Leech's pleading eyes. 'I'm not sure. What happened to the potion I gave you? Did she have it all?'

Tears started to creep down Mr Leech's cheeks. 'No she didn't. Art accidentally dropped the bottle.'

'Why didn't you send for more?'

Tim's shoulders collapsed and he wiped his face with his free hand. 'We didn't want... I didn't want... no witchcraft in my house. I'm sorry.'

Mollie looked over to the window behind the children where Wendy almost had her whole head inside.

'It's not witchcraft, Mr Leech. I told you this last time!'

'I'm sorry. It was stupid, I know. Can you help her?'

Mollie huffed and knelt on Margaret's other side. 'I'm not sure. Have you been giving her plenty of water?'

'A little. What good will *that* do?'

'Trust me,' Mollie said. 'She's burning up and needs water in her body.'

'Go on, Art.' Tim nodded to Arthur. The eldest boy scooted off to fetch some water.

'Now I'm going to give her some of this green suff,' Mollie told them. She looked from Leech to Leech as she spoke, making sure they were all listening. 'It tastes terrible but it's good for the blood.'

The three remaining children took a step back when she withdrew the bottle full of green liquid from her pocket.

Wendy rolled her eyes from the window. 'I told you!' she spoke into Mollie's mind.

Mollie ignored the horse and turned her attention back to the children.

'Who can guess what is in here?'

Arthur walked back in at that moment. He carried a pail of cool water and placed it down next to the bed.

'Lizard guts?' answered Lottie, the second eldest girl.

'No, not lizard anything. Tell me,' asked Mollie, 'is there any Aloe Vera around here? You know, the pointy plant with the juice inside?'

'Yep,' said Arthur. 'Grows thick out the back of our place. Why?'

'Well this green potion is mostly just Aloe Vera juice. I also mashed up some rosemary, some nettle and some ginger. Who likes ginger here?'

Lottie's little hand shot up in the air.

'Well, Lottie, ginger is very good for you, even when you aren't sick. I mashed all of the *herbs* together to make this little potion. No witchcraft,' here she looked at Tim, 'and no lizard guts.'

Mollie poured some of the green sticky liquid onto her spoon and gently pressed it into Margaret's mouth.

'Now this next potion,' Mollie said as she fished out her second bottle, 'is very good to have when you're very sick, like your mother here. It's red, so what do you think is in it?'

'Lizard blood!' Lottie shouted. The rest of the children took another step back.

'It's a lost cause,' said Wendy from the window.

Mollie took a deep breath and fought the urge to tell them how idiotic they all were.

'No, Lottie. No lizards. This is red because it has lots of berries in it. You can taste it if you like. It's delicious.'

Lottie shook her head and closed her mouth tight. The other children did the same.

'I'll taste some,' said Mr Leech. He learned over the bed and opened his mouth.

Mollie smiled and poured some onto the spoon and tipped it into Tim's mouth.

His eyes immediately lit up.

'That is delicious,' he said, smiling to the children. 'Strawberries and raspberries, and something else. It's tickling my tongue.'

'Fennel!' said Mollie. 'She looked back to the children. 'Just fennel. No Lizards. No witchcraft. Just some plants that make you better if you mix them together. Now we need some water.'

Art went and got Mollie a cup and she filled it in the bucket, then slowly poured water between Margaret's parched lips. She gave Wendy a wink at the window and gathered the elements around her. She made a show of being slow with the water, but really Mollie was buying herself some time. She knew that some herbal remedies might have cured Margaret last month, but now Mrs Leech would need something a little more substantial. She would need the magic of a sorceress.

Inside Margaret's body, a fire was burning away: a fever which Mollie knew needed to end before Margaret would ever recover. Mollie took the water element that she was pouring into Mrs Leech and sent it to every part of Margaret's body. Every organ, every limb and every cell was being doused with Mollie's water spell. When Mollie finished with one cup, she emptied in another and worked her magic again. It was like trying to put out a million tiny fires with a million drops of water. It was exhausting work for Mollie, but she kept at it.

'She's sure drinking a lot,' said Art.

Tim gave his son a frown.

'She needs a lot,' Mollie replied. 'Her skin is dry and hot. See how it's peeling?'

At last, when Mollie thought that she had the fever under control, she dropped the cup and sat back down. The pail at her side was empty.

The children stood silently and watched for a while, but when they saw that nothing remarkable was going to happen, they each left the room. Wendy took her head out of the window and gave Mollie and Tim some privacy.

'Thank you,' Tim said, patting Mollie's shoulder from over the bed.

'You're welcome.'

'Do you think she will... make it?'

Mollie looked at Mr Leech's eyes. They were the same eyes as Sprout's: scared and hopeful at the same time.

'I do.'

Mr Leech let out a long shuddering breath as tears ran from his eyes again.

'As long as you keep the water up and give her three spoonfuls a day of the potions until you run out.'

Tim nodded. 'I will,' he blurted. 'I will! And I'm so sorry for not trusting you from the start. I never should have believed all that witch nonsense. Can you forgive me, please?'

Mollie nodded. 'Of course.'

At that moment, Sprout walked in the room—her steps as timid as a rabbit's. She looked exhausted and even dirtier than usual. Her hair was pasted across her forehead with sweat.

'I beat you here,' Mollie said with a smile.

'You have a horse! It's not fair!'

Then Sprout did something that Mollie had never seen her do before: she smiled. Her face was split in two by a row of perfect, white, shiny teeth.

'Mamma looks better!' she said as she pointed at Margret. 'You did it!'

Mollie looked around and saw at once it was true. Margaret's skin and lips had more colour, and her breathing was louder than it was before.

'Thank you so much!' Sprout said, and she ran over and threw her arms around Mollie Adkins.

Mollie smiled and squeezed her back, enjoying the only hug she'd ever had from anyone other than her mother.

'You're very welcome, Sprout. Anytime.'

8

THE DEPARTURE

'Do you still think it's a bad idea?' Mollie asked Wendy as they made their way back to the cottage.

The sun was glaring down at them from the heavens, and the morning that had started out so mild had now disappeared. The clouds that Mollie had played with earlier had drifted on, leaving only a blazing blue sky. The bugs and insects that usually buzzed about in the grass had burrowed somewhere cooler, and the entire countryside felt as unnaturally silent as the Leech household had been.

'No, not anymore,' Wendy replied. 'When you first told me you were curing people using potions, I thought you'd gone mad. But the way you turned that whole family from witch-hunters to Mollie-lovers was so very smart. Was it just the potions though? I saw you wink at me and guessed you were using more than mashed up berries.'

'I had to use a spell! Did you see that poor woman?'

'I did.'

'She wouldn't have made it through another week.'

'That's what I thought. But won't they get suspicious when she suddenly gets better after a few sips of berry juice?'

Mollie shook her head. 'She won't suddenly get better. It will take Mrs Leech a long while to get on her feet again. And even after she is walking, it will take many more months to get enough strength back to do all the things she used to do.'

By the time they got home, Mollie was sweaty and so thirsty she joked that she too could drink an entire bucket of water.

'You just kept pouring it into her!' said Wendy. 'I thought she was going to burst!'

Mollie smiled at the thought of it, but the grin fell away when she and Wendy rode around to the back of the cottage. It was there she saw Whitestaff crawling desperately towards the barn. His face was full of fear, and the way he was clawing himself forward made it look as though he was trying to escape some horrible monster. The young sorceress leapt off Wendy and dashed over to her dragon.

'What's wrong, Whitestaff? What are you doing?'

'Mollie!' he gasped as he craned his neck to face her. 'Help me!'

'Help you what? What's the matter?'

'I need to get to the barn! To the egg!'

Mollie nodded and started to lift and push the dragon along the ground as though he were a heavy log that was blocking a path.

'WHAT ARE YOU DOING?' Whitestaff yelled. 'USE YOUR MAGIC!'

'Sorry!' Mollie cried, clearly flustered.

She gathered enough air to levitate her friend and float him over to the barn while she ran along behind. Wendy, scared by Whitestaff's terrible shouting, followed nervously at a distance.

'What is it? Why do we need the egg?' she asked, her voice becoming panicked. 'Is it time to go?'

'No, just let me down next to it!'

Mollie did as the dragon asked and knelt beside him.

'What is it, Whitestaff? Please tell me. You're scaring me!'

The dragon's frantic eyes searched the egg. 'Hello?' he called. 'Susset? Olfar? Can anyone hear me?'

He paused to listen. No reply came.

'Uncle, say something if you can hear me! Uncle!'

Not a peep came from the egg.

'WHY WON'T YOU TALK TO ME?' he hollered.

'Maybe they're just not near the portal?' Mollie suggested.

'No,' Whitestaff shook his head. 'I heard them, right enough. They were calling me. It sounded terrible. I couldn't get to the egg fast enough because of this stupid spell!'

'Calm down, Whitestaff. Tell me what happened from the beginning.'

The dragon closed his eyes as he tried to compose himself.

'You and Wendy had left,' he began, 'and for a moment I thought I heard Susset.'

'The sorceress from Sorteya?'

'Yes. But she sounded far away. She sounded frightened. And then I heard my uncle. His voice was all muffled, but I could tell there was something wrong with him too.'

'Could you make out what they were saying? Were they talking to you?'

Whitestaff shook his head.

'No, I couldn't hear it from out near the stream. It just sounded ... wrong. Then there was a noise like a rumbling of thunder—or a... a... mountain collapsing! And then it all stopped. I think I heard a scream. I've been trying to get myself closer to the egg all this time.'

'I'm sorry I wasn't here. Do you want to take a quick trip though the portal and make sure the others are fine?' Mollie inspected the egg. 'Everything looks normal from this end.'

Mollie was right; everything did look normal. The smooth golden eggshell had emerald-green flecks across its surface. It lay on a pile of straw and hadn't moved since Mollie and Wendy had liberated it from Cudgel. It was open in a clam-like way, and in its mouth lay a large pearl of shining light: the doorway to Sorteya. It was a special portal that connected the two worlds, and Whitestaff was the only one who could use it.

'I think I have to,' Whitestaff said. 'I wanted to hold out for as long as I could, but there is something wrong in Sorteya. I have to go. I have to see for myself.'

'But you can just come right back, can't you?'

'I don't think so.'

'Why not!'

'Because, Mollie, I know something terrible has happened there. I don't know how I know, but I can *feel* it. It must have something to do with being a Kai'dahl. And anyway, I don't want to waste the dragon essence I've been storing.'

'But this isn't how I wanted to say goodbye. Will you come back?'

Wendy stepped forward. 'Please come back,' she said.

Whitestaff looked from horse to sorceress. 'I *have* to come back, girls. Unless I can break the spell on this damn egg that keeps me a Lili'dahl, I'll keep having to come back to recharge. I just want to go home and stay there! Latos!' He shook his head at Mollie. 'Sometimes I wish your father would just magically appear and fix this portal.'

'You don't know how many times I've wished for Merlin to magically appear...'

'I'm sorry, Mollie, I—'

'But he never does. So we will just make do.'

'I didn't mean it like that. And I didn't mean that I want to stay in Sorteya and never see you again, or you, Wendy. I just need to know where home is and stay there.'

Mollie nodded and hugged him tight around the neck. Wendy walked forward and nuzzled them both.

After a while, Whitestaff broke their embrace and told them once more that he had to go.

'One last thing, before I leave. You two have been terrific. I'm sure that I will be back, but in the meantime, take care of my egg. Don't leave it out of your sight. If I can, I will shout through and tell you that I'm safe and that everything is well. If you don't hear from me—'

'Don't say it,' Wendy demanded.

Whitestaff carried on, his voice low but firm. 'If you don't hear from me, know that the gift of your friendship has been the thing most precious to me. It saw me through some terrible times on Sorteya, and it made the good times even better. I will treasure the day that I met both of you.'

'This is all happening too fast!' Mollie said. 'We were supposed to send you off properly this time. Don't go just yet.'

'I have to, Mollie. Its the duty of the Kai'dahl. I have to make sure the Palal are safe.'

With those words, Whitestaff reached out and touched the portal. He gave them one last look before he disappeared.

Mollie turned her back on the egg and hugged her face into Wendy's cheek. She sobbed wildly for a long while, until at last her crying stopped and she wiped her eyes dry on Wendy's coat. Without speaking, they both eased down next to the egg and waited in silence. They had hoped to hear Whitestaff's voice from the void, telling them that all was well and the noises he heard were just his active imagination, or better yet, see him walk through the portal and tell them that Sorteya didn't need him after all. But none of that happened. The sun went down and the moon came up and Mollie fell asleep on Wendy's flank. And the dragon stayed gone.

9

HULUM

The port city of Hulum was two and half days' ride from Nalib. It was slightly greener than the capital, but it had none of the opulence or style. Hulum was a city of necessity, not luxury. Its sole purpose was to provide trading ships safe harbour and nothing more. There were taverns, inns, stables, and two very large ship repair facilities where vessels could berth and have their hulls scraped and masts mended. Everything had a sense of practicality about it; shop fronts were bare, furniture was sparse and decoration minimal. What Hulum did have, however, was people. They filled the streets like an endless double line of marching ants, either heading to the ships or away from them. And it was here that Pip and Balad found themselves being carried by a current of people all headed for the docks.

'There it is, young Prince,' Balad shouted over the noise around them. 'That's the ship we are looking for. The Black Dart.'

Pip followed Balad's finger and knew at once his guard was right.

'It's the only black ship in the harbour,' Pip yelled in reply.

'Not black exactly, Prince,' Balad called over his shoulder. 'That is tyshwood. It is brown, but you can only tell if the sun is shining directly on its grain. See?'

Pip narrowed his gaze, and as they were jostled closer, he could make out the colour more clearly.

'Tyshwood?' Pip shouted.

'A very rare commodity. An entire ship made out of tyshwood! I never dreamed there was enough in one place.'

'What?' Pip asked over the noise.

'I said it's rare. It's valuable.' Balad took a gold coin out of his pouch and held it up so that Pip could see. 'Worth a lot of this.'

'What are you doing, Balad? Shadowclaw! Put it away!'

The tubby guard chuckled. 'You forget your lessons with Pukami, Honoured One. It's safe to trade in gold here. The Scourge can't smell it over the stench of the sea and the dead fish.'

Pip did recall being told that once, but he felt a lot more comfortable when Balad made the coin disappear back into the pouch.

'Where does tyshwood come from?' Pip asked, his voice barely carrying to Balad's ears.

'An island that used to be a mountain of fire.'

'A what?'

'An island that used to be a mountain of fire.'

But Balad's voice was drowned out by the throng of people around them. Pip gave up trying to talk. Instead, he allowed himself to be pushed along the jetty behind his guard until they reached the gangplank to the Black Dart. They were about to board the ship when they were met by one of the tallest men Pip had ever seen. The Prince came up to the man's chest and Balad's eyes were only level with his stomach. It was very difficult to see the man's face properly as it was half hidden by shaggy blond hair.

'Hallo?' said the stranger. He moved his lean body to block them from walking across the plank and onto the Dart. 'Got business here or should you be moving on?'

At first glance, the man looked calm enough, even friendly, but when Pip looked closer he could see that the stranger had ever so slightly shifted his weight to the balls of his feet. His fingers were half curled and ready to form fists at any moment.

'We do,' said Balad, drawing himself up as tall as he could go. 'We are here to see the captain of this vessel.'

'Captain don't like to be bothered.'

'Nobody does,' answered Balad. 'But we are here to see him and our business is urgent.' The royal guard tried to step around the man, but the stranger matched his steps and used his body to keep Balad from passing.

'Makes no difference if the business is urgent or not. Captain don't like to be bothered. Maybe you can bother the first mate instead?'

'Where is he?' asked Pip.

'You're talking to him. But talk fast before I lose interest.'

'That is no way to speak to a Prince!' said Balad, his right hand reaching for the sword at his hip.

Pip put his hand on Balad's shoulder and stepped forward.

'My name is Pip Ael of Nalib. I understand that my father, the sultan of this land, has arranged passage for me aboard your ship. My friend and I would be very grateful if you let us aboard.'

On hearing Pip's words, the stranger's body relaxed slightly. 'You must be the precious cargo Captain was on about. Come aboard, mates, come aboard. The Captain will be glad that you're here.'

He put an arm around each man and escorted them onto the deck.

'My name's Rio. Pardon my bad land manners and all, but Captain don't let just anyone aboard his precious Dart. Everyone wants to have a look at her up close and captain don't like sneaks.'

'I can see why they'd want a better look,' Pip said as he inspected the Dart. 'She is a beautiful ship.'

It was no exaggeration on the Prince's behalf; the ship was immaculate. The decks were clean, the ropes looked new and free of tangles, the sails were down, of course, but Pip could see they were in good repair and well stitched. Even the sailors themselves looked ordered. It seemed that everything had its place on the Dart and everyone knew their job. The ship had the same air of effortless efficiency that Pip's father had cultivated in the palace of Nalib, and Pip couldn't wait to meet its captain.

Rio guided the two below the quarterdeck to the door of the captain's cabin. The door itself was a foreboding piece of artwork. Evil, impish faces were carved into its front, and its brass handles had been moulded into the shape of snarling beasts. It wasn't made of tyshwood, but Pip guessed it was the next best thing. It looked as though it would take a battering ram to break it down.

Rio gave seven even knocks on the door and waited.

Must be a coded knock, Pip thought.

Presently, a voice from within invited them to enter, and Rio opened the door and ushered Pip and Balad inside.

Pip's eyes searched the entire cabin with unconcealed interest, and he found that the cabin matched the rest of the ship in terms of order and neatness. It was a spacious cabin, with shelves on either side that held thick, ageing tomes. A blue rug spread across the entire floor. It was soft and had a picture of two black throwing darts crossing each other to form an 'X' woven in its centre. In front of Pip was a heavy looking desk that held a pot of ink and several rolled-up maps. Light shone through two large open windows and the rear of the cabin, so it was hard for Pip to make out the figure of the captain who sat at the desk. As Pip's eyes adjusted, however, he saw that the man was the exact opposite of what Pip had expected him to be. His black beard grew wildly, like a tangle of vines competing for space on his cheeks and chin. His clothes were patched and ragged and his hair seemed to be allergic to scissors. It struck Pip that the captain put order and neatness into everything but himself.

'Welcome aboard the Black Dart, mates,' said the captain as he stood to shake hands with Pip and Balad. 'You must be the Sultan's son. It's good to meet you, Prince Ael.'

'Thank you, Captain Blackbeard,' said Pip as he had his hand crushed in the bigger man's mighty paw. 'You do us honour to have us aboard.'

The captain laughed and exchanged a look with Rio, who gave a slight nod in return. 'Please,' he said with a wolfish smile, 'from now on it's best if you call me Bob.'

10

THE KRAKEN

As soon as the introductions were made and everyone was
comfortably seated, Bob told Rio to get the crew to cast off and
make for the ocean. Before long, Pip could feel the ship moving
slowly out of the port and down the river, on its way into the ocean
beyond. The captain spread out a large map over the desk for all to
see.

'Now correct me if I'm wrong, Prince, but your father wants
you to go here?'

Blackbeard pointed to the continent at the Northern side of
the map. It was a land that Pip knew almost everything about thanks
to its ambassador, Robert Dugasi. Mr Dugasi had been boastful
about its Queen and its people, and he felt the need to lecture
everyone in the palace on every aspect of life in his home country.
So much so, that most of the palace servants had learnt to avoid eye-
contact with Dugasi, lest they became trapped and forced to listen to
one of his long and patriotic monologues. The only criticism he ever
gave of his homeland was of the dreary weather, which he
passionately despised. Dugasi's country was known as Albion in

many places, but Robert referred to it always as the 'Mother Country'.

'Yes,' Pip said. 'My father has instructed me to go there. Have you ever been there before?'

'Albion? Many times. Lot of business for me there.'

'Is there anywhere on this map you haven't been?'

'One or two places. Maybe even three,' he gave his guests a brief smile. 'Why don't I show you the route we'll be travelling?' Bob picked up his quill and used the feather tip to point. 'Here we are right now, making our way from Hulum down the Hulum River. From here, we hug the coast all the way up, like so.' He traced the line from the Sultan's land so the others could see. 'Then we head east, along this coast—'

'Why don't we cut across the sea here?' asked Pip, pointing to the large body of water. 'Won't this be quicker?'

Blackbeard frowned and nodded. 'Through the middle of the Pohmin Sea? It looks quicker, Prince, but it's death to go through the middle of *that* water.'

'How so?'

'There is a monster that lurks in there. A tentacled beast of the waves that tears ships apart with its eight horrid legs and eats whatever is inside.'

'A sea dragon?' asked Balad.

'A kraken,' replied the captain. 'I'd love to go the short way, mates, through that patch of water rather than around the edges of it.

But I know first-hand what lives there and I ain't going back. No sailor will.'

'Going back?' asked Pip.

'Aye. I was about your age and I was already First Mate to Captain Fogharty aboard the Night Jewell. Nice ship, held a good line and could catch any type of wind. No Dart, mind you, but still a beauty of a ship. About this time some sailors were talking about some monster in the deepest part of the Pohmin. Fogharty paid no heed. He was an old sea-dog and he'd seen all there was to see on the sea. Well he took us straight though the guts of it,' here Bob drew an arrow with his pointer in the middle of the Pohmin Sea.

'And what happened?'

'Nothing to begin with. The wind was good and the waves were small and we were making beautiful time. We'd crossed the middle of the sea and had no problems at all. Then at about an hour till dusk, we got a gentle bump. Something you'd barely notice on any other day. But I had been tense for the whole voyage and I felt it. I was working the deck and I looked straight up at Fogharty who was at the helm. The other sailors mustn't have noticed, because they were going about their work and some were singing songs and making jokes. But I could tell old Fogharty felt it. His face went the colour of sea-foam and he just looked at me. 'Twas the first time I ever saw him scared.

'It seemed like he was frozen for a few moments, then I think he was about to give an order or something when we got another bump, only this time it was big enough for everyone to feel. It felt like we had run aground, which confused the Latos out of everybody, because we were in the middle of the blasted sea. Then, not a bump, but a *crash*! 'Twas so hard my teeth cracked together and I bit my tongue. Everyone was panicking and shouting and suddenly the Jewell was lifted out of the water!'

Blackbeard closed his eyes for a while and took a deep breath before continuing. Balad and Pip were on the edge of their seats, eager to hear more of the tale.

'Next thing we saw was octopus arms coming over the bulwarks. Only these arms were as thick as the main mast! Fogharty threw a knife at one, sinking the blade deep, but I don't think the monster even felt it. We got four arms on either side and that's when we heard the splintering of the wood. The kraken was ripping the ship *apart*! Fogharty yelled for us to abandon ship while he started hacking at the arms with his sword. I jumped at the same time the monster tore the ship in two! I was flung high into the air and then splashed into the sea. When I came up to the surface, all I could see was a frenzy of arms and whitewater as the kraken feasted. 'Twas a horrible sight to behold.'

There was silence for some time as Pip and Balad took the extraordinary tale in.

'Amazing,' said Pip after a while. 'How did you get back?'

Bob nodded at the question and cleared his throat. 'Luckily for me, when the monster had eaten its fill, it swam away. I clung to some driftwood and made my way back to what was left of the Night Jewell. In the middle of the wreckage was a lifeboat, right side up

61

and completely untouched. It was just bobbing up and down on the water like nothing had even happened. Well I climbed in and waited, hoping some of my crewmates survived. But, alas, none ever returned to the surface. So I took the driftwood and used it for an oar. I was scared to paddle at first because I didn't want the kraken to come back. But as it got dark I had no choice. I paddled that blasted boat all night and all the next day. The currents did most of the work, and eventually a ship found me and took me aboard. I told them what I'd been through and no one has ever been up the middle of the Pohmin since. Especially not me. That's why we have to sail around the edge of it rather than go straight across. The water is too shallow for it on the coast.'

Pip blew out a breath and leaned back in his chair. 'Amazing. A kraken! And you survived.'

'Aye, I'm here to tell the tale.'

'In that case,' said Balad, 'we'd best not go through the sea. We have a monster of our own to worry about, young Prince. And the Scourge of Aldallah is more than enough problem for us.'

At this the captain stood. 'I'm interested in hearing about your monster,' he said. 'But I think it will have to wait. By the pull of the ship I reckon we have just made open water, and that means I need to take the helm from Rio. I'll show you your cabins first and you can settle in. We've got about two weeks of sailing ahead of us, mates. Let's hope it's all smooth.'

11

THE ARRIVAL

Whitestaff hated leaving Wendy and Mollie early, but as he made his way through the blackness, he knew he'd done the right thing. The dragon made his way forward, determined to see if his dragon friends were safe or in need of him. As he did so, the world of Sorteya took shape around him. But the more Whitestaff saw, the more concerned he became. He was supposed to walk forward into Susset's peaceful dugout, with its glass shelves filled with books and its large comfortable cushions. His portal was meant to be the centrepiece of the dugout, its shimmering light illuminating the room. However, as he made his way further through the portal, Whitestaff noticed his surroundings were not that of Susset's home. With each anxious step it became more apparent that he was, in fact, outside—and on the ground!

The Sorteyan wind blew fast across its dusty surface, howling as it made its way though the bases of spires. Yellow balefruit grew like lumps of pus nearby, and with each passing second Whitestaff felt his body surge with new strength and energy.

His body expanded and grew like a blossoming golden flower until his paws cracked the dry earth below with his weight. The dragon let loose a thunderous roar as he flexed his muscles and spread his wings. He looked behind him, and sure enough, there lay his beautiful portal, glimmering and shining in the dirt.

Latos! What has happened?

With a mighty leap, Whitestaff took to the skies to get his bearings. He beat his now-massive wings furiously until he broke through the layer of cloud that permanently blanketed the lower sky of Sorteya. It didn't take him long to spot a familiar pattern of spires in the distance.

Home!

Whitestaff sped to the spires he recognised.

There's the library,' he said to himself. 'And there's the hatchery. Past that and around the fat spire should be Olfar's.'

He was about to call out to let the other dragons know he was home, but something made him stop.

This isn't right, he thought. *Where is everybody?*

Whitestaff slowed himself in the air and hung back; his squinted eyes desperately scanned for signs of life. He spotted movement around one of the tallest central spires and his hearts beat with excitement. But the excitement turned to dread as he looked closer. There *were* dragons flying in and out of the spire dugouts, but their movements were like hasty squiggles and their shapes were small and dark. And there were too many of them.

Nazoor!

Whitestaff's first urge was to shoot forward to claw the beasts to shreds and find out where the Palal were, but he resisted, knowing that he would be heavily outnumbered. With a growl of frustration, he clung to the side of a nearby spire instead and watched.

From his vantage point, Whitestaff could see that the tallest spire, which used to be the home of Cracone and Nap, was being used as some sort of command centre. Nazoor were flying in and out of it in small teams. They seemed to be searching every dugout in every spire. When a thorough search was made, the team would leave and fly back to the command centre. One such team was flying down to what Whitestaff knew to be the hatchery.

The Lili'dahls! I have to get there first!

The golden dragon knew that if he flew to intercept the Nazoor, he'd be spotted by the rest of the mini-dragons and beaten in no time. So he did the thing that no Nazoor would do—he headed straight down.

Whitestaff figured that he was safe below the fog, as no Nazoor would get so close to the ground below. He flew wildly around the spires and tried hard to recall a mental map of his home. When he thought he'd found the spire for the hatchery, he pulled himself up and flew back above the blanket of cloud.

Yes! he thought as he saw the Wyvern above him. *They're going for the hatchery, right enough.*

He watched as the group of seven Nazoor swooped into the open mouth of the hatchery, hissing as they flew. They were closely followed by an eighth Nazoor, only this one was different to the rest.

He appeared much larger than the others, and with a shock, Whitestaff registered that *this* dragon had scales instead of skin.

An Alpos! Audgar!

With new determination, Whitestaff pumped his wings harder to catch up, both of his hearts pushing blood and adrenaline through his body. He heard yelling and screaming from above—a dragon in pain. Whitestaff flew faster still and rocketed into the hatchery, the memories of his own encounter with these deadly creatures fresh in his mind.

His entrance was met with an immediate attack. Three Nazoor came at him, claws outstretched and beaks biting. Unfortunately for the Wyvern, Whitestaff was still charged with energy from his portal. The mighty Kai'dahl knew that he could not afford to hesitate and so smashed the face of his first attacker with a bunched paw, sending the Nazoor crashing across the room. The second Wyvern received the back of Whitestaff's tail. It cracked along the small dragon's neck and pounded him into the ground, never to move again. The last Nazoor that came at Whitestaff met the golden dragon's teeth. Whitestaff bit down hard with no mercy into the side of the horrible beast. He shook the Nazoor like a dog would shake a toy and threw it out of the hatchery entrance. Its broken body fell like a stone.

With his attackers out of the way, Whitestaff took a second to catch his breath and survey the second fight. It looked as though the eggs had been piled up at the back of the dugout and were being protected by two Re'dahl. The four remaining Nazoor and Audgar were fighting the red Palal, who appeared to be losing.

Whitestaff roared once more and launched himself into the fray. This time he stomped one the nearest Wyvern and felt its bones cracking beneath his paws. His tail once again came whipping around from his hind and smacked one of the Nazoor on the side of the head and sent it sailing into Audgar.

'Whitestaff,' shouted one of the Re'dahl. 'I never thought I'd be glad to see you!'

Whitestaff looked around to face Nap. The red dragon had blood trickling down his chin and scratches along his chest.

'Nap?'

The red dragon nodded and leapt to the aid of his comrade. He pulled a Nazoor attacker off his Re'dahl friend and threw it at Whitestaff.

'You deal with this one,' he said.

Whitestaff nodded and sent a heavy paw smacking into the stomach of the flying lizard, who promptly collapsed and rolled around the floor, hissing in pain. The sound made Whitestaff queasy. The defeated Nazoor's tail squirmed back and forth, and it looked so hurt that Whitestaff stopped his attack.

Audgar saw this and gnashed his needle-like teeth. He pushed his way to the Kai'dahl, trampling the Nazoor that Whitestaff had just hit. Audgar grabbed at Whitestaff with his two massive legs, lifting them in the air while he balanced on his tail. Whitestaff caught the legs in his front paws and wrestled with the massive

Alpos. Audgar was using all of his muscle to slash at Whitestaff's face with his claws, and Whitestaff was straining to hold them back. At first it seemed that the two were evenly matched in strength, but Whitestaff brought his own tail around and smacked Audgar's tail out from under him, making the beast topple over. Without thinking, Whitestaff heaved the Alpos off the floor and threw him into the wall, sending tapestries sailing from their hooks. Audgar had hit the wall at full force, but that wasn't enough to stop him. He got up, groggily flapped his wings and half-flew, half-stumbled towards the dugout opening as fast as he could manage. Whitestaff watched as the huge Nazoor beast blindly dropped out of the entrance and flew crookedly away.

Behind Whitestaff, the fight was almost over. It was now down to two Re'dahl and two Nazoor. In a matter of seconds, Nap had dropped them both to the ground. He gave one a shattering shoulder charge and pierced the other one through the chest with the barb on his tail. The Nazoor shrieked with agony for a second, and then its black eyes rolled back and it fell in a silent heap.

Whitestaff let out a long breath of exhaustion, and the Re'dahl next to Nap groaned and slid down the wall.

The room around them was a disaster area. Feathers floated down from torn cushions, glasses of balejuice were smashed at their feet and the floor was littered with the bodies of the defeated Nazoor. The eggs at the back of the hatchery remained intact.

'Nap,' Whitestaff panted as he wiped blood from his brow, 'what in the Latos is going on here?

12

THE REFUGE

Nap walked over to where his Re'dahl friend was slumped and sat
next to him.

'It started at dawn, right Ugos?'

The other red dragon gave a weak nod.

'I was in the common room of my dugout with my father. We
had just woken up and were about to have some breakfast. The first
thing we noticed was the sound of them. We didn't know what it was
right away... sometimes the wind plays strange sounds with the
mouths of the dugouts. Then Luzahmin came in looking all scared.
All she could do was point outside. We rushed over to the entrance
and saw thousands of Nazoor filling the sky. The noise they made
became deafening. Imagine the beating of thousands of pairs of
wings and the hissing of thousands of tongues. It was disgusting.

'I stood there gaping like a tooker but father knew what to do.
He told Luzahmin to spread the word for everyone to fall back to the
Court. He told me to grab the best Re'dahl fighters and come here to

evacuate the Lili'dahl and their mothers while he prepared his Re'dahl for war.'

'And now you're here? With *one* other fighter?'

'No,' Nap replied. 'That was about two hours ago. I came here with Ugos and Briss and Sojat. At first the Nazoor had no plan, they were just attacking everything and anything. I sped here with my Re'dahl and told the Bo'dahl we were under attack. We each carried two or three hatchlings back to the Court and left the eggs, fighting as we went.'

'You fought while carrying hatchlings?'

'It was easier than it sounds. The Nazoor really had no plan of attack. They seemed unorganised and forgot to take us on in numbers. Their blood must have been up or something. Or they were just feeling extra bold.'

'You have to remember,' Ugos added, 'that we've had two decades of peace. The first dragons to attack would have been the young and inexperienced or were trying to make a name for themselves. They flew at us usually one or two at a time and were easy to knock out of the sky.'

Nap nodded in agreement. 'Whatever the reason, the initial stages of the battle went well. We were able to get most of the Palal to the safety of the Court and we managed to get the Lili'dahls out of here.'

'What about Olfar, and Armay and Graggy?'

Nap shrugged. 'I didn't do a headcount, Kai'dahl.'

'Why did you come back here? Shouldn't you be with the others?'

'Ugos and I wanted to come back and see how many eggs we could carry. Father told me not to come.'

Whitestaff's shoulders slumped. 'And now we will have to abandon them?'

'Why?' asked Nap. 'Let's start taking them to the Court.'

'We can't. That Alpos will tell the others that we're here. I expect we'll have Nazoor breathing down our neck very soon, right enough. We'll have to grab as many as we can and leave.'

Nap snorted. 'Shows how much you know. Their Alpos are all brawn and no brains. Audgar can't even speak. And even if by some miracle he can actually make a sentence, by the time he gets to the others he will have forgotten what to tell them.'

'He's right,' Ugos said. 'We should be safe for a while.'

'Can our Alpos speak?' asked Whitestaff. 'It's just, I've never seen a Palal Alpos.'

Nap pointed to a curtain over on the far side of the dugout. 'Yes, they can speak. But we still put them through there.'

'I remember this,' Whitestaff said quietly. He made his way to the curtain and pulled it aside. The room behind the curtain was tiny, only big enough for a small dragon to stand in. In the middle of the room was a metal stand that looked like the head of a giant pitchfork. At the centre of the prongs was a black sphere that hovered in mid-air. It looked like Whitestaff's portal, but it contained none of the colour.

'Don't get too close or you'll get sucked into it,' Ugos warned.

'Graggy told me about this once,' Whitestaff said. 'He said that we put our Alpos into it? How could we?' He turned to face Nap. 'Where does this portal lead?'

Nap shrugged. 'Random places. The middle of a sun, a remote planet somewhere. No one knows.'

'But *why*?'

'For the safety of our race, Kai'dahl. See those eggs over there?' Whitestaff looked to the large pile and nodded. 'Well, they're all white. They have white little hatchlings in them. They're safe.'

'Mine isn't white.'

'Of course not. Yours would be gold,' Nap scoffed. 'That's how we can tell a *king* is on the way.'

'Don't be so hard on him,' Ugos said. 'He wasn't born here.' The other red dragon looked at Whitestaff. Ugos was more heavily built than Nap. His scales weren't the same blood-red as Nap's; they were lighter, almost pink, and his face held none of Nap's anger. 'Your egg would be mainly gold with flecks of green, am I right?'

Whitestaff nodded.

'Well, Alpos eggs are silver with flecks of black. If we see such an egg, it goes through there,' Ugos indicated the portal with his head. 'We do this because every Alpos is more dangerous than a thousand Wyvern.'

'Olfar told me that they were dangerous, but he never let me know why.'

'They're insane,' said Nap.

'Unfortunately, yes,' Ugos agreed. 'They're all born blind too; Nazoor skin where the eyes should be. And they can control the elements. They can burn you or freeze you or blast you into pieces.'

'They can do *magic*?' Whitestaff said, aghast.

'Terrible magic,' Nap answered. 'All they do is use it to kill. They're all mad. We should never have crossed bloodlines all those years ago.'

'So Audgar can do magic?' Whitestaff asked in alarm.

'Of course not! Why do you think he didn't just annihilate us a moment ago?'

'Let's go back to the start,' Ugos suggested. 'Whitestaff, an Alpos is just another name for what you get when you mix a Nazoor with a Palal. If the Alpos hatches from a Nazoor egg, it's the size of a Palal, has twice the strength but none of the brains. They can't think or even speak. If an Alpos hatches from one of our eggs, they have Nazoor skin and can control magic, but they are totally blind. They are either born mad or go that way very quickly.' He blew out a long breath. 'Either way, it's a disaster. Our ancestors very soon figured this out and stopped mixing the bloodlines. It's a mistake we're still paying for today. One we never should have made in the first place.'

'I see,' said Whitestaff. 'No we shouldn't have. Not if this is the result.' He gave the portal a look of distaste and let the curtain fall back in place.

'We should get these eggs out of here anyway,' Nap said. 'Scoop up as many as you can and get ready to fight your way out.'

Whitestaff went over to the eggs and cradled as many as he could in his front legs.

'We won't have to fight our way out though,' said Whitestaff and he curled his tail around a few more eggs.

'Why not?'

'We'll just sneak out of here.'

Nap blew through his nose. 'And how do you suggest we do *that*, Golden One?'

'Same way I got here,' said Whitestaff with a smile. 'We go down and then up.'

13

OPEN WIDE

'Good plan,' said Ugos as he flew in beside Whitestaff. 'They'll never
dip down here below the clouds. We should get to the Court
without any troubles. Provided you know the way.'

'I know the way, right enough. I've spent the past months
dreaming about Sorteya, trying to remember every single detail.'

'It's just like you to bring us closer to the ground,' Nap said.
'Must run in the blood.'

Nap's front legs were cradled around a bunch of eggs, but
even encumbered in this way, he was still a graceful flyer. And even
as he was being insulted, Whitestaff couldn't help admire Nap's skill
in the sky.

Ugos shook his head at his friend. 'What does it matter, Nap?
As long as we get the eggs to safety.'

'Exactly,' Whitestaff agreed. 'Besides, that's the spire we want
up ahead. Your honour will be safe from the dreaded ground soon
enough.'

The golden dragon led them to the spire he had picked out
and slowly drew himself up close to its surface. As he broke up

through the cloud layer, he could see the King's Court above him. It was an entrance unlike any other. Instead of just a gaping hole, the Court entrance had been fitted with the head of a dragon that had enormous emeralds for eyes and scales of pure gold. Its fangs were formed of sparkling silver, and its mouth was usually wide open, allowing entry. But as Whitestaff flew closer to the head, he panicked. The mouth was shut tight and it was surrounded by Nazoor.

The Wyvern had been batting into the dragon-head entrance, scratching it and trying to pry open the jaws. One of them spotted Whitestaff and the two Re'dahl and shouted to the rest, who turned their attention to the newcomers.

'Get ready to fight!' called Whitestaff. He felt his muscles tense around the eggs in his grasp. His eyes scanned the Nazoor numbers and he knew that his team would be easily outmatched, even if they weren't all carrying eggs.

'No fighting this time, Kai'dahl,' Ugos said. 'What you'll need is speed. Follow Nap.'

At that moment, Nap shot up and away from the cloud of Nazoor. Ugos closely followed, leaving Whitestaff with no choice but to try and match their pace.

Up he surged, pumping his wings like mad as the two red dragons in front put on even more speed. He watched them from behind and they made no sign of slowing down, until at last they hovered in the sky, high above the Nazoor. There they turned to face their enemy.

Why have we stopped? Whitestaff wondered. *Aren't we trying to get away?*

The Wyvern had now gathered together and readied themselves for a fight, turning their backs on the Court entrance. Whitestaff was close enough to hear them calling to each other, hissing for blood. The Nazoor had the numbers; they knew they'd win.

But the numbers didn't seem to bother Nap, who all of a sudden thrashed his wings for speed and then pulled them in close to his body, allowing gravity to hurl him downwards. He speared at the Wyvern horde, letting himself free-fall at them. Ugos did the same. He lowered his head to use it as a battering ram. The Nazoor were not expecting this type of attack, and Whitestaff could almost see the gleam fading from their eyes. The first few dragons managed to clumsily flap out of Nap's way, but the Nazoor behind weren't so lucky. Nap sent them flying like skittles with his skull. Ugos did them same, cutting a path for Whitestaff to follow. The Kai'dahl dropped his head and pulled the eggs closer to his body. Down he soared, like a falling boulder. He launched into the Nazoor and felt them bouncing off his broad scales. They were hissing and clawing at him as he went past them, but he was travelling too fast for them to do any damage.

From his squinted eyes he could see Nap and Ugos in front. They had broken through the cloud of Nazoor and were heading for the mouth of the Court.

What are they doing? They'll be killed, Whitestaff thought. He winced as Nap dived at the mouth, expecting the Re'dahl to smash right into the golden jaws. But that didn't happen. Instead, at the very last instant before impact, the jaws opened and snapped Nap and Ugos up with one bite.

Whitestaff almost slowed down with relief and shock, but forced himself to continue spearing forward, hoping that the mouth would open for him too. As he broke though the Nazoor blockade, his vision filled with the gigantic face of the dragon. He aimed at the closed mouth and realised that even if he wanted to pull up, he couldn't. He was moving much too fast. He put his head back down and braced for impact as he shot at the closed mouth. He expected to smash into those golden jaws and silver teeth. He closed his eyes and... *SNAP!*

The jaws opened right at the last second and closed after him. He was inside the vast expanse of the Court.

Whitestaff shot his wings out instinctively in order to slow down, but he was a big dragon and had too much momentum. His surroundings went by in a blur. The massive amphitheatre and the front benches for the Council whizzed by, and when Whitestaff looked up he saw that he was on a collision course with the King's throne! He beat his wings forward but it was no use—he was going to crash!

Suddenly, Ugos and Nap jumped up from beneath him and tackled him around the stomach, pulling him and his eggs to the floor. The eggs went spilling and rolling in every direction and the dragons tumbled together in a heap. Whitestaff skidded along the red carpet that led to Cracone's throne before finally lurching to a halt. When he opened his eyes, he saw his face was inches away from the thick metal base of the throne.

Whitestaff couldn't move for a few minutes. Nap and Ugos had knocked the wind right out of him. It hurt, but without their quick thinking, he knew it would have been worse.

Other dragons moved around him and collected the eggs that he, Nap and Ugos had brought back. A few helped him to his feet.

'Whitestaff! You're back!' someone shouted.

'Whitestaff?'

'Look, it's the Kai'dahl.'

'Thank heavens.'

'We'll need him more than ever now.'

'He's back!'

'It's really him!'

Whitestaff looked around and nodded to his fellow Palal. 'I wish it could be under better circumstances,' he said, his breath tight and ragged. He straightened himself and turned his attention to Nap, who had managed to untangle himself from Ugos. 'I think I need to speak to your father, Nap. Can you take me to him?'

'He's the King, Whitestaff. Unless you haven't noticed, we're at war. He won't have time for you.'

'He will want to know I'm back.'

'Then *I'll* go and tell him.'

Whitestaff was about to argue when Susset appeared.

'Oh, Whitestaff! Thank goodness you're here.'

Nap snorted and rolled his eyes. 'Our saviour,' he mumbled.

Susset ran to the golden dragon and threw her arms around his neck. When she withdrew, Whitestaff had a good look at her. She was still a remarkable beauty, but it looked as though she'd been through a war herself. The hooded robe she wore was torn, her hair was messy and there was a bruise on her right cheek. She was also sporting a fat lip.

'What happened to you?' Whitestaff asked.

'All in good time, Kai'dahl,' she told him. 'But first things first; you need to speak to Cracone. You are on the Council after all, and he's been waiting for you.'

Nap huffed at this and shook his head.

Susset ignored Cracone's son and took Whitestaff by the arm and led him to an arched doorway, which led to the rooms at the back of the Court. Before he disappeared through the arch, Whitestaff looked over his shoulder at Nap.

'Coming?' he asked.

Nap looked up with surprise. It took him a second to register what Whitestaff meant. 'Sure,' he said after a moment, 'I mean, I suppose so. If it shuts you up.'

Whitestaff looked to Susset and gave her a sly wink. 'Nothing ever shuts *me* up.'

'Don't I know it,' said Nap as he came after them, wearing the closest thing he had to a smile.

14

THE CUNNING PLAN

There were two rooms at the back of the Court. One was for the King himself. It contained sleeping cushions and a work area, should matters of the Court keep him from going home. The other was for the King and his Council to meet and discuss matters not suitable for the Court to hear. It was known as the Private Chambers, but it had now been converted into a makeshift war room.

In the middle of the room was what used to be a huge table, around which members of the Council would sit and argue about new ideas or Sorteyan laws. Now, however, the table was covered with a three-dimensional map of the Palal section of Sorteya. Whitestaff recognised it immediately, including the deep trench of the Dire Channel which separated his kind from the Nazoor. A Gra'dahl was busily sculpting more spires with dirt, trying to make the map as accurate as possible. Whitestaff was impressed to note that the model spire for the Court even had a miniature dragon head moulded onto it.

The assembled dragons sat on cushions around the map and were having a heated debate when Whitestaff entered. It took the dragons a moment to realise that the Kai'dahl was even in the room.

'Whitestaff!' called a familiar Gra'dahl above the shouting. 'Thou has returned!'

The old green dragon rose to hug his nephew, and one by one, the Councillors fell quiet.

'Olfar! It's good to see you.'

'And thee, my boy.'

Whitestaff turned to the head of the table where Cracone sat. 'Your Majesty. I came as soon as I could.'

Cracone nodded. 'It's good you're here,' he growled. 'We're in need of all the muscle we can get.'

'I can see that, right enough. The Nazoor are outside the jaws of this dugout right now, clawing to get in. If it wasn't for your son and Ugos, I'd still be out there facing them on my own.'

Cracone moved his head to the side to look at Nap with his one good eye. 'That's my boy. Always good in a scrap,' he grinned.

'I learned from the best,' Nap said, returning his father's smile.

'If it pleases the Council though,' Whitestaff said, 'could someone tell me exactly what is happening and why? I mean, I can see that we're at war, but what started it? Was there any warning? Have we had any communication from Mezelga or Cross?'

Olfar cleared his throat and looked to Cracone. 'May I?'

The King nodded and let his good eye drift over the map in front of him. The ruby slab covering his bad eye glinted.

'What we know, Nephew, is that the Nazoor have attacked in massive numbers. Judging by the sheer size of the invasion, the Nazoor have been planning this for some time. Does thou remember when we flew out to the Dire and saw the Nazoor swarming the banks?'

'Yes I do.'

'Well, I don't think the Nazoor were actually trying to provoke us into a war after all.'

'No?'

'No. I think that there were so many of them that they no longer all fit on their side of the border. They were overflowing, so to speak.'

'They've run out of room!'

'Don't sound so surprised, Whitestaff. We were having the same problem, remember? It is my guess that they have nowhere else to go, and so decided that the best hope for their survival was here.'

'What about the Tournament? What about the treaty?' Whitestaff asked.

This time, Cracone answered. 'If Olfar is right, and they have no spires or balefruit left, then they are desperate. They probably figured that as long as we can put forward a fire-breathing Kai'dahl Champion, then they'd always lose.' Cracone looked Whitestaff over

83

from top to bottom. 'And they're right. What hope would they have against you one-on-one? Even if they did use their Alpos.'

Olfar agreed. 'Yes. Their main hope was to secure rule over Sorteya with the Tournament. I suppose they realised that was a false hope.'

Whitestaff mulled this over in his head. 'If they have increased in numbers, why didn't they come to us and ask for more land?'

'Ha!' shouted Cracone. 'The Nazoor don't ask for things. They take them. Besides, we don't have the space to give them.'

'What happened to the other Palal?'

'The King made an excellent decision to fall back here and close the Court mouth. He bought us some time to regroup and to strategise.'

'Olfar, did Armay and Graggy—'

'They made it out, Nephew. They're in the next room: the King's room. Only now we're using it as an infirmary. Thou can see them when we're finished here, but it's thy cousin thou should be worried about.'

'Luzahmin? Where is she?'

'Hmmmm,' said Olfar, 'that's what we were discussing when thou came in. It seems we are missing three of our Palal, and my daughter is one of them.'

'I thought she was with you, father!' Nap said. 'I'll go and find her. If they've harmed a scale on her body I'll—'

Cracone shook his head. 'Not so fast son. I sent her to warn as many Palal as she could and tell them to fall back here. It seems she got held up.' Cracone pointed at the green dragon who was busy moulding spires with dirt. 'Cartogras here has made this map and we've been matching the returned Palal with their dugouts.'

'Yes,' said Olfar. 'So far we have everyone accounted for, except Luzahmin, Kurt and Sophiena. Kurt and Sophiena live here,' he rested a claw on a spire to the west of the Court. It is our guess that Luzahmin is with them.'

'Fine, let's go and get them. I'll take all the Re'dahl we have,' said Nap as he turned to exit.

'Not yet,' said a Gra'dahl on Olfar's left. 'We need to be discreet about our position. If we all leave now then the Nazoor will all know where we are hiding.'

'So?' said Nap. 'Umdir, you know the Court entrance has been enchanted by Merlin himself! Once the jaws are shut, they'll only open for a Palal.'

'The jaws are not the problem,' Umdir replied. 'If the Nazoor know we are all in here, they'll simply dig their way in. I'm surprised they haven't thought of that already.'

'They're still searching the spires one by one,' Whitestaff said. 'They're using your old dugout as a base, Cracone, and from there they're sending out scouting parties to each spire. The last time I saw them, they were looking through the hatchery.'

Cartogras cleared his throat to speak. 'That means, Majesty, that they are at Kurt's dugout now. If we draw a line from your dugout to the hatchery like so, then assume that they're working from the centre outwards, they have already covered this area.' Cartogras drew a light circle around most of the spires. 'This demonstrates very deliberate and strategic thinking on their part. It's almost as though they have their own map of our environment. They chose your spire, your Majesty, because it's central and offers a view of all the other spires, owing to its height. Either way, Kurt and Sophiena are just at the border of the circle, which statistically means they have been caught by now.'

'Blast them to Latos!' Cracone thundered. 'How do they have such a good knowledge of our half of Sorteya?'

'Cross?' offered Umdir.

'I doubt it,' said Olfar. 'He only ever got access to my dugout for diplomatic reasons.'

'Have we ever had reports of Nazoor close to us?' asked Cracone.

Nap and Whitestaff shared a look. They had both seen Nazoor under the clouds long ago.

A scouting party? Whitestaff wondered.

Nap seemed to be thinking the same thing. 'Could they have flown below the fog and mapped it from there?' he asked. 'Whitestaff showed me a similar trick just before.'

Olfar scoffed. 'Not likely they'd get so close to the ground. But still...'

'They do seem to have either good luck, or good planning on their side,' Umdir added.

Nap and Whitestaff avoided each other's eyes.

'We're getting off track,' the King said. 'We need to decide if we're going to mount a rescue, now that we have a reasonable idea of where they are. How many are we going to send?'

'I don't think it's a good idea,' said Umdir.

'I'm with the King,' said Olfar. 'We send a massive force to bring Luzahmin and the others back.'

'That's because she's your daughter, Olfar,' said Umdir. 'It's clouding your judgement. Revealing our position isn't wise.'

'They already know our position,' said Whitestaff. 'There are dozens of them outside, remember.'

'Yes,' replied Umdir. 'But they don't know we have the *entire* population of the Palal in here. If they knew then they wouldn't be wasting time doing searches. They'd be tunnelling in as we speak.'

'I agree with Umdir,' said a Bo'dahl Councillor. 'A rescue mission would be unwise.'

At her words, the Council broke out into argument again, each shouting over the other. Cracone banged his sceptre and bellowed as hard as the rest of them.

'We should stay here and think ourself lucky to have only lost three,' said one.

'If it was your daughter, you'd want her rescued,' retorted another.

Nap joined the debate, even though he wasn't on the council. He yelled so hard that his blood-red scales turned an even deeper shade of red!

'ENOUGH,' shouted Whitestaff at last. 'ENOUGH!' His roar echoed through the chamber.

The Councillors huffed and snorted but closed their mouths to hear what Whitestaff had to say.

'I have listened to both sides and I think I have a solution. We can go and get Luzahmin and keep our position low-key. But Latos! We need to stop arguing and start thinking. We are at war here, and the only way we can hope to keep our scales is to work together.'

Some of the Councillors nodded at his words while others looked at the floor, suddenly ashamed.

'Very well,' said Cracone. 'What do you propose we do?'

15

THE DREAM TEAM

'My suggestion,' said Whitestaff to his fellow Councillors, 'is to do what we hope that the Nazoor *aren't* doing right now. We tunnel! We dig through this dugout and hollow out a nice little exit at the back of this spire.'

'How does that help?' asked Umdir. 'That would give the Nazoor even easier access. We'd be doing their hard work for them!'

'We tunnel all the way below the fog. Or better yet—we make our exit in the middle of the fog. That way they won't spot it.'

'Good thinking,' bellowed Cracone. 'Then we take a large force and engage the enemy with a surprise attack! Excellent!'

Whitestaff nodded. 'Yes, to my way of thinking, if Luzahmin and the other two have been caught, then they've been dragged back to the Nazoor base—Cracone's old dugout. But I don't think a large force is the right thing to do, Your Majesty.'

'No? And why not? We need to hit them hard!'

'We may have to soon. But for now the main objective is getting to Luzahmin, Kurt and Sophiena. I say we send a small force to rescue them. That way we have a greater chance of avoiding detection.'

'Why not engage the dirty Wyvern now?' Nap demanded.

'Because we'd lose,' Whitestaff replied.

'What makes you so sure, Kai'dahl?' Nap asked. 'You've never seen the mighty Re'dahl army fight before.'

'No I haven't. But I've taken on several Nazoor at once and nearly lost. They outnumber us ten-fold if what I saw was any indication.'

'Thou has fought the Nazoor—'

'Not now, Uncle. I'll tell you about it another time.' Whitestaff gave Nap a meaningful look. 'What's important is that for every one of us there are *ten* of them. We'd fight, we'd thin their ranks right enough. But in the end we'd lose everyone.'

'Then what hope do we have?' a Bo'dahl Councillor asked.

The assembled dragons looked to Cracone, who shrugged his shoulders and gestured to Whitestaff. 'Ask him.'

The dragons turned their attention back to the Kai'dahl.

'I'm hoping that my small rescue party may also find out some valuable information about Mezelga's whereabouts.'

'Their Queen?' said Umdir. 'How would that help? I don't follow.'

Cracone gave a vicious smile as he traced the outline of the scar on his chest. 'I do. Mezelga is the key to this. We kill her, then we kill this war. Isn't that right, Whitestaff? The same tactic Frendrek used last time?'

The room grew silent as everyone looked to the golden dragon.

'Yes,' he said. 'We find the whereabouts of the Queen, and we end this madness.'

Everyone cheered but Umdir, who waited patiently for the commotion to die down. 'I hate to bring facts into this plan,' he said, 'but how exactly are you going to find this information? It's not as though the Nazoor are going to tell you.'

'No, you're right,' said Whitestaff. 'That's why I need a small party, just a few dragons.'

'You'll still be seen!' retorted Umdir.

Whitestaff looked at Umdir, then settled his gaze on Susset, who had been patiently standing next to the King the whole time. Everyone followed Whitestaff's gaze and looked to the sorceress. Whitestaff gave her a toothy grin and waited for her to catch on.

'Oh,' she said at last, giving up a glowing smile. 'Not if I turn them all invisible!'

'My thoughts exactly,' said Whitestaff.

There was more cheering as the rest of the Councillors came to understand the plan.

'Good thinking, my boy,' said Olfar.

Cracone smiled too, but soon had to bang his sceptre and demand silence. 'It's a good plan,' he said. 'I like it. Now we have to get to action before it's too late. Umdir, get some tunnelling happening now.'

'Yes, Your Majesty.'

'In the meantime, the rest of you either help build Whitestaff's back door or check in with the infirmary in the next room. I'm sure Nightgale could use all the claws she can get. Whitestaff and Susset, pick your rescue team, but leave room for me. I want to go out there and see what we're facing.'

Whitestaff nodded. 'I already know who I'm taking,' he said as he went to the infirmary to find Graggy and Armay.

The King's room was almost as spacious as the Private Chamber, and it too had been turned upside-down by the war. Large cushions were set in rows of six, and the injured Palal sprawled over them and tried to make themselves comfortable. Nightgale was busy administering poultices she had made from the pulp of yellow balefruit, while Armay and Graggy were helping other dragons with bandages. Armay was the first to spot the Kai'dahl enter, and she cried out with joy.

'You're back! Graggy, look!'

The green dragon's head snapped up to see his friend, and his face beamed. In an instant, Graggy was up on his long legs and bounding towards Whitestaff—Armay close on his tail. They reached Whitestaff at the same time and hurled themselves at him. A smaller dragon would have been bowled over, but Whitestaff's big frame and strong tail kept him upright. He hugged his dragon friends, one front leg around each.

'It's good to see you too,' he said with a laugh.

'I'm so glad you're here,' Armay said as they all stood back and looked at each other properly. 'Now I know everything will turn out all right.'

'It's good you came back early,' agreed Graggy, his voice extra fast with excitement. 'Now all we need to do is point you at the Nazoor and you can do your fire-breathing trick all over them.'

Whitestaff shook his head. 'I don't think I have *that* much fire in my stomach.'

'Guess not,' said Graggy. 'Did you *see* them all? They filled the entire horizon! Who knew there could be that many?'

'Never mind the Nazoor,' said Armay. 'How have you been, Whitestaff?' She traced a claw around his cheek.

'I've been good, Armay,' he said, giving her a wide smile. 'I've been eager to get back here to you. I mean, to you all. To Sorteya, is what I mean.'

Graggy laughed. 'Whitestaff, are you turning into a Re'dahl?' he asked, 'Or are you just blushing?'

'Leave him alone,' said Armay. 'I'm sure he missed you too.'

'I did,' agreed Whitestaff. 'There was no one on Earth who laughs like a choking cat.'

Graggy laughed at Whitestaff's remark, and then starting laughing at the sound of his own peculiar, snorting laughter. It was too much for Armay and Whitestaff—they began laughing too, until Nightgale came over and politely told them that an infirmary was no place for frivolity, and to please take the reunion elsewhere.

Whitestaff led his pals back into the war room where they took turns in telling each other what they'd been doing for the past five months. Graggy's shoulder had mended nicely thanks to the juice and pulp of the yellow balefruit, and it was now ready for action.

'On the upside,' Graggy said, 'I got my fair share of attention from Nightgale. Made the pain worth it.'

Armay gave him a friendly shove and told Whitestaff that she had been trying to convince the Bo'dahl councillors to adopt Whitestaff's plan to utilise the spire space lower to the ground.

'They're much more open to the idea,' she told him. 'Especially since that's where all the yellow fruit is. They've been using it for all sort of ailments on the Lili'dahls, from teething to temperatures. It really is wonderful. I think some of them are beginning to feel silly that we've let it sit there for the past however many decades.'

'As they should,' said Graggy.

After they all had their turn, Whitestaff drew them back to the more serious matter at hand. He gave them an overview of his plan and showed them on Cartogras's map where his tunnel was being dug and where he thought Luzahmin and the others might be.

'So Susset is turning you and the others invisible, so that you can find your cousin and maybe Mezelga?' Armay asked.

'Yes. Cracone has insisted on coming, and I thought I'd take you two with me as well. You were both chosen Contenders for the

Tournament, so I know you have the speed and strength for a quick getaway if we need it.'

'Excellent,' said Graggy. 'The team is back together.'

'Perfect,' said Armay.

Whitestaff gave them a grin and nodded. 'But before you get too happy, I have another companion in mind.'

Graggy arched a questioning green eyebrow.

'What would you think of Nap joining us for this one?'

16

THE WAGER

The sun was making its way above the horizon, spilling its brilliant rays over the surface of the sea. The wind was blowing west across the deck of the Black Dart, bringing with it the warmth of the new day, and the crew adjusted the main sail to catch as much of it as they could. Pip marvelled at how Bob's men could make the ship sail north while the wind blew in a different direction, but he supposed they'd had years of experience and to them it was nothing unusual.

To the Prince, everything about being at sea was new and exciting, so the journey had been a memorable experience. To Blackbeard's crew, however, the voyage was one of many, and so they were constantly looking for something to relieve their boredom. They played dice, cards, drinking games and sang songs while they worked. They gambled a lot with each other too and were always thinking up the most extraordinary bets.

As Pip made his way to the forecastle deck, he noticed that one such gambling event was about to take place.

'But tell me, Garth. How many shots do I get?' Rio asked.

Garth scratched his head and looked to his mates. 'Three? Does that sound fair?'

'Four,' said Rio. 'And if I win, I get two captain cards from everybody.' Rio looked down and noticed Pip had joined them. 'You're just in time to watch me lose another bet, Prince Pip.'

Pip laughed as he joined the circle of shipmates. 'What's the bet?' he asked.

'The crew here have bet that I can't shoot down a Pohmin Gull with my bow. If I win, I get three Captain Cards off of everybody.'

'Hey!' yelled Garth, 'you said *two* cards before!'

Rio gave Garth a smile. 'So I did. My mistake. Two it is.'

'What's a Pohmin Gull?' asked Pip. 'Is that them?'

Garth followed Pip's gaze upwards where a flock of birds wheeled around looking for prey.

'Aye. The big ones are the Pohmin Gulls. Plenty of fat on them this time o' year. If he hits one, I'll gladly give over two cards and we'll eat it for supper.' Garth held up a card to show he meant it. 'Though I doubt he'll be able to even see them with all that hair covering his eyes.'

Garth was the unofficial bet-master aboard the Dart. He was almost the complete opposite of Rio, in that he was short and wiry and constantly craning his neck to look up at people. There was a cheerful mischief in his eyes though, and Pip took a liking to him. Garth also had a reputation for winning the most Captain Cards aboard the Dart, and he carried his stash with him at all times.

Blackbeard had explained to Pip and Balad on the first night of the voyage what the cards were. To a ship's captain, a gambling crew meant trouble. Too often Blackbeard had seen brawls break out over gold or rum, which is what sailors usually gambled with. A bored crew can be just as difficult though. As a compromise, Bob allowed gambling—as long as no money was used. If you wanted to make a bet, you had to use a Captain Card. These were special cards that Bob had paid an artist to make. They were the size of a normal playing card, but instead of a suit or a number, they all had a picture of the Black Dart on them. Each crew member was given ten at the beginning of each voyage and had to return his hand when the ship had reached its destination. Seeing as though the cards weren't worth anything, nobody ever fought over them, yet they helped make the bets interesting and this kept the crew amused.

Garth licked his lips as Rio knocked an arrow and aimed it high. The big First Mate squinted his right eye and picked out the fattest bird in the flock.

TWANG!

The arrow soared at the birds. Pip and the others watched it as it sailed high. It seemed to be heading for a direct hit, but the arrow lost pace too soon. It completed its arc well below the white bellies of the birds, turned and fell, and splashed down into the water.

'One!' the crew yelled as the arrow was swallowed by the sea.

Rio shook his head and fitted another arrow. This time he drew the string back with all his might until the bow creaked with the strain.

TWANGGGG!

Up the arrow shot, even higher than before! But this time, the wind came into play. It blew the arrow off course. Even so, Rio's shot still fell short of the juicy birds up above, and was lost to the waters below.

'Two!' chanted the crew.

'What if I climb up to the crow's nest?' Rio asked the crew. 'I can't get enough height from here.'

'I picked you 'cos you're the tallest,' Garth quipped. 'Take it from someone who knows, you don't need the extra height, by Latos. But if the crew say so, then it's fine by me.'

The crew cheered and agreed to the new terms of the bet, their stomachs aching for the taste of Pohmin Gull.

'You can only have two shots though!' Garth insisted. 'Otherwise the Captain will have our hides for wasting good arrows.'

Rio agreed and took two arrows in his teeth, slung his bow over his shoulder, and climbed the netting up to the crow's nest above.

The crew watched from the deck below as the First Mate shot both of his arrows at the birds above. The arrows now had the height, but none of the accuracy. Deflated and empty-handed, Rio climbed back down.

'It's no use,' he said when his feet landed on the deck. 'The wind is too strong up there. The ship rocks too much and the birds are all flying this way and that. It's impossible!'

'Pity,' said Garth. 'Pohmin Gulls are the best eating bird in the world.'

His shipmates all said aye in agreement, their stomachs growling with disappointment.

'I'm a good shot with the bow,' Pip offered. 'I could climb up there and hit one.'

Garth laughed through his nose. 'Ahhh, maybe you didn't understand, Prince Pip,' he said. 'The wind is strong and the boat is rocking. It'd be near impossible to hit a *still* target, let alone a flying bird.'

'Aye,' said Rio. 'I only took the bet for fun. There was no way I was going to actually hit anything. I was just hoping for a fluke.'

Pip looked at the birds overhead and judged the distance from the crow's nest to their white, succulent bellies.

'I could hit you a gull,' he said. 'I've hit harder targets in my time.'

The crew mates on the deck raised their eyebrows at each other or rolled their eyes.

Garth was about to say no, but the Prince looked hopeful and the birds looked delicious. He shrugged his shoulders and gave Pip an arrow. 'I guess it can't hurt to try.'

Rio nodded and offered his bow.

Pip took them and asked Garth, 'How many Gulls would it take to feed the crew?'

'Ahhh, about seven, I should think. If we all wanted to be full,' he replied. 'Why?'

Pip looked around at the crew and gave them a broad grin. 'Then I best have six more arrows,' he said.

17

THE GULL FEAST

Amid the singing and drinking and sailors cheering, Pip chewed his first mouthful of Pohmin Gull and decided Garth was right: it was the best tasting bird that had ever taken to the skies. The sun had long left the heavens and the crew were feasting in the mess on Pip's delicious game. He was sitting at a long table with Balad on one side of him and Rio on the other. Blackbeard was at the head of the table and Rio was recounting Pip's efforts with the bow.

'He was amazing, Captain,' Rio said. 'None of us believed him when he said he'd get us a bird.' He made an apologetic face to Pip. 'Sorry, Prince. But we thought we'd give him a shot anyway. Next thing, he asks for more arrows. Well Garth didn't want to refuse him, did you Garth?'

'Who am I to refuse a royal request?' Garth smirked. 'Though I thought you might take the arrows out of me pay, Captain.'

'By Latos, I would have,' said Bob with a laugh.

'So we give him the arrows and he climbs up the nets like he's been doing it all his life. He gets in the nest and quick as you can think, down fall seven Gulls, arrows sticking plum through their tasty little hearts.' Rio turned to face the Prince. 'How did you do it? I was up there and I know how hard it would have been to hit just one bird. But seven? Latos, can everyone shoot like you in Nalib?'

'No,' Balad answered for Pip. 'The Prince of the Sands is unique in that way. Ever since he was old enough to walk he has had perfect aim. I remember a time when he was eight and we had an invasion of rats in the palace. The Prince decided to use his toy sling on any rats he could spy. After two weeks, all the rats were dead. If he wants to hit it, he will. Same with knives, darts, and as you saw, arrows. That is why we take him hunting all the time. We know we'll never go hungry with the Honoured One.'

Blackbeard gave his royal guest an appraising look. 'What's your secret then, Prince? Do you have magic in those bandages around your arms?'

By now the entire crew was listening to their conversation. Pip blushed and looked down to his forearms. 'No, no magic here.'

'The bandages are a gift from The Scourge of Aldallah,' Balad boasted. 'The Prince fought a dragon near Nalib, and now he wears the scars to prove it.'

'The Silver Scourge?' asked Blackbeard.

'You have heard of him?'

'Yes, Balad, I have. You mean to tell me that *you* fought a *dragon*?'

Pip nodded.

'Not only did he fight it, but he beat it! Sent an arrow right into its face!'

'You killed the Silver Scourge?' asked Blackbeard, half rising in his seat.

'No, Bob. I only chased it away. I wish I'd killed it.'

'Still...' Blackbeard let out a slow breath and sat back down. 'I heard about this silver dragon. It roasted a whole city, didn't it?'

'Aldallah,' answered Pip. 'Some of my father's people saw it happen. They're lucky to still be alive.' He thought of Jumba and everyone at home and missed them suddenly. 'That's why we're aboard your good ship, Captain. Balad and I are going to Albion to find weapons, or people, to fight the dragon.'

'Why Albion?' asked Rio.

'Didn't they have a war with the dragons long ago? Didn't they drive them all away?'

'They did,' said Bob. 'Long before I was born. But you think they might have some secrets that will help you defeat it once and for all?'

'Yes,' said Pip. 'The Scourge will come back eventually. And when he does, we need to have something to fight back with. Something powerful. Otherwise my home will be a burnt-out shell like Aldallah, and I will be a Prince without a home.'

Pip's words had a sobering effect on the crew. Unsure of what to say, everyone dipped into silence, and so it fell to the ship's best singer to lighten the mood. Drake was one of the youngest members aboard the Dart, but he was the most popular and not just because of his voice. Drake had a way of turning a foul mood into a pleasant one, and he decided that the feast needed him. From under his seat he produced a tambourine and pounded a beat to get everyone's attention. The rest of the crew brightened straight away as Drake began to give the table an impromptu shanty. He sang:

Heave Ho, and off we go,
I'd die for a taste of that Pohmin Gull.
A juicier bird never took to the sky,
Oh I wish they'd never learned to fly!

Heave Ho, and off we go,
I'd die for a taste of that Pohmin Gull.
But we can eat only their shadows,
Until they meet Prince Pip's arrows!

Heave Ho, and off we go,
I'd die for a taste of that Pohmin Gull.
Each arrow could hit the eye of a bull,
So tonight I bunk with my belly full!

Drake's mates laughed at the song and clapped the young man for his cleverness. He had reminded them of the wonderful food on their plates, and so they returned their attention to the feast that the cook and his helpers had made for them. Of course there was the Pohmin Gull, enough meat for everyone, but the cook had also boiled some vegetables, baked some bread and uncorked some of the ship's wine. Soon the sounds of scraping knives and clattering plates filled the air again. With the superb food in front of them, and Drake's song still in their ears, the mood became jolly again. Garth made everyone take silly bets and somehow ended up with even more Captain Cards, and Blackbeard told some stories of life aboard Night Jewell under Captain Fogharty. At the end of the meal, Drake gave them another song. This time it was a slow and wistful shanty that had a soothing effect on the sailors, and soon after it was finished, each member aboard the Dart went to his bunk with a full stomach and smile on his face. Only Blackbeard, Pip and Balad were left at the table.

'You know,' said Bob, breaking the empty silence that remained, 'the only things I ever heard about the Silver Scourge seemed too strange to be true. I mean, a silver dragon that can burn a whole city with just its breath? Is that really what happened?'

'No,' Pip answered, 'not with its breath. Shadowclaw can wield magic. It can burn or freeze, push or pull, smash or throw. It doesn't even have to lift a claw. It uses magic to do all of its bidding.'

'Magic, you say?' said Bob, leaning in a little closer. 'Real magic?'

'Very real,' said Balad.

'The type of magic that can make a person invisible, say?'

'That's exactly it!' said Balad. 'Shadowclaw makes himself unseen, then he appears right out of the air. He did that to us before we left Nalib; the day it left the Prince in those bandages!'

Blackbeard thought for a moment and then took a long drink of ale from his mug. When he finished, he wiped his mouth with his sleeve and chuckled to himself. The longer he chuckled the louder he became, and soon the laughter grew until Bob's body shook and the mess echoed with it. Pip noticed there was a faraway look in the captain's eyes, and even though Bob was still laughing, the noise of it didn't sound happy.

Balad looked at his Prince, then back to the captain.

'What is the joke, Bob?' the royal guard asked. 'What is funny? Maybe you have had too much ale?'

Blackbeard let his chuckles die down, shook his head and gave a dismissive wave with his hand. 'No, that's not it. I got an idea. A perfect idea. Some puzzle pieces just matched up in my brain, and when that happens, I can solve all our problems and it makes me happy.' He put an arm around each of his guests, pulled them in close and lowered his voice. 'What you have is a dragon that can do magic, you say?'

Balad and Pip nodded.

'And you're going to Albion to find an army?'

'That is our plan. And our only hope.'

'Well you don't need an army, mates.'

'We don't?'

'No. See, the only way you can fight magic, is with more magic.'

Balad considered this. 'That makes sense. *Use a thief to catch a thief,* as my mother would say. What an excellent idea! And do you know where we can find magic in Albion?' he asked.

Blackbeard gave another little chuckle and his eyes shone. 'That I do, me mates. That I do.'

18

THE GRITBOLES

'Maybe we should go and check on them?' Wendy suggested as she flicked the summer flies with her tail. 'They might be sick and need your help?'

Mollie scoffed. 'Lovesick, you mean.' She patted the spot on the horse's cheek and softened her voice. 'I'm sure they'll call for us soon. We need to give them time, Wendy. Besides, I know you're dying to see Bramble.'

'I am,' Wendy admitted theatrically. 'I don't see why *he* has to stay? Terry and Esmae need their privacy, not a horse! He should come here and keep us company. Maybe I'll just trot on over and suggest it. There's room in the barn now that Whitestaff's gone.'

At the sound of the dragon's name, Mollie's insides sagged. It had been lonely enough without her mother around, and now that the dragon had left too, she only had Wendy for company. The cottage felt empty and hollow. Every now and then she'd think of something to tell her mother, then remember mid-breath that it was no use calling: her mother wasn't there. She felt herself about to give in to Wendy's demands. Another horse would be nice for company...

Suddenly, Wendy's ears went stiff and her neck tensed.

'I can hear the cart!' she said in an excited whisper. 'I can hear his hooves!'

Mollie hugged her horse and gave a squeal of delight. 'I'll put the kettle on!' She dashed inside the cottage and set the table and started a fire in the little iron stove on which to boil the water. She then ran outside just in time to see Terry and her mother riding towards them, side by side, in Terry's little cart. Bramble pulled them steadily along, but Mollie could see he was going a little faster than he normally would. They pulled up outside the cottage and hopped off the cart and into Mollie's waiting arms.

'Greetings Mr and Mrs Gritbole,' she said with a smile. 'How is the old married couple on this fine day?'

Esmae laughed at her daughter. 'Cheeky! We couldn't be any better now that we're here with you. How have you been? I've worried about you this whole time!'

'I hope that's not true,' Mollie said. 'Your mind was meant to be on other things! Like your new husband for instance.'

Esmae began to blush. 'Well he has managed to distract me a few times.'

Terry blushed also and made himself busy unfastening Bramble from his cart, unable to look mother or daughter in the eye. As soon as Bramble was free, the horse nuzzled Wendy and the two galloped off—chasing each other and neighing with joy. Mollie took her mother and step-father inside, and soon they were seated and sipping freshly-brewed tea.

'You didn't really worry about me, did you, Esmae?' Mollie asked.

'Of course I did,' Esmae replied.

'She did,' Terry agreed. 'She'd ask me five times a day if I thought yer was fine. I told her it's not Mollie yer have to worry about. Save yer sympathy for the poor blighter that gets in her way.'

Mollie gave Terry a knowing smile. Mr Gritbole had certainly grown on her since that night at the Gibbon Fair, and now that he had the affection of Esmae, he always looked clean and smelled of soap. But as her mother had shown her, it wasn't a person's looks that revealed their character: it was their actions. Terry had been the only person in Danmurk Shire to ignore gossip and superstition and offer the 'witches' a ride in his cart. He had earned Mollie's respect that night, and had maintained it since.

'You needn't have worried, but I am glad you came when you did. Whitestaff had to go back in a hurry and I've been anxious about him.'

'Why? I thought he was going to stay for a while longer yet.'

Mollie shrugged her shoulders. 'I'm not sure. He was in a panic when Wendy and I came back from the Leechs'. Something about a feeling he had? His duty as a Kai'dahl? To be honest, it's all a bit of a blur now. It happened so suddenly.'

'That's no good,' Esmae said, taking her daughter's hand. 'Wait a minute. What were you doing at the Leech place?'

Mollie explained to the newlyweds her new plan of making potions to cure ailments. She told them about Margaret Leech and how sick she was and how she'd used the potions to make her well again.

'I know you think it's a bad idea, but they're going to call us witches no matter what we do, Esmae. This way we can show them our 'magic' is just a few herbs and crushed berries. Maybe we can avoid the pitchforks?'

Esmae was silent for a while, her brow furrowed. Presently she looked to her husband and said, 'That does explain a few things, doesn't it?'

Terry nodded. 'The flowers yer mean?'

'Yes. And not only that. All the smiles and waves we've been getting.'

'I told yer it wasn't just me.'

'What are you talking about?' Mollie asked.

Esmae shook her head as if to clear it. 'It's nothing really, Mollie. It's just that the people of Danmurk Shire have been especially nice to me lately. I thought it was just because of Terry's influence.'

'And I kept telling yer that no one ever leaves flowers at me door. Or waves and tells me to have a good morning.'

'Then it's working!' Mollie declared.

'Maybe so,' Esmae agreed. 'The Leechs' don't have much, but they have a lot of mouths.'

'Mouths that could say a lot of nice things about us to an awful lot of people,' Mollie added. 'That was the whole plan. I wanted to spread another kind of rumour about the witches of Danmurk. A good rumour this time. And do a little good along the way.' She gave her mother a brilliant smile.

'Well this calls for a real celebration,' Esmae said, returning her daughter's smile. 'Terry, would you mind using that bow of yours and catching us something tasty? Mollie and I will stay here and prepare a small feast.'

Terry's face lit up. 'Since I married you, Esmae, I haven't eaten so often or so well. I shall be delighted—nay, honoured to catch us a juicy morsel or two.' He marched outside to get his quiver and bow and set out into the woods.

'I love it when he pretends to be a gentleman,' Esmae laughed. She waited a few moments and got up, poked her head outside and looked around.

'What are you doing?' Mollie asked.

'Making sure he's gone. I needed to get rid of him for a bit,' Esmae replied in a whisper and sat back at the table.

Mollie was shocked. 'What do you mean? Isn't everything going well?'

'Shh, of course it is. I just need to tell you something and I don't want Terry to hear.'

Mollie placed her cup on its saucer and leaned closer to her mother.

'What is it?' she whispered back. 'Tell me.'

'It's your father,' Esmae blurted. 'Merlin!'

Mollie felt the blood drain from her face. She hadn't thought about her absent father in a long time. 'What about him, mother?'

Esmae's face crumpled and she bit her bottom lip before she answered. 'How do I say this Mollie? The other night when I was with Terry I looked out the window and thought I saw Merlin looking in. Mollie, I think your father has come back!'

19

IN THE TUNNEL

Deep inside the spire of the King's Court, the excavation of a secret tunnel had been completed with great haste. It began at the side of the Gra'dahl section of the Court and spiralled down under the Chambers, finishing roughly in the middle of the Sorteyan fog. The tunnel was wide enough for Whitestaff and Nap to stand face-to-face in the gloom, though the Kai'dahl did have to stoop to avoid scraping his head on the roof.

'What's the catch? You going to feed me to the Nazoor?'

'Nothing like that, Nap. I just think it would be better if you were with us,' Whitestaff said. He put a heavy paw on the Re'dahl's wiry shoulder and looked him in the eye. 'I know that since I got here we've been on the wrong side of each other. But we're at war, Nap. We could lose everything. Our homes have probably already been destroyed and that's just the beginning. This is bigger than me being King and you not liking it, or whatever your problem is.'

'You're doing it now,' Nap hissed.

'Doing what?'

'My problem! Taking charge. Owning everyone. Look around you. This tunnel was built because you snapped your claws. I hate it how you can just appear out of nowhere and have all the things the rest of us have to work for. Being allowed in the Tournament, having your own Council, having everyone love you and cheer for you. It's not fair. I had to *work* for my place. My father had to *work* to be the King. He didn't just expect it. It wasn't just handed to him because of his colour!'

'And you don't think I've worked?' Whitestaff asked.

There was silence in the narrow corridor. Because every Palal dragon was in the Court, it was hard to get any privacy. After the tunnel had been dug, Whitestaff sent for Nap so that they could do an inspection and go over the plan. Really, Whitestaff just wanted to get Nap alone so they could talk openly. Susset had lit the tunnel with glowing orbs of magic, and the light of them swam slowly around the two dragons.

'How have you worked?' Nap spat.

'Where do I start?' Whitestaff replied. 'I lost both parents, I've been separated from my kind for most of my life, I've spent years in a cage without even knowing who or what I was. Then I *fought* to get *here*. When I arrived I *fought* to win the Tournament!' Whitestaff paused and took a deep breath. 'Can't you see, Nap? My whole life has been a fight. And now I'm home at last, only to find that I have to fight again! And I'll do it, Nap. I'll fight every last Wyvern that wants to take my home and my fellow Palal away from me. I've always fought in one way or another. I just don't want to fight with *you*.'

After a long pause, Nap looked to the ground and nodded. 'I'll come with you,' he said. 'Only to make sure Luzahmin is safe.'

'Great. I'll get the others and tell them we're ready.' Whitestaff made his way past Nap and back through the tunnel towards the Court. He was greeted by Umdir at the tunnel's entrance. The Gra'dahl wanted to know if Whitestaff approved of the tunnel.

'Perfect,' Whitestaff assured him. 'Exactly what I had in mind.'

The green dragon looked pleased with this and he pointed his claw to the newly constructed war room. 'They're waiting for you in there.'

Whitestaff gave him a nod and entered the room. Susset and Cracone were hunched over the three-dimensional map in the middle of the room and were deep in conversation. Armay and Graggy walked over to their friend.

'How did it go?' Graggy asked. 'Is he coming or was he too proud?'

'He's coming,' Whitestaff said. 'More for Luz than for me. But I hope I gave him something to think about.'

'What did you say?' asked Armay.

Whitestaff shrugged. 'I told him I want us to get along, more or less.'

'I don't know what his problem is,' said Armay.

'I do,' said Whitestaff. 'I just need to get him to see things from my point of view.'

'Impossible,' said Graggy. 'He only sees what he wants to see.'

The three made their way over to Cracone and Susset.

'Are we ready? Susset asked.

'This is who you've chosen?' Cracone asked, looking Graggy and Armay over.

'Almost,' said Whitestaff as Nap entered the room and made his way over to the group. 'I also asked your son to join us, Your Majesty. We may be in need of that sharp tail of his if things get heated.'

'Excellent,' said the king, clearly chuffed. 'No better Re'dahl in a scrap than this one. Fighting since he was a Lili'dahl.'

Whitestaff gave Nap a wink. 'That makes two of us.'

Susset put her hood over her head and cracked her knuckles. 'I'm not sure I can bend the light around so many all at once. I'll need you to stay together. If you drift away from the group, then you may be out of range for the spell. Do you understand?'

The dragons nodded and told her they were ready. They arranged themselves into a tight bunch so Susset could practise her sorcery.

Susset closed her eyes and wove her magic. Whitestaff watched as he and his companions became shielded in a gigantic bubble. From inside, the room around them looked hazy, as though it were behind some poorly made glass.

At that moment, Umdir walked in. His eyes searched for the dragons he knew to be in the room, but of course he couldn't see them. Behind the veil of magic, Nap smiled at Umdir's confusion.

Umdir cleared his throat. 'Your Majesty? he said, looking directly at Cracone. 'Where are the others?'

'Blast it!' said Cracone. 'How come you can see me?'

The old Gra'dahl's expression became even more perplexed. 'Because you're standing right in front of me, of course. Where did the others go? I only just watched Nap walk in.'

Cracone turned to Susset. 'Why can he see me and not you lot?'

Susset let go of the spell and the magical wall disappeared. Umdir's face brightened as the other Palal came into view.

'Of course!' said the old Gra'dahl. 'The plan to go invisible! Well done, Susset.'

'Not really, Umdir,' Cracone barked. 'You could see me!' He turned back to the sorceress. 'Why didn't you do your trick with me too?'

'I thought I did,' said Susset. 'Oh, wait.' She marched over to the Re'dahl king and pointed to his chest. 'The Royal Medallion. You're wearing it.'

'So?' said Cracone, looking down at his chest.

The medallion was a disc on a heavy gold chain. On the disc was the outline of a rearing silver dragon. Around the silver dragon were strange markings that looked like they belonged to some ancient and forgotten language.

'So?' Susset replied, 'Don't you remember that the wearer of this can't be touched by magic? That's how Merlin made it. My spell won't work on you as long as you wear it.'

Cracone took the medallion from around his neck. 'Of course,' he said. He handed the treasure to Umdir. 'Keep this safe for me. Susset, let's try again.'

Once more the Palal bunched up together and were encased in Susset's magical bubble.

'Can you see any of us this time?' Susset called out to Umdir.

'No,' the Gra'dahl replied. 'It works perfectly. Though you do sound very far away.'

The sorceress let the spell fall again, revealing the dragons once more to Umdir's eyes. 'Excellent. It traps noise a bit too it seems. That could be very useful.'

The others agreed and congratulated Susset on her abilities.

'Right then,' said Cracone. 'Let's get this started.' He gestured to Whitestaff to lead the way, then followed the golden dragon down through the tunnel with the others.

Nap hesitated at first and was about to protest at Whitestaff being at the front, but something made him stop. Nobody seemed to be ready to listen to him anyway, so instead he followed the rest of them without complaint. By the time they had reached the tunnel exit, Whitestaff had gone over the plan one more time and reminded them to fly together, no matter what.

'I want to find Mezelga as quickly and quietly as possible,' he told them. 'Then, I want to finish her and her madness. I want us to end this war without another drop of Palal blood being spilled.' Nap cheered along with the others at that remark. The red dragon was so thrilled at having his own part in the plan to end the war, and so eager to rescue Luzahmin, that his complaint about a Kai'dahl taking the lead was all but forgotten.

20

NOW YOU DON'T

The sky was turning a dull purple as the Sorteyan sun sank below the spires. From inside Susset's bubble, the world looked blurred and murky. Not only did the spell keep them hidden from sight, Whitestaff noticed it kept the wind from racing over his scales too. It was like being in a void and he didn't like it at all. The five dragons flew in a tight formation, with the sorceress riding on Whitestaff's broad back. None of them spoke above a whisper.

Soon enough, the towering spire of Cracone loomed in front of them; the dugout mouth seemed open wide in pain.

'What have they done to the place? They've made the entrance bigger,' said Nap as they flew closer. 'They've dug it all out. Why?'

'Hold it! Slow down,' Whitestaff hissed to the others. 'Look at them!'

Without warning, an army of Nazoor burst from Cracone's old dugout, taking to the sky like bats flying out of a cave at twilight.

Their horrid screeching filled the air, and the sound of their beating wings was like a million trees thrashing in a hurricane.

'Where are they going?' Nap asked. 'Oh, no. They're coming this way!'

The Palal watched while the massive flock of Nazoor came rushing at them—a thick, dark cloud of pointed teeth and angry claws.

'Down,' shouted Cracone. 'Fly down!'

The small party dipped down to avoid colliding with the Nazoor.

'How can they see us?' the King demanded.

'They can't,' yelled Susset over the noise. 'Look!'

Everyone looked up to see the Nazoor horde fly straight over their heads and onward, completely unaware of the Palal's existence.

'You're right. They didn't see us. Otherwise we'd have been torn to shreds,' said Whitestaff.

'So many of them,' said Nap, his jaw agape. 'Just so many.'

'Too many,' agreed Graggy as they watched the thick column of Nazoor pass. 'Where did they all come from?'

'And where are they going now?' said Cracone.

'Why don't we ask them?' said Whitestaff pointing back to the dugout.

At the dugout entrance, Whitestaff spotted a group of remaining Nazoor. The mini-dragons stood and watched as the army headed out, clearly satisfied with how the war was progressing.

The Palal waited until they were sure the army had left, then flew up to Cracone's dugout and hovered at the entrance, just in front of the ten Nazoor that stood in the mouth. They were close enough to hear them speak.

'Excellent,' one of the Nazoor said, completely unaware of the five dragons that were flying just in front of his beak. 'We shall have this planet all to ourselves soon.'

'Soon, Tithe,' agreed another. 'Glory to the name of Mezelga.'

'Queen Mezelga!' chorused the other dragons.

'Tell us where she is!' growled Cracone under his breath. 'Then we'll see who owns this planet!'

Whitestaff raised his paw at Cracone for silence as the Wyvern were joined by two more dragons, one of which was Audgar!

'Audgar,' said the Nazoor who had spoken first. 'Excellent work in there. Pity you'll forget your good service in about five seconds.' The other dragons hissed in laughter.

The Nazoor that had arrived with Audgar spoke. 'Now that we have what we want from the prisoners, Tithe, what do we do with them?'

Whitestaff looked back to the first Nazoor. 'The one they call 'Tithe' seems to be in charge,' he whispered to Graggy. 'He's the one we need to question.'

'Kill them,' Tithe replied lightly. 'Get Audgar to do it if you wish. He seems to enjoy killing Palal. I'm sure if he had the brains to speak he'd tell us as much.' He began to hiss at his own joke.

Palal? Whitestaff thought. *They must have Luzahmin and the others.* He turned to his team and was about to tell them to get ready to fight, but before he had a chance to speak, Nap shot forward out of the invisibility spell and headed straight at Audgar.

'No one touches Luzahmin!' the Re'dahl screamed as he hurled into the Alpos.

Nap slammed into Audgar and sent him crashing against the dugout wall.

The other Nazoor were stunned for a few moments until Tithe snapped at them. 'Don't stare! Kill him!' he ordered.

The Nazoor hissed and sprang onto Nap, biting and clawing at his blood-red scales. Whitestaff flew forward to help, but Cracone beat him to it. The old king swooped down on the Nazoor from above. He crunched one in his jaws while his tail bashed two Nazoor aside with one blow. He caught another by the tail and swung it around, then let it go to send it smacking into Audgar, who had just picked himself up off the floor. Whitestaff couldn't believe what he was seeing! Cracone was like a red whirlwind of terror!

At the sound of the fight, ten more Nazoor came flapping from deeper inside the dugout to join in the fray. Whitestaff, Armay and Graggy shot forward and met the newcomers with claws, tail and teeth. Whitestaff used his massive frame to gather three enemies in his front legs and crush them in a binding hug. Graggy used his speed to charge from one to the other, knocking them this way and that with his skull or his shoulder. Armay's fighting style was much smoother. She kept perfect balance as she struck out with her tail and

125

claws. Some of the Nazoor targeted her because she was blue. This was a mistake, for the Bo'dahl taught them not to judge a Palal by its colour. Her precise tail-whips and claw-slaps made sure it was the last lesson they would ever learn.

After a few ferocious minutes, the melee was all but over. Only Audgar and Tithe remained of the Nazoor, the rest were a crumpled heap on the floor—their dragon essence drifting out of their bodies and into the gloomy sky.

Armay and Graggy seized Tithe, pinning him to the floor by his wings, but Audgar refused to yield. He didn't seem to understand that the fight was over. The mighty Alpos charged at Nap, who was still trying to untangle himself from some lifeless Nazoor. Audgar leapt at Nap with his claws outstretched.

'Watch out!' Whitestaff called.

Nap turned around a moment too late, and Audgar's claws caught him right in the face. Nap yowled in pain and brought his front claws up to defend himself. At the same time, Susset conjured a Magic Missile and hurled it at the Alpos, who was driven hard off Nap as the energy smacked into him from the side. The powerful blast sent Audgar crashing into the dugout wall again, in the same spot he'd bashed into before. Only this time, he did not get up.

Cracone rushed over to his son, who was holding his two front paws over his left eye.

'Nap. Show me your face, son. Did his claws get you?' Nap winced in pain as his father gently took his paws from his face. 'Hmmmm,' said Cracone. 'Bad. Susset, if you could?'

Susset glided over next to the king and inspected Nap's wound. The scales around Nap's eye had swollen, and three deep cuts could be seen where Audgar had scratched at the Re'dahl's eye. She lifted the lid of the eye and prodded it with care. After a few moments she said, 'I can close the injury, Your Majesty, but the eye won't see the light again.'

Cracone grunted. 'Latos! I thought as much. Like father, like son, eh Nap?' His voice was heavy.

Nap gave a weak smile, his eyes still closed. 'I learnt from the best.'

'You need to stay still while I work some magic,' Susset said to him. 'This may not be a pleasant sensation.'

Whitestaff left Susset and Cracone to work on Nap and marched over to the helpless Tithe.

'Tithe,' he said. 'You have some of my dragons. You need to take me to them now, or I'll tear your wings off and throw you out of this dugout, where, after a few thousand feet of falling, you'll hit the ground head first. The choice is yours.'

Tithe looked into Whitestaff's eyes and saw he wasn't joking. His black forked tongue squirmed in his beak as he imagined crashing into the dreaded ground with no wings to save him. For a Nazoor, it would be the worst death possible.

Tithe lifted a claw and pointed to a tunnel on his right. 'They're through there,' he said. 'I'll take you straight to them.'

21

THE RESCUE

Graggy and Armay held one of Tithe's wings each as the Nazoor led them through a twisted corridor and down into a newly dug tunnel. Whitestaff followed behind, his claws ready to swipe in case Tithe had any ideas of escape. The change to Cracone's dugout that they witnessed on the outside was nothing compared to the complete reconstruction that had taken place inside. Everything had been hollowed out and tunnelled so that the spire could house the entire Nazoor army. Furniture had been removed or smashed and wall-hangings had been torn down. There was nothing left to suggest that the Palal King and his son had ever lived within. As they walked further down into the dark passage, Whitestaff could hear a dragon sobbing. He pushed past the others and bolted towards the sound.

'Luzahmin!' he called. 'Is that you?'

His question was answered moments later as the tunnel gave way to a massive circular chamber. Tied to the wall were three Palal and two Nazoor—all had their legs and wings bound. In the middle of the chamber was a fire that gave off no heat or smoke, and somewhere in the back of his mind, Whitestaff knew that Olfar's dugout had been looted and desecrated too. The Nazoor had taken the only place the Kai'dahl had ever really felt at home.

He rushed over to his cousin and ripped through her bindings. When she was free, the slender Bo'dahl hugged her cousin tight and then turned to help the Palal next to her. After being untied, Kurt and Sophiena collapsed into a hug of their own, nuzzling each other and crying.

'What happened here, Luz?' Whitestaff asked.

'It was terrible,' she cried. 'They just kept scratching him until we told them.'

'Scratching who? Told them what? Start at the beginning.'

'We don't have time,' Luzahmin shouted as tears rolled off her face. 'They caught the three of us and brought us here and tied us up. They wanted to know where the other Palal were and I wouldn't tell them so they started scratching Kurt until I couldn't take it anymore and I told them everything!'

Whitestaff looked over to Kurt and could see the long dark scratches on his scales. At that moment, Nap, Cracone and Susset entered the chamber. Luzahmin moaned and ran over to Nap, her own pain forgotten. She held his face in her front paws and examined his wounds.

'What have they done to you?' she asked.

'Nothing compared to what I did to them, Luz. It's all right.'

'No it isn't,' Luzahmin insisted. 'Your eye is...'

At that moment Cracone intervened. 'Here,' he said to his son, taking off his own ruby eyepatch. 'It's time I passed it on anyway—now that you've earned it.'

The scales under Cracone's eyepatch were dark and twisted. Without the patch, Cracone looked even more ferocious, and Whitestaff, who had never seen the Re'dahl King without the ruby slab covering his bad eye, was tempted to ask him to put it back on. However, Nap beamed as he took his father's patch and placed it over his own newly-lost eye.

'Susset has fixed most of it up, Luz. But the eye itself is lost.' He gave Luzahmin a forced smile. 'Do I look that bad?'

Luzahmin shook her head. 'You'll never look bad to me!'

The two hugged tightly and curled their tails around each other.

Whitestaff allowed them a minute and then interrupted. 'Luzahmin,' he said softly. 'You were telling me what happened here. Why were they hurting Kurt?'

The Bo'dahl released Nap quickly and she turned to face the others. 'That's right,' she said. 'You all have to leave now! You have to get to the court before the Nazoor do.'

'The Court?' Armay said. 'We just came from there.'

'And now you have to go back,' said Luzahmin. 'They know where we are. They're going to start digging through. I had to tell them or they were going to kill Kurt. I'm sorry but we have to go!'

Whitestaff nodded in agreement. 'Susset, you take all these dragons back with you. Kurt, will you be able to fly?'

The wounded dragon stretched his wings and gave a nod.

'What about these two?' Whitestaff pointed a claw at the two Nazoor dragons who were still tied up.

'I don't know about them,' Luzahmin said. 'They were like that when we got here.'

'Fine. I want to talk to them,' Whitestaff strode over to the helpless Wyvern and untied their beaks. 'Why have they done this to you? Who are you and why are you here?'

As soon as the rope was gone, the smaller of the two Wyvern took in a huge gulp of air and thanked his Palal rescuers through ragged breaths. 'You have no idea what has been going on in here,' he told them as he loosened the bindings around his wings. 'My name is Kigg and I'm with the Party for Peace. I was spying for Cross with Xenos here,' with his head he indicated the Nazoor tied up next to him, 'but Tithe found out.'

'Cross, you say? Where is he now?'

'The whole party is in Mezelga's dungeon,' Tithe answered for him. 'Mezelga's new law. Any dragon talking about or supporting peace will be incarcerated. For life.'

'How many are there in the Party?' Whitestaff asked, addressing his question to Tithe.

'Just under a hundred,' he said. 'But it doesn't matter. They've all been caught and sent to the dungeon and no one lives long there.'

'Disgusting,' Kigg said. 'We could have found another way, Tithe. We don't need war!'

'No we couldn't,' Tithe snapped though his beak. 'War *is* Peace, Kigg. If we wipe out the Palal with this war, we will have exactly what you and your Party want. A peaceful Sorteya. No fighting. No Tournaments. Just us. It is Queen Mezelga's vision and we are all part of it.'

'Not all of us,' said Xenos.

Tithe laughed and looked at Cracone. 'It doesn't matter. It's too late. The army is on its way to your Court and this will soon be done.'

'Then we have to leave now,' said Susset. 'Maybe I can create some sort of magical barrier around the Court? I might be able to hold them off for a while?'

'Good idea,' said Whitestaff. 'Susset, you make these dragons invisible and take them with you to the Court. Do what you can to keep the Nazoor from digging in.' The Kai'dahl began to untie the rest of the ropes that bound Xenos, the larger of the captured Wyvern.

'Aren't you coming?' she asked.

'Not right away. I'm taking these two to Mezelga's dungeon. When I get there I'll free Cross and his Party.'

Tithe laughed again. 'You'll never be able to rescue them,' he said. 'Some of our army stayed back to protect the Queen, should you get any ideas of emulating your late father...'

Whitestaff growled to himself in frustration. The Nazoor had thought of his plan before *he* had. Taking out the Queen would have meant a quick victory to the Palal, but the Nazoor accounted for this manoeuvre and were one step ahead. At that instant he recalled a conversation he'd had with Olfar long ago about the Nazoor. "Never underestimate their minds either," Olfar had told him when he'd met Cross. "Sometimes I think they are much smarter than us." *You hit the nail on the head, right enough, Olfar,* Whitestaff thought to himself. *They've thought this whole thing through and they already have us on the run.*

Tithe's laughter made Whitestaff growl to himself again. Only this time the growl kept going after the Kai'dahl had stopped. He looked to see where the noise was coming from. The other dragons were looking too; their eyes all fell on Sophiena at the same time. The Bo'dahl was crouched down low, her teeth were bared and her sights locked onto Tithe.

The Nazoor faced her—his black eyes gave nothing away, but Whitestaff thought he saw a flicker of fear spark in those dark pools.

'He's the one who hurt Kurt!' Sophiena said.

'Not me,' said Tithe. 'It was Audgar and Friy.'

'You told them to!' With that, Sophiena leapt at the Nazoor. She hit him so hard that he was yanked out of Armay and Graggy's paws. The Bo'dahl trampled Tithe into the ground and finished him off quickly with a snap of her jaws before any of the Palal could react. Kurt dashed over to Sophiena and pulled her off the crumpled Nazoor. He tried to soothe her with some whispered words, but the Bo'dahl was trembling with rage.

'Take them out now,' Whitestaff said to Susset.

The sorceress nodded, knowing that Kigg and Xenos might be next if Sophiena wasn't made to leave in a hurry.

'I'm going with you, Whitestaff,' said Cracone. 'If they still have some numbers on their side of the Dire, you're going to need my claws.'

'I'm coming as well,' said Nap.

'Not with your eye,' Whitestaff said.

'I still have *one*,' said Nap, 'and one is all I need. Besides, it's not up to you.' He turned to Cracone. 'I'd like to come, father.'

'And come you shall,' said Cracone, throwing a front leg around his son's shoulders.

They both looked at Whitestaff, daring him to disagree.

'Well, I suppose between the both of you, you have a perfect pair of eyes,' he said. Then he turned to Graggy and Armay. 'Stay below the clouds. Even though you're invisible, you must be cautious. Get everyone in the Court ready to fight. Susset, try and keep them out for as long as you can. I have a plan.'

They all agreed to the Kai'dahl's wishes and bade him farewell.

'Come back to me in one piece,' said Armay as she nuzzled his chest.

'I always do,' said Whitestaff.

Susset cast her bubble of invisibility and set off with Kurt, Sophiena, Luzahmin, Armay and Graggy. Only Whitestaff, Kigg, Xenos, and Cracone and his son remained.

The gold dragon turned to the two captured Nazoor. 'Kigg, I need a very direct answer from you. Do you know where the Queen is? Can you take us to her?'

Kigg shook his head. 'They knew you would do this,' he said. 'They knew you'd try and find her, so she had herself hidden away. No one knows where she is. But wherever she is hiding, she'll have many guards. More than you can kill with such a small number.'

'Thank you,' said Whitestaff. 'I would do the same in her position. Next question. If I free Cross and the Party for Peace, will they fight with me?'

Kigg closed his eyes and thought. 'Fighting is what we've tried to avoid, Whitestaff.'

'I know, but you have to choose a side. If you don't, Cross's Party, and everyone in it, is finished. Do you think Cross will understand this and tell his Party to fight?'

Kigg nodded. 'It's true what you say. I can see that perfectly. We either have to fight now or die from Mezelga's claw anyway. But only the leader of the Party could ask them to fight, and it isn't really Cross's Party at all.'

'I thought he was the leader?' said Cracone. 'He's the one who we speak to. He's the one that calls himself the leader.'

'That's what we wanted you to think,' said Kigg. 'That's what we wanted Mezelga to think too. We're peaceful, but we're not stupid. We knew the day might come when Mezelga wanted to silence us, so we kept the true leader a secret.'

'Well if it isn't Cross, who is it?' Cracone asked, clearly perplexed.

'You just rescued him,' said Kigg, pointing at Xenos.

22

THE STORY OF TYSH

After almost two weeks of sailing aboard the Black Dart, Prince Pip Ael of Nalib was glad that his journey was nearly at its end. He'd gotten on well with Bob's crew and had proved to be a popular passenger since he'd filled their grateful stomachs with Pohmin Gull. But one or two strange things had happened since leaving Hulum, and Pip began to feel that the sooner he had the dirt of Albion under his feet, the better.

Every now and then, a whale would come close to the ship and inspect the Dart out of animal curiosity. The first time this happened, Pip nearly jumped out of his skin. He was strolling on the main deck and stuck his head over the bulwarks to watch the spray of the sea as the bow cut through the water. Suddenly, a massive dark shape slid out from under the ship. Pip was horrified as the tremendous beast turned white as it rolled on its stomach and burst through the surface of the sea.

'Monster!' he had called in alarm. 'The kraken is on us!'

Rio sprinted to the starboard side and brushed his hair out of his face so he could look to where Pip was pointing.

'No, Prince,' he said with relief. 'Just a whale. Coming to give us a little show and keep us company, by the looks.'

'Whale?' said the Prince, trying to recall the lessons that Pukami had given him on zoology. 'I didn't picture them this big!'

Rio nodded and clapped a hand on Pip's shoulder. 'This is one of the biggest I have seen. Look at him blow!'

A spray of water and froth burst from the whale's blowhole and shot up into the air. The sound of it made Pip jump. The whale disappeared briefly and then launched out of the water, splashing down with a mighty crash, only to emerge a moment later and slap the water with its fins. The two watched the wondrous show for a few minutes before the whale lost interest in the ship and began to swim away.

'He's going,' said Pip in dismay.

Rio laughed. 'There will be more to see on our journey, I can almost promise you.' He thought for a second and then un-looped a spyglass that was tied to his waist. 'Watch him for a bit longer if you like, but don't drop my glass. Captain would keelhaul me.'

Pip beamed and took the precious spyglass from Rio and put it to his eye. It took him a moment to locate the whale, but when he had it centred he kept it there and continued to watch the creature happily splash about for a few more minutes. As the whale disappeared from view, something else came into the focus of the glass. It looked to Pip like three other ships. They looked similar to the Dart in shape and size. Pip knew that ships at sea flew flags to identify them, so he squinted through the lens to see if the ships were running any colours. He nearly dropped the spyglass when he saw the the three ships all had identical flags: two crossed darts on a blue background. He was about to look more closely when Rio firmly took the scope away from his eye.

'Whale's gone now,' Rio said. 'And I'd better have this back before it comes to any harm. The sea is about to turn rough.'

Turn rough it did. Until that point, the journey had been a smooth one, and Pip had begun to fancy himself as a seaman at heart. That changed with the storm that crashed on the ship only an hour after the whale had disappeared on the horizon.

The skeleton crew that remained on deck had lashed themselves to the mast, or in Rio's case, the wheel. The others had gone into the mess for some food or to their bunks to catch some sleep before it was their turn to go on deck. Pip didn't like his chances of sleeping with the constant rise and fall of the ship, so he found himself squashed between Balad and Blackbeard in the mess.

Pip winced with each groan and sigh of the wood around him as the ship was buffeted by the waves.

'Don't fret none, Prince,' said Blackbeard with a laugh. 'The Dart ain't likely to buckle in a storm such as this.'

'Yes,' Balad chimed in. 'A ship made of tyshwood will hold a thousand storms, right Bob?'

The captain hummed in agreement; the corners of his mouth turned up in pride.

'You told me something about tyshwood in Hulum, Balad. Apart from the dark colour, what makes it so different to other types of timber?' asked Pip. 'I had not heard of it until we saw this ship at the docks.'

'Tyshwood comes from the ruined city of Tysh,' said Balad. He looked to the captain for confirmation. Bob shook his head and took over the story.

'It didn't come from Tysh exactly,' the captain said. 'It came from a small island off the coast of Tysh called Hasti's Back. You see, Tysh was a wonderful seaside city. The docking bays were nice and wide and the houses on the hillside were all made of white stone. I remember the first time I saw it with old Fogharty. The city shone in the sunlight. Very nearly tossed aside my sea-legs and settled down in Tysh. I was only a boy really, but I was excited by the place and by the people. They had some wonderful stories and beliefs. They used to worship Hasti, the god of the sea. In their culture, Hasti was a big whale that lived off the coast. When waves came breaking in over the docks, they'd say that Hasti was slapping his tail on the water out at sea.'

Pip remembered the whale he'd seen just an hour before and thought their explanation of big waves was feasible enough.

'But Hasti wasn't always a good god. Sometimes he'd send fierce winds with his blowhole, and sometimes his blowhole would shoot up fire and smoke so high and so thick that Tysh would be covered in ash for days.'

'Like a volcano?' asked Pip.

'Exactly like a volcano,' said Bob. 'There were a few underwater volcanoes near Tysh. The small island off the coast was the remains of rock thrown out by the volcano. From a distance it looked like the back of a gigantic whale, which is how it got its name: Hasti's Back. No one knows why, but the trees that grew on the island were almost as hard as steel. And the metal that was below the trees and in the rocks took days to melt down.'

'Metal?' said Balad. 'I didn't know there was metal too.'

'Yes, it was called *Hastine* by the locals. But the rest of us call it Tyshsteel. Remarkable stuff. None of it left now, but there weren't much to begin with. Only enough to make a couple of swords once that they used in Albion to fight the dragons.' Bob caught the look on Pip's face. 'No Prince Ael, you won't find the swords over there. They're long gone. Lost forever I'd say, just like Tysh.'

'What happened to the place?' Pip asked.

'A terrible fate in the end. It turns out that the predictions of Hasti came true. The locals protected the island off their coast, you see. They knew that the wood and the metal was valuable and they thought it was a gift from their great whale god. Their legends said that if all the trees were chopped down and all the metal taken away, then Hasti would destroy the city of Tysh and all those in it. As you can imagine, other nations heard about the wood and the metal and plundered their little island. They'd come in the dark and take what they could and sail off before the sun rose. And sure enough, one morning the locals woke to find Hasti's Back bare. It was then that the island revealed itself for what it was: a dormant volcano. I spoke to some sailors who were on their way to the city of Tysh and saw the eruption. Lucky for them they were still a fair way out to sea and lived to tell the tale. They told me Hasti's Back exploded with the force of a ten-thousand powder kegs or more. No warning, mind. Fire rained down on Tysh for hours until the city was no more. They said that the water boiled with the heat of it. Another volcano to a seasoned sailor, but to those poor souls of Tysh it would have looked as though Hasti the whale god was blowing fire out of his blowhole and punishing them for not taking care of his gifts. He buried them—and the tyshwood—forever.'

The rolling and lurching of the ship continued, and claps of thunder sounded somewhere close by. Pip and Balad looked at each other in silence, both wondering the same thing.

'I can see what you're thinking,' said Blackbeard. 'Where did all this tyshwood come from?' He spread his arms to indicate the wood around them. 'Was I one of the pirates that plundered the Hasti's Back?'

Pip couldn't meet the gaze of the fierce captain; he was too embarrassed that Bob had guessed his thoughts.

'Well I'll have you know that I'd never have stolen from the good people of Tysh. I wanted to live there, remember? In fact, Captain Fogharty and me sunk a few pirate brigs that were heading away from the island, their holds full of stolen timber. The ruler of Tysh let us have a quarter of the wood we returned as a reward. Fogharty and I stashed the wood further up the coast and set sail for home. We had big plans to build a new ship with the wood on our return, but that was the voyage where we met that blasted kraken in the middle of the Pohmin Sea, and you know the rest of *that* tale.'

'We do indeed,' said Balad sadly.

There was a moment for quiet around the table as each man thought about the sad fate of Tysh. Pip wondered how people could be so greedy as to take what wasn't theirs and ruin the lives of those they'd never met. He made a silent vow to be the sort of ruler who put people before wealth, and he would encourage his subjects to do the same, much like his father.

'Well lads,' said Blackbeard at last, breaking the reverie. 'Many thanks for the company, but I'd best go and relieve Rio before he falls asleep and gets washed overboard. Try and get some shut eye.'

Pip and Balad thanked the captain and raised their tankards to him. When he was sure the captain had left, Pip leaned in and whispered to his royal guard.

'Do you believe him?' Pip asked.

'About Tysh?'

'About the wood? Do you think he stole it?'

Balad shrugged. 'I don't know. I guess it doesn't matter one way or another. Tysh is gone now and this ship is about all that's left.' The guard looked more closely at his friend. 'What else is bothering you, Honoured One?'

Pip took a breath and told Balad about the other ships he'd seen earlier and how they were flying flags with darts painted on them—the same design as the rug in Bob's cabin.

143

'What does that matter?' asked Balad.

'I'm not sure,' said Pip. 'But don't you think it's strange that we have ships following us flying flags with black darts on them. After all, isn't *this* ship the Black Dart? And if those other ships are part of Bob's fleet, why are they hanging back behind us?'

'It could be a coincidence?' Balad suggested.

'Maybe, but Rio did *not* want me to see them, that much was clear.'

Balad thought for a moment, then said, 'Perhaps we'd better keep our eyes open on this voyage and our mouths shut, young Prince. I have noticed one or two suspicious things too, but I can't put my finger on what is afoot.'

Pip thought back to the night Blackbeard had come up with his brilliant plan, and the horrible mad laugh he'd given after. 'I know what you mean,' the prince said with an uneasy shudder. 'Sometimes I get the feeling that Bob is a big spider of the sea, and we've just been caught in his watery web.'

23

A SINGLE STEP

'What do you mean? How could Merlin be back?' Mollie huffed and rubbed her forehead. 'I mean, I know *how* he could be back: he can travel through time and he could show up wherever, or whenever, he wants. But why now?'

'I don't know,' Esmae answered, her words coming out in a rush. 'It was all very strange. Terry and I had just finished dinner and stoked the fire. We were sitting at the table and I was facing my new husband, when all of a sudden, there at the window right behind Terry, was your father. Our eyes met for the briefest second, but the shock must have shown on my face for Terry spun around to see what I was looking at. Only Merlin was quick to read the situation and made himself invisible in the blink of eye, thank heavens. Terry asked me what was wrong and I lied and told him I thought I saw an owl at the window. It was a stupid lie but it was the first thing that I could think of!'

Mollie relaxed back into her chair. 'Maybe it was your imagination?'

'I had that same thought too, Mollie. Maybe I hoped it was my imagination. But no, it was Merlin. He looked as though he hadn't aged a day—not like me—but it was your father, as sure as I'm sitting here now, just as I remember him. I haven't told Terry. We've practically only just said our vows and I'm already lying to him.'

The Adkins women sat in silence for a moment and finished their tea, each lost in their own thoughts of Merlin's return, and what it could mean.

'It's strange how he's still here even when he *is* gone,' said Mollie. 'Remember how Whitestaff told us it was Merlin that made the portal in his egg? And it was Merlin who helped the dragon leave all those years ago. It's like everything is always connected to him somehow, even though he's never here.'

'I know what you mean,' said Esmae. 'It makes moving on so much more difficult.'

 What do you think he wants?' asked Mollie after a while.

'I don't have a clue. He looked lost. Just like the first time we met. I wish he had've picked another time to show up out of the blue. Maybe I could have spoken to him, explained things...'

'You've nothing to explain, Esmae,' Mollie chided. 'He made a choice and we all had to live with it. You had to carry on without him.'

'Don't be cross with him, Mollie.'

'Why not?' Mollie asked. 'He left you plain and simple. You can't feel bad that you've moved on.'

'I gave him permission to leave, Mollie. It's different. It's complicated.'

Mollie was about to argue the point when there was an awful clatter at the door. At first she thought Terry had forgotten something and made his way back to the cottage. She turned to the entrance, half expecting to see Mr Gritbole falling through the door, his bow slung over his shoulder and his quiver on his back. But it wasn't Terry that had crashed into the Adkins cottage. It was an entirely different man altogether. Mollie looked right into his face and she knew from that moment on, her life was to change dramatically.

Pip Ael was glad to have his feet firmly planted on the ground. Bob had sailed them around the Pohmin Sea and up the coast of Albion. He skipped the country's biggest ports and anchored in a place called Lareborough, which used to be a coastal fort but now served as a minor stop for ships and trading vessels.

'This is the place you want,' Bob told them as he escorted the pair down the gangplank and off the ship.

'This is the home of the one we seek?' Balad asked.

'Not exactly,' Bob admitted. 'But this is the closest I can take you with the Dart. The rest of the way is through there.' Blackbeard pointed at a mountain range behind the town of Lareborough. 'There is a nice wide trail up there that's easy to find. You follow it as far as you can and it takes you to the town of Gibbon. You'll see the place from the mountain track, so you can't miss it.'

'And the sorceress is in Gibbon?' asked Pip.

'Last time I saw her she was in Quilshire, but the *first* time I saw her she was in Gibbon. Go to a place called the Barren Arms. It's a yellow Inn at the centre of the town. The Innkeeper there is named Jake. Talk to him, he seemed to know more than his fair share about the girl.'

'Girl?' said Pip. 'You said she'd help us kill Shadowclaw—'

'And she will,' said Blackbeard firmly. 'You need magic and this girl's got it. Fight magic with magic, remember? She's worth more than any army, I'll wager. Half the townsfolk up there live in fear of her and her mother.'

'Still,' said Pip, 'when you told us a sorceress lived here, I'd pictured a powerful mage living in a castle. Not some girl in a town that you can only get to through a mountain track!'

Blackbeard was about to argue more but Balad stepped in.

'Let's not allow the blowing sand to blind us, Honoured One. Your father sent us here to find a match for the Silver Scourge. If the girl can weave magic better than the dragon, then that is what we need. If she can't, then we continue to the Queen and hope she can spare some knights, or weapons, or something. Either way, if we return with more than what we left with, your father will be happy.'

'A *girl*, Balad!'

'Yes, Prince, and you are but a boy. But you did more damage to the Scourge than anyone ever has.'

Pip couldn't think of a retort. He sighed and nodded. 'Very well. The least we can do is meet her.'

'Excellent,' said Blackbeard. 'I'll be here to take you back when you return. I'd say two days there, two days back and one for safety. Five days?'

Pip's brow creased. 'Five days you say? What makes you so certain she'll even come? Perhaps she will refuse. Or maybe we will have to visit the Queen after all.'

'Refuse you?' said Bob. 'You think a girl from some spot of a village is going to say no to the Prince of Nalib? Besides, you haven't looked in a mirror lately, Pip, have you?'

'Mirror? No. Why? What makes you ask?'

Blackbeard laughed as a reply, only it wasn't a joyful laugh. It was that same horrible everlasting roar that he gave on the ship when he first told them of his plan. His face went red and his hands held his belly.

Pip looked at his guard who shrugged and picked up his pack. They left the small docks of Lareborough and made their way into the town to purchase some supplies—Blackbeard's horrible laughter fading behind them.

The town of Lareborough reminded Pip of a smaller and friendlier version of Hulum. Where Hulum was strictly business though, Lareborough was largely residential. It had stores, a ship repair yard and all the other conveniences you'd expect to find in a seaside town, but it also had an open nature, where all the locals knew each other and where visitors were welcome. The people passing by all greeted Pip and Balad with a smile and a wave, and Pip liked the town at once.

Soon he spied a supply store and he and his guard made their way across the street to it and entered through the open door. The inside of the shop struck Pip as bizarre. It was like the nest of some giant bird who'd gathered bits and pieces from all over the world and arranged his treasures in the most decorative way he could imagine. Nets hung from the roof, wooden carvings hung from the walls, and rows of strange objects lined the shelves. Pip saw books and children's toys on the same shelf as a sword and a chest. There was no apparent order of things.

'Morning to you both,' said the lady behind the counter. 'After anything in particular?'

'Whatever we're after, I'm sure you have it,' laughed the Prince.

The lady cackled back and made her way over to them. She stood much shorter than Balad, owing to her stoop. She had twinkling eyes and a mischievous smile on her mouth. Her hair was thin and as white as sea-salt.

'We're on our way to Gibbon,' said Balad, 'and we were after some supplies. Some dried food, some tea, and a water bladder if you have one? '

'And some bandages,' said Pip, looking at his arms. 'These ones need changing. And maybe some arrows too? Two dozen if you have that many.'

The shopkeeper nodded her head. 'I can fix you up with all of that. You'll need the arrows if you're going to Gibbon. Is it just the two of you?'

'Yes,' said Balad. 'Is there a reason to ask?'

'Bandits,' said the lady as she made her way around the shop collecting the order. 'If you're heading to Gibbon on the mountain path, you'd best find an escort. There's a small group of bandits that have been giving the track some trouble lately. On second thought, they'll most likely leave you two alone though. Not to offend you, but they're after gold and you two don't exactly look like royalty.'

Pip and Balad gave each other a grin. After such a long voyage, their clothes were wrinkled and in need of a good wash. No one would suspect Pip was heir to an entire kingdom.

'They mostly attack the merchant carts that come down here from Gibbon and Quilshire,' the shopkeeper explained. 'The merchants bring their goods here to be shipped out of our port. Sometimes goods arrive here to get taken up there,' she jerked her thumb in the direction of the mountains. 'Usually it's good business, but lately these bandits have been ambushing any haul that looks valuable. Bad for the merchants. Bad for me too, I suppose. Ah, here are the arrows. Goose or turkey fletchings?'

'It doesn't bother me,' said Pip.

The shopkeeper nodded and gathered up all of their items and placed them on the counter. Balad paid the woman and the two left the shop and headed for the mountains.

24

THE BARREN ARMS

'Say what you will about Blackbeard, he sure knows how to give directions.'

'True, Prince,' said Balad. 'There is the town, just as he promised. And that yellow building must be the Barren Arms.'

From their vantage point at the top of the mountain track, the town of Gibbon was easy to navigate with their eyes. It looked smaller than Lareborough and not as well kept.

'Everything is so green in this part of the world,' Pip said half to himself.

'It is.'

'And it's not half as hot here as it is in Nalib. We've still got more than half our water supply.'

The journey along the mountain track had taken the prince and his guard all day. They had walked the winding track without incident, and decided to make camp for the night. Pip had baulked at making a fire at night for fear of attracting the group of outlaws, but Balad had found wisdom in the words of the shopkeeper.

'They won't bother us, Honoured One. Two men sleeping on the side of the road isn't worth the trouble. Nevertheless, why don't we take turns in resting? Me first, then you.'

Pip agreed and sat first watch, feeding the fire as needed. Nothing happened for a few long hours, then the prince thought he heard something close by. He had the feeling of being watched and the hairs on the back of his neck prickled and made him shiver. He strained his ears for what seemed like another hour, but heard nothing more. He woke Balad soon after for guard duty and allowed himself to sink into a deep sleep. The earth was warm below him, and his body seemed thankful that there was no rocking as there had been aboard the Dart.

In the morning, he awoke to find that Balad had brewed some tea over the fire. He drank it with relish and watched as Balad stowed away their few belongings in his pack and buried the fire.

They set to walking once more and found Gibbon below them soon after.

'If we had have kept walking last night, we could have made it to Gibbon and rested in a bed,' said Pip.

'Well now we know,' said Balad. 'Let's go straight to the Inn. Maybe we can get a drink and rest there. Maybe even buy something to eat. I'm sick of these dried out biscuits already.'

'Good idea,' said Pip. 'He might be more helpful after we've spent some coin in his establishment, and I think I could use a bath.'

'Remember the hot tubs at home?' asked Balad. 'Oh to be there now.'

Pip closed his eyes. 'Stop it, Balad. You're teasing the both of us!'

Of course, the tub at the Barren Arms held no hot water. In fact it was the only bathtub to serve the guests at the Inn, and it looked as though it had never been used. The stable boy fetched the water from a well nearby and filled the tub with chilly water. Pip washed his clothes first and then himself, but he felt no cleaner afterwards. Balad did likewise and the two stood in the sun behind the stables until their clothes felt dry to touch.

'Let's hope the beer is better than the bath,' Balad said as they made their way back into the Inn. The ground floor of the Barren Arms also served as a bar, and Pip wondered why anyone would choose to drink in such a gloomy place. It stunk like old tobacco and the ground was filthy. As old sawdust stuck to his boot, he began to regret having a bath. *I'm going to be dirty again in two minutes anyway*, he thought.

'Two beers,' said Balad as they approached the bar.

The bartender looked closely at Pip through the hazy air. 'Old enough?'

'For beer?' asked Pip.

'Yes, for beer. I'm not asking if you're old enough to marry me, am I?'

Pip shrugged. 'If I'm old enough for the ale in Nalib, then I'm old enough for the beer in Albion.'

'Very well,' the bartender nodded. 'Nalib, you say? Never heard of it. Long way away, is it?'

'Weeks of sailing and a few days riding. But the ship that got us here is the fastest there is in all the seas.'

'That's a wild boast,' said the bartender as he poured the beers. Pip desperately wanted to ask for a cleaner glass, but bit his tongue. 'I know a thing or two about ships, and I can name the ten fastest brigs and schooners on the water.'

'Really,' said Pip. 'What would you say is the quickest brig about?'

'Easy. There's no ship faster than the Black Dart!'

'Strange of you to say. That was the name of the very ship that brought us here,' said Pip.

The bartender nearly dropped the glass he was filling. 'True? Then you be friends of Blackbe— Bob?'

'Yes. Captain Bob saw us here very safely. My name is Pip and this chubby bearded man is Balad.'

'Not chubby,' Balad growled. 'It's all muscle.'

The bartender gave them a nervous grin and offered his hand. 'Well met to the both of you. My name's Jake. Any friend of Bob's, is a friend of mine.'

Balad and Pip exchanged glances.

'Good to meet you too, Jake.'

'What brings you all the way to Gibbon of all places?' he asked.

Pip's original plan was to find Jake and ask him outright about the sorceress, but something about the man's manner made him reconsider. Balad must have picked up on it too, for he kept his

155

mouth shut. Pip figured instead it would be best to get Jake talking without arousing his suspicions.

'Just passing through to bigger and better places,' Pip answered. 'There was a lady in Lareborough that warned us about bandits. Is there anything else we should be wary about as we travel through this land?'

Balad gave Pip a surreptitious wink of approval.

'Doesn't know what she's talking about,' said Jake. 'The bandits don't really exist.'

'She seemed to believe they do.'

Even though the bar was empty, Jake made a show of looking around to make sure he wasn't going to be overheard. He leaned in close to his guests and lowered his voice. 'She's half right. The bandits do exist but they aren't real bandits.'

'How do you mean?' Pip whispered back.

Jake licked his lips and looked around again. 'Well, have you ever heard of the Witches of Danmurk?'

Pip shook his head.

'Of course you haven't, you're not from here. Well, halfway between here and Danmurk Shire live a pair of witches. Horrible crones that have been terrorising the townsfolk for years.'

'Women that can do magic? That's terrible,' said Pip. He looked to Balad, who was doing his best to keep a straight face.

'Yes it is!' Jake continued. 'I had to house one here on Blackbea— I mean, Bob's request. But he doesn't know them like I do. One day, about a year and a half ago now, they went too far.

They stole some poor gentleman's horse and gold from the Quilshire Fair and rode back to their den. Well that fine fellow, Cudgel is his name, he vowed he'd get even with them both in the end, and that's what he's doing.'

'I don't follow,' said Pip. 'How's he related to the bandits?'

'Like I said,' grinned Jake. 'There are no bandits. Cudgel has hired some men to help him search for the witches. He knew they lived around here because he remembers them from when he was in Gibbon. This is where he first met them.'

'But haven't they been robbing merchants?' asked Balad.

Jake shrugged. 'Got to pay his men somehow, hasn't he?'

'How do you know all this?' asked Pip. 'And why haven't you told anyone?'

Once again Jake made a show of being discreet. 'I know because he came in and got drunk last night and blabbed that whole story. Good thing he did, too.'

'Why is that?'

'Because I had the information he needed. I told him exactly where the witches live. Like I told you, halfway between here and Danmurk. You have to go west at the crossroads. Five miles that way.' Jake winked at them and pointed south.

Pip and Balad looked at each other, wide-eyed.

'Why, I bet he's on his way there now, ready to kill them once and for all. And good riddance to them too. The world is a better place without witches!'

Pip was too stunned to speak. All he could think of was that he'd come so far and failed. Then his stomach turned at the thought of two women being killed by a group of thugs. *We're too late!* He thought.

Balad was the first to compose himself. 'Well I hope he gets them!' he exclaimed. 'Magic only causes mayhem, as we say in Nalib.'

'A truer word was never spoken,' agreed Jake.

'Well, now, Jake. It was an honour to drink in your establishment, but my young friend and I must be off. Do you know where we can get some horses? A pair of very fast horses?'

25

AN OLD ENEMY

As Pip gripped the reins of his galloping horse, he couldn't help but wish it was Jasper underneath him, rather than the skinny nag Jake had sold him. Back at the Barren Arms, the bartender had offered his two horses on the spot when he saw Balad's gold coins. They bought them without doing a proper inspection, and as a consequence, had paid twice their worth.

It doesn't matter, Pip thought. *We'd have paid triple. Let's just hope we're not too late.*

Pip and Balad sped south in the direction that Jake had pointed. The horses' hooves kicked up the dust and the arrows in Pip's quiver rattled with every stride. Soon they came to a crossroad, and Pip followed Balad as he turned west without hesitation. They charged furiously down the dirt path, spurring their tired horses, until at last, a small cottage came into view. The Guard and the Prince pulled up their horses and flung themselves from the saddles. Pip nocked an arrow in his bow and charged into the cottage, Balad on his heels.

Through the entrance they clattered, ready for a fight with Cudgel and his band of cut-throats. But Cudgel wasn't there and there was no fight to be had. Instead they found two women sitting at a table and sipping tea. The women both had hair the colour of ink. Their wide, blue eyes looked shocked at having two men charge into their home. Pip looked to the younger one and was about to offer an apology and an explanation, but his words froze up when their eyes locked.

She didn't cry out. She didn't scream. She just looked at him with surprise, then cool curiosity. He couldn't help but smile under her gaze. He lowered his bow, his cheeks turning red.

'What is the meaning of this?' asked the elder of the two. 'Who are you and what do you want?'

Pip couldn't take his eyes off Mollie, so it was up to Balad to do the talking.

'Forgive us, please,' he said, returning his curved sword to its sheath. 'We were told there was some trouble here and we came to help you.'

'Help us?' asked Esmae. 'Trouble from who?'

'Forgive us. My name is Balad and this is Pip Ael. Are you two the Witches of Danmurk?'

'We have been called such things. But we usually go by our *actual* names. I am Esmae and this is my daughter, Mollie. Now what is this trouble you were speaking of and why are you in my home?'

Before Balad could answer, there came a loud command from the back of the cottage, and Cudgel's men began their charge. They came through the windows and burst through the back door. Esmae reacted quickly and summoned a magic missile. She blew one attacker back through the door and into a man behind him. They tumbled a few meters in the air before landing in a heap.

Pip raised his bow and caught a bandit in the shoulder. He howled with pain and stumbled towards the prince. Pip hit him across the head with his bow and knocked him unconscious. Balad took out two men by hitting them with the butt of his sword, once each on the forehead, and they dropped like lead. One fat little man charged at Mollie with a mace held over his head. Quickly Pip nocked another arrow and shot it at the weapon. The force of the arrow hitting the mace yanked it out of the man's grip, so that when he brought his fist down it was harmlessly empty. Mollie finished the job by lifting him in the air with invisible magic, then hurtling him to the ground with a dull thud. At the same time, she used an ice spell to hold the three remaining attackers where they stood.

Balad seized the opportunity and bashed one over the head with a wooden chair, smashing the furniture to pieces and spraying ice everywhere. Esmae, Mollie, Balad and Pip had grouped in the middle of the cottage and were standing back to back. Around them were men on the floor, dropped weapons, broken bits of furniture, somebody's tooth, a torn shirt, and two frozen men who could pass for blue statues. For a moment after that, everything was silent. Then, all of a sudden, Mollie gathered the air around her. She used its power to pick every thug up off the ground. One by one, she flew them out the back door and sailed them into the sky. Some of the men came to and screamed in fear as they shot high above the trees, then splashed down into the lake behind the cottage. Only one man remained. He was the one that had tried to hit Mollie with his mace.

Mollie Adkins walked to him and knelt over his body. The man tried to get up, but it was as though his muscles were made of jelly. 'What happened?' he asked. 'Did we win?' He was still seeing stars from when he'd been slammed to the floor. Soon enough though, his vision returned, and a look of pure fear crossed his face when he saw the young Adkins above him.

'Cudgel,' said Mollie sweetly. 'We meet again.'

'Y-y-you!' he stammered. 'You're the witch what took me horse an' dragon! I want em back!'

At that moment, Terry came sprinting inside. He had *his* bow drawn and ready to fire. When he saw his wife and Mollie were safe, he dropped his bow and relaxed his shoulders. He scanned the room and took in the damage.

'Who are these people?' he asked. 'And why were there men flying through the sky just now?'

'A good question,' said Esmae. She turned to look at Balad. At the same time she pinned Cudgel to the ground with her magic, making escape impossible.

Balad introduced himself and his ward a second time. 'These men that attacked you are the same bandits that have been terrorising the mountain path between Gibbon and Lareborough. You named this one *Cudgel*. That is the name of their leader. His true purpose was to find you two ladies and finish you off. Revenge for stealing from him, or so he says.'

Cudgel turned white as Esmae looked down at him.

'Is that so?' she said. 'Terry, my dear, I think you may have to escort Mr Cudgel here to Danmurk. Tell Sir Layton that we've found the bandit leader. He will take it from there.' She bent down and spoke directly to Cudgel. 'Mr Cudgel here is going to confess everything, aren't you, Cudgel?'

Cudgel's eyes went from Mollie to Esmae and back again. He nodded vigorously.

'Good,' said Esmae. 'With a bit of luck, you'll have the whip instead of the dungeon. But if I ever see you near me or my daughter again...' She leant close to Cudgel and whispered in his ear. Mollie never found out what her mother said to Cudgel, but by the way the man's face went a horrid shade of green and his legs began to twitch, she felt that it was a good enough threat to keep him away for an enternity.

Terry tied Cudgel's hands behind his back with some rope and led him to the cart outside. He bade them all farewell and set off with his prisoner for Danmurk, leaving the Adkins women alone with the two strange heroes.

'Now that that is dealt with,' said Esmae, 'perhaps you two had better explain your role in all of this, before I get my daughter here to make you fly over the trees too.'

26

A STUPID QUESTION

As Whitestaff flew across the Dire Channel with the King, Nap, Xenos and Kigg, he couldn't help but remember the first time he'd cast eyes on this fantastic roaring landscape. The Dire was a massive body of water that split the main landmass of Sorteya in half. Tidal surges and currents pulled the seawater one way, then the other, and the effect was like a giant saw of water that constantly cut into the land. The cliffs that towered on each side showed just how far the water bit down. The wind howled through the Channel, and every now and then, massive chunks of rock splashed down from the cliffs as the wind and water eroded them. The Sorteyan sun was lightly touching the horizon, and the sea-spray took on a yellow shimmer as it shot up the rocky walls.

Whitestaff called his party to a halt and raised his voice over the din. 'From now on, you lead the way,' he told Xenos. 'Take us to a safe distance from the dungeon. I want to see what we're up against.'

'Of course,' said Xenos. 'Though I suggest we wait until the sun has disappeared. When the light hits your scales, you glint and light up like a golden warning beacon. Mezelga's scouts will spot you easily.'

Whitestaff nodded and the dragons dipped down into the Dire so they wouldn't be seen. They found a small alcove in the cliff and waited for dark. Nap fiddled with his new ruby eyepatch and scanned the sky with his one good eye, keen to resume the mission. When all agreed that the light was dull enough, they set off once more for the Wyvern Queen's lair.

They flew up and over the cliffs, above the blanket of clouds, and entered the Nazoor side of Sorteya. Whitestaff strained his eyes to take in as much as he could. He was curious about his rival dragons and wondered how different their lives were. The first thing he noticed was that the Nazoor spires were honeycombed through. Where the spires on the Palal side housed only one or two dugouts, the Nazoor spires seemed to be full of holes. Not surprisingly, some of the spires were so over-tunnelled they had collapsed in on themselves. Next he was struck by the barrenness of the Nazoor land. His side of Sorteya was almost blindingly purple; balefruit shone in the sun and faintly glowed in the dark. But here all the balefruit were gone. There was no purple glow because there was no fruit at all. There was just the muddy coloured dirt of the spires. To Whitestaff's eyes, the Nazoor land looked dead. It was as if a swarm of locusts had flown in, devoured everything, and flew away. It was silent here, but Whitestaff figured that most of the Nazoor were over his side of Sorteya, ready to devour his land too. The rest must be with the Queen, wherever that was.

Xenos flew them low, skimming the blanket of fog with their tails. He made a long arc left into a narrow opening in one of the standing spires. He pulled up short once he was inside, and the dragons following him bumped into his back.

'Shhhhh,' he told them. 'Follow me. We will be able to see the Queen's palace soon.'

Xenos took the party through the dugout. The Palal dragons had to crouch low as they walked, wings tucked in and tails straight. Obviously, the dugout was not constructed for dragons as large as the Palal. Whitestaff had the most trouble getting through. Sometimes the tunnel would narrow so much that his body would scrape against each side of the spire, widening the gap for those behind him. After much twisting and turning, the dragons came to another opening on the opposite side of the spire. The dugout widened again at the entrance, and all of the dragons could stand side-by-side.

'There it is,' Xenos said as he pointed out Mezelga's spire. He needn't bothered though, because it was obvious where the Queen of the Nazoor lived. As far as spires go, this was the biggest Whitestaff had ever seen. It was several hundred metres higher than the other spires, and about twenty times as round.

'How is that possible?' Nap asked. 'It's huge!'

'The palace? Well,' answered Kigg, 'when the other spires are dug out, we take the leftover dirt to Mezelga's servants. They add it to the outside of her spire and it gets bigger. Simple really.'

'Why didn't we think of that?' said Cracone. 'Imagine how much bigger the Court would be!'

'Necessity is the mother of invention,' said Xenos. 'We need to reuse everything because there are so many of us. You probably just throw whatever dirt you tunnel down to the ground.'

'We do,' admitted Cracone. 'Though now it seems stupid.'

Xenos smiled; his razor-like teeth shining in his beak. 'You just don't have the need that we do. I used my party to petition Mezelga to ask you Palal for your leftover dirt. With it we could have made our spires larger and we wouldn't have all these collapses. She wouldn't hear of it though.'

'Our party wanted to open up trading arrangements like this,' added Kigg. 'We give to you, you give to us. Every dragon benefits. But Mezelga's plan is always to take, never to ask.'

'I see,' said Cracone. 'Your party had many good ideas, it seems.'

'But none adopted,' said Xenos.

The dragons stood a while longer and watched the massive palace. The activity was minimal; a lone guard would fly a lazy circuit around the spire every now and then before disappearing back inside. Whitestaff noticed something different about the Nazoor guards, however.

'What do they have on their heads?' he asked.

'Helms,' replied Xenos. 'The guards to the palace all wear armour.'

'That should make things tougher,' said Cracone.

'Perhaps, but I don't think there are many guards here,' said Xenos. 'No one cares about the Party of Peace, so Mezelga would never have predicted anyone would want to rescue them. I'd say we'd only have to face about thirty guards at the most.'

'Thirty versus five,' said Nap. 'That doesn't sound good, but we have the element of surprise.' He clapped Whitestaff on the shoulder. 'And we have a flying volcano.'

Whitestaff returned Nap's smile. 'Ready for a fight, Re'dahl?'

Nap brought his tail around and ran a claw over the sharp barb on the end of it. 'I think you already know the answer.'

27

THE CHASE AND THE FIRE

Whitestaff was pleased with Nap's answer and he knew that each of the one-eyed Re'dahls would be worth five Wyvern in a fight, but he worried about the two Nazoor that were with him. *Will they fight their own kind when it comes to the crunch?* he wondered. *Or is this some elaborate trap of Mezelga's, and Xenos and Kigg are luring us to our deaths?*

The team of dragons watched the huge spire and waited for an opportunity to attack. Xenos gave the order to follow when he saw the dugout mouth empty of guards. The mini-dragon flew like lightning towards the entrance, staying low and then shooting up the face of the spire so he could avoid being spotted from above. The other dragons followed, close on his tail. Xenos shot into the palace entrance and immediately attacked the first Nazoor guard he saw. Whitestaff entered behind, just in time to watch Xenos claw at the guard's neck and finish him off with a whip of his tail. The force of Xenos's blow sent the guard's helmet spinning through the air. Any doubts Whitestaff had about Xenos's ability, or willingness to fight, disappeared in an instant.

At that moment, more guards appeared from inside and Whitestaff's team charged at them. Mezelga's guards were caught completely by surprise and only managed to put up a weak resistance before being trampled by the intruders. With the entry guards out of the way, Xenos took the lead once more.

'Follow me!' he shouted as he charged through the tunnels and down to the dungeon. The other dragons had little choice but to follow. Through the narrow tunnels they twisted, dispatching any stray guards they saw along the way. Down and down they spiralled, until suddenly the tunnel opened up to an enormous hollow.

The team spilled into the chamber and saw at once that they'd made a terrible mistake. Every member of the Party of Peace was shackled to the wall of the circular dungeon. Next to each dragon was a flaming torch, making almost one hundred flaming lights in all. In the centre of the dungeon was more than sixty of Mezelga's guards—double the number that Xenos had guessed! The firelight shone on their helmets and gave sparks to their black eyes. They turned at once to the intruders and hissed.

'Palal!' shouted one of the guards. 'Kill them!'

Quicker than Whitestaff had thought possible, one of the guards pounced onto Cracone, slashing at his chest with a hooked claw. Another followed soon after, and before Whitestaff could even think, the Re'dahl King was buried under a pile of Wyvern.

A cry of pain from the King jolted the others into action. Nap was first to reach his father. He stabbed the Nazoor mercilessly with his barbed tail. Kigg dove into the fray too, pulling the dragons from Cracone's body. Whitestaff moved to help, but the guards had sprang at him too, overwhelming him with their numbers. He swatted at them and bit down on whatever guard was unlucky enough to be in the way. Unfortunately, he crunched down hard on one of his attacker's helmets and threw his head back in pain. The rescue mission was failing fast.

Thirty Nazoor in armour would have been difficult, thought the Kai'dahl, *but this is impossible!*

'RETREAT,' roared Whitestaff over the screeching of the Nazoor. 'GET BEHIND ME AND BACK INTO THE TUNNEL.'

Using his mighty size and strength, Whitestaff hurled himself before the tunnel mouth. He yanked Cracone and Nap backwards by their necks and tossed them up the tunnel and out of the dungeon. He glanced back to see Xenos and Kigg had joined them, then he used his body to block the opening. Now *he* was all that stood between his team and and sixty royal guards. The Nazoor regathered themselves and fanned out around him, crouching low and hissing.

'What now?' asked Nap from behind. 'We're outnumbered.'

'I want you to run back the way we came,' answered Whitestaff, not daring to take his eyes off the Wyvern in front of him. 'Run as fast as you can and don't stop until I give the order.'

'But they'll chase us down—'

'Not now, Nap. Don't argue, just do as I say. RUN!'

At the Kai'dahl's command, the small party of dragons scurried back up the tunnel and away from the dungeon. Whitestaff gave a mighty roar, stunning the guards for a few moments, then he too turned tail and fled.

Behind him he could hear the Nazoor giving chase. They crammed themselves in to follow, and in doing so, tumbled over each other, buying Whitestaff a little more time. His large body slowed him down, however, and he knew that soon he would be caught.

'Keep running!' Whitestaff called to those ahead. 'Don't stop until we're almost at the top.'

'And then what?' hollered Nap back.

'You'll see.'

The echoes of the hissing Nazoor snaked through the tunnel. The Wyvern guards had unblocked themselves from the back opening and were half sprinting, half flying after their quarry. Whitestaff desperately wanted to look over his shoulder, but the tunnel wasn't wide enough for him to do so. Instead he kept his head down and ran. Soon though, he could feel the Nazoor just behind him, and the proof came when he felt something sharp swat at his tail.

'We're here,' called Nap from in front. 'We're at the start.'

By now the sun had gone and it was too dark for Whitestaff to see anything, but he could tell that Nap was right. The tunnel was getting wider again as it came closer to the mouth.

Grateful for the extra space, Whitestaff stuck his wings out to the side. But instead of taking flight, he used them as breaks to stop himself from moving forward. He took a deep breath and spun himself around to face his attackers.

The Nazoor guards pounced at him: their needle teeth sharp and ready to bite, their claws ready to scratch.

Whitestaff watched them leap at him through the air. He saw the delight shining in their black eyes quickly change to horror when they saw Whitestaff's chest glow with molten fire. Some of the Nazoor tried to stumble backwards and away from the Kai'dahl's open mouth, but the Nazoor coming from behind pushed them forward.

Whitestaff opened his jaws as wide as they would go and breathed out long and hard as fire erupted from his mouth. It came out as fast as a raging geyser, right into the faces of the closest Nazoor. The heat of it turned them to ash and melted their helmets in a second. But it wasn't just the first lot of Nazoor that suffered. The fire-stream travelled along the length of the tunnel, roasting and burning all of the Nazoor guards as it went. Their cries and screeches were drowned out as Whitestaff belched more flame down the tunnel, giving it all he had.

Cracone, Nap, Kigg and Xenos watched from above, shocked by the ferocity of Whitestaff's breath. The golden dragon gave it one more awesome jet of fire, then collapsed where he stood, sucking in cool air in between coughs. The other dragons pulled him to the dugout mouth and away from the super-heated tunnel.

173

Presently, Whitestaff's breathing became normal again. Smoke and dragon essence from the dead Nazoor began to trail back out of the tunnel and into the night air.

'Do you think it's cool enough for us to go back down?' asked Nap.

'Best give it another few moments,' said Cracone.

The dragons slumped to the ground, glad for the excuse to lay down. Their bodies hurt from the fight down below, and their minds were still trying to comprehend what they had seen. It's one thing to know that a dragon can breathe fire, but to see one dragon roast sixty others is another.

'That was some plan,' said Nap at last. 'I have to hand it to you, Kai'dahl; you know how to fight.'

'The tunnel did most of the work,' Whitestaff replied, his voice coming out with a croak. 'I just wish there was some other way. That was awful, killing them like that.' He turned to Xenos and Kigg. 'I'm so sorry. They were your kind, even though you believe in different things. No dragon deserves to die in such a way.'

Xenos looked at Whitestaff for a moment, then nodded.

'Yes, they were still my kind. And it's because you're the kind of dragon that is sorry that I can order my party to follow you. Mezelga would never have apologised. Even at war you are compassionate—a trait we Nazoor seem to have lost.' He picked himself back up off the dirt. 'But let's not forget the reason we came here. There are a hundred more of my kind chained to the walls of the dungeon down there. Let's set them free.'

28

THE NEW ALLIANCE

Each of the shackled Nazoor seemed to be in different stages of exhaustion. Some collapsed straight to the ground as Whitestaff released them, while others firmly shook tails with him and pledged their undying loyalty. The ones that were strong enough helped to unshackle the other prisoners, and before long, the Party of Peace members were all free.

They rubbed their skin where the shackles had been and cursed Mezelga's name as they did so. Some had more than just chaffed skin to worry about; they had scratch marks where the royal guards had been interrogating them, or hurting them just to relieve their boredom. They gathered around Xenos who stood in the middle of the dungeon. He motioned them to be quiet so that he could be heard.

'Party members, I'm glad to see you all alive. Today has indeed been a black day, not just for our Party, but for every Nazoor dragon. For today, our brothers turned against us. They struck us down and chained us. They beat us and they broke us.

Today, the very thing our Party wanted to avoid has occurred. We are at *war*! Mezelga has flown against the Palal; our brother race. Her plan is to smash them into oblivion. She wants to crush them and wipe them from the face of this planet.'

Xenos scanned the dragons in front of him. Every ear was hanging on his words, and Whitestaff could now see why Xenos was their leader. *This is a dragon that understands the power of a good speech,* Whitestaff thought as Xenos continued.

'She wants to destroy them the same as she wants to destroy us! And so now we are left with no choice. We too are at war. Only, our war is with Mezelga and her tyranny. We will join forces with the Palal and strike back at our Queen. We will finally speak to Mezelga in her own language: the voice of war!'

The Party members cheered at Xenos's words and hissed to each other of revenge. But Whitestaff wasn't so sure that whipping the Party up into a frenzy was such a good idea. He whispered in Xenos's ear and asked if he could address them. Xenos nodded and brought his dragons to order. When it was quiet again, Whitestaff spoke.

'Party members, I'm sorry for the loss of your brothers. We thought that there would be fewer guards here and we were hoping to keep the fighting to a minimum. My only aim was to free you quickly so that you may be spared. You and I share no blood, but we have the same ideas. I too have sought peace on this planet in my own way, and it saddens me that Mezelga has unleashed this madness.'

The Party members agreed with him and hissed.

'But you must know this before you join the side of the Palal. Ours is a losing side. Your Queen has hidden herself away, and I must return to my own kind, because as we speak, Mezelga's army is attacking my fellow dragons at the Court. There are only a few thousand Palal, but there are ten times the number of Nazoor at least. The Palal will fight to the death to save ourselves. However, we are sure to lose.'

Some of the Nazoor began muttering amongst themselves.

'If you wish,' Whitestaff spoke over the top of them, 'you may leave now. You are a Party committed to peace and if war sits ill with you, then I won't stand in your way if you want to leave.' He pointed a claw to the exit.

Some of the Wyvern nodded and broke off into urgent, hushed discussions as they considered Whitestaff's offer.

'What are you doing?' Cracone whispered in the Kai'dahl's ear. 'We need every claw we can get!'

'Think about it, Cracone,' he answered. 'Xenos has got them ready to fight now, but what about when the first battle comes? Will they still be willing to fight? If not, it's better that they leave now than turn tail on us when it gets tough. Or worse—change sides! If they don't, or won't fight, then we don't want them.'

'Hmph. True, I suppose,' growled the King.

The discussions seemed to be over, and it looked as though about half the Nazoor were slowly heading for the exit, but no dragon wanted to be the first to leave.

There was a quiet, tense moment when Whitestaff was sure some of the older, weaker Nazoor were going to break. He knew that as soon as one Wyvern left, many more would follow. But in Whitestaff's mind, he'd rather they left now than turned on him when it was clear his side was doomed.

'Before you make up your mindsssss,' someone shouted, breaking the silence. 'You should know that leaving issss not really an option.'

Everyone looked around to face the speaker, but Whitestaff recognised the voice instantly.

'Cross!' said Whitestaff. 'I wondered if you were in here.'

'Unfortunately I am. But I'm also alive, thanksssss to you.' He gave the Palal a wink and spoke directly to his fellow Nazoor. 'You can't leave,' he said. 'The offer Whitestaff hasssss generously offered you can't be accepted.'

'And why not?' retorted one of the older Nazoor. 'We don't want war, we never have. Why should we go and kill ourselves now?'

'Becaussssse,' Cross hissed. 'You haven't thought it through. What do you think our Queen will do when she finds out we have escaped? She will hunt us down! You know it. From this day forth you will be sought after and harassed until you are found and killed, or worse! Like it or not, Whitestaff hasn't saved ussss at all. He hasss prolonged our life a little. He hassss risked his neck for ussss and if I'm going to die then I want to die with honour. Fighting for the *right* sssside. Standing by my oath to the Party.'

He let his logic sink in with the Nazoor. It didn't take long. Their quick minds saw at once that Cross was right. They were doomed anyway, and dying for the Party and for Whitestaff was much more honourable to the Nazoor than running and being hunted down later.

Cross licked his beak with his narrow forked-tongue. He folded his wings around his body, the way a bat does, stood up straight and spoke once more. 'I pledge my allegiance to the Party of Peace. My ssssole aim will be to protect and preserve life at all costssssss, though I know it may be difficult.' The other mini-dragons had all taken the same oath, and so joined in with their own voices.

'The only time I will raise my claw,' they all chanted in unison, 'is if I see my brothers are being cut down, or the chance of peace is being assaulted. I pledge this to my Party. My life for Peace.'

When the oath was recited, the Nazoor unfolded their wings. 'My life for Peace!' declared Xenos again. 'Our brothers *are* being cut down. Peace *issss* being assaulted! We all made an oath, now let'sss die keeping it.'

He raised his claws above his head and his Party cheered for him.

Nap too was caught in the moment and cheered also. 'To war!' he growled. 'Follow Whitestaff!'

'Follow Whitestaff!' the other cheered.

Whitestaff looked around the dungeon at the small army he had acquired. Their needle teeth shone in their beaks and their eyes

179

were full of fervour and readiness to fight. It gave him a small glimmer of hope that maybe his race wasn't going to lose this war as easily as Mezelga had planned.

'Let's go!' he roared over the cheers. 'To battle!'

He led the charge back up through the tunnel and on the way back to the Court, where an army of Nazoor was waiting, ready to fight.

29

A SMALL IDEA

Whitestaff flew over the Dire Channel with Nap, Cracone and his newly formed Nazoor army. The Sorteyan moon took up almost half of the sky. It was ten times as large as the moon he used to spy from his cage on Earth, and it shone with the sun's light so brightly that true darkness never fell on Sorteya, even in the dead of night.

Past the Dire, purple balefruit began to appear. They too shone with moonlight, and the Nazoor plucked and devoured them as they flew past.

'They haven't eaten ssssince yesterday,' said Cross as he caught up to Whitestaff at the front of the pack. 'So much of it is left on your side.'

'I don't think it's our side any longer,' said Whitestaff. 'Who decided on sides anyway? Why couldn't we all live together when we left Earth?'

Cross thought a moment. 'If my hisssssstory is correct, we did try. Right at the start. One of your Kings and one of our Mezelgas did co-exist in early Sorteyan hisssstory...'

'Ah, yes. Hence the Alpos. I'd forgotten.'

'It never worked out asssss you know. The planet was divided.'

'Can I ask something?' said Whitestaff. 'Something I've been wondering?'

'Of courssse.'

'Why is there a Party of Peace at all? If you joined Mezelga, you and Xenos and the rest, the planet would be yours by now. Why defy your Queen? Why did you all take the oath?'

Cross gave a hissing laugh, though there was no humour in it.

'We all have different reasons. Take Xenosss for example—hisss father died in the last dragon war, just like yours did. Nazoor don't usually have close kin relationssshipss like you Palal, but Xenosss cared very much for his father, poor Gamoss. The old dragon was lame when he went into battle. In fact, he isss the one that gave Cracone that terrible ssscar all those years ago.'

'Xenos's father fought Cracone?'

'Yesss, with his good claw. He didn't want to fight that day, and Xenos begged Mezelga's guards not to make him. With his right wing and claw almost uselesss, they both knew he'd be dead within minutes of battle. But when Mezelga orderssss you, you have little choice. She basssically sent the old Gamoss to his death.'

'And now Xenos is fighting alongside Cracone? Extraordinary.'

'We all have similar stories. It would be easy enough to blame the Palal and hold a grudge, but if you dig a bit deeper, you can sssssee that it is the Tyrant Queen who issss to blame. That's why the Party wassss started. We wanted to try another way of living.' Cross sighed deeply. 'But look at where it's got ussss. War tearing usss apart again. No wonder the Chin chose a different location.'

'Who are the Chin exactly?' asked Whitestaff. 'I keep hearing the name but haven't been told much about them, other than they're large.'

'Masssssive,' hissed Cross. 'Though I've never seen one, of course. All I know is that they didn't come with usssssss on Exodus Day. Your kind would know more than the Nazoor. They made sssssome deal with your great wizard.'

'Merlin?' Whitestaff grunted. 'It seems as though everyone has made a deal with him. Whether they want to or not.' Suddenly, Whitestaff was struck with an idea. 'Excuse me, Cross, I need to ask the King something.'

Cross bowed his head and glided back to Xenos's side.

The Kai'dahl tilted his wings and veered over to Cracone, making sure he got the side with the good eye. The King was flying with his son and Whitestaff squeezed himself between them.

'Cracone,' he said. 'Can you tell me everything you know about the Chin?'

'Whitestaff, we're about to fly into the last fight any of us will ever have. Now isn't the time for idle chat! You want to talk? Let's talk about flight formations and battle tactics, not long gone dragons!'

'Yes, you're right,' said Whitestaff. 'We need to come up with a plan for the next battle. Nap, do you think you can do that?'

Nap smiled in return. 'That's all I've been thinking about since we left the dungeon.'

'Good,' said Whitestaff. 'Then organise this lot, I'm putting you in charge of preparations.'

'That's the King's job!' barked Cracone. 'I give the orders!' He glared at the Kai'dahl. 'Nap!'

'Yes, Father.'

'Do as he says. Get these Nazoor into some sort of formation and tell them whatever strategy you've cooked up.'

Nap's eyepatch glinted in the moonlight as he nodded. 'Right away.' He swooped off to find Xenos.

'Now, Kai'dahl. Make it quick. What do you want to know about the Chin?' And why is it so important?'

'Allies,' replied Whitestaff. 'Take a look around, Cracone. We've lost this war, and the only hope we've got is making new allies, right enough. Just like we did tonight.'

Cracone's eyes brightened for a moment, then he shook his head. 'It's a good strategy, boy, I'll give you that. But it can never happen.'

'Why?' asked Whitestaff. 'That's the part I need to know. Where are they and how can I get to them?'

'It's no use. They went to another planet, that's why. I was taught that when the dragons left Earth, after the war with the humans, we were all supposed to come here: to Sorteya. But the

Chin were so disgusted with us, with our fighting, they asked Merlin to send them elsewhere. To a barren planet. A dead planet. Beyond our reach.'

'But not beyond Merlin's? Surely if he sent them there, he could get them back?'

'I suppose he could. But we don't have Merlin, Whitestaff. We have you and me and Nap and a hundred half-starved Nazoor. Get your head out of the clouds, boy. You want something to think about? Think about how you're going to survive a million Nazoor talons scraping at your scales.'

Whitestaff followed Cracone's eyes to the jagged scar on his chest. In the distance he could hear the chatter and hiss of the Nazoor army as they flew closer to the Court. The sound made the blood in his veins turn to ice.

30

WHAT MONEY CAN'T BUY

Balad had to do the talking once again, as Pip couldn't manage a single sentence without tripping over his own tongue. He explained the whole situation to the Adkins women, from the attack at Aldallah by Shadowclaw, to the sea voyage with Blackbeard. Esmae listened as she cleaned up the wreckage in her cottage, while Mollie boiled some more water for tea.

When Balad had finished his tale, the cottage was clean, the tea was ready, and Esmae spoke.

'It seems you have quite the spot of bother in your land, Prince Ael. But I don't see what this has to do with us? Mollie and I have enough trouble trying to survive in a small place like Danmurk Shire. What could possibly motivate us to come and help you slay a dangerous dragon?'

Balad thought for a moment. 'Money? Yunas, our Sultan, has more gold than you can count. You could use it to buy a big house. You could live anywhere or go to whatever place you want! You could live like Queens!'

The Royal Guard's face fell as Esmae laughed. 'My dear, Mollie and I can weave magic to our heart's content. We can gather any element that exists just by thinking about it. If it's gold we wanted, we could summon a wagon full as easy as we could blink.'

'And trust me,' added Mollie, 'I've often thought about it.'

Esmae gave her daughter a frown. 'But gold doesn't make life any better. In some cases it makes it worse. Like with your great aunt, Mollie. Or do I need to remind you of her story?'

Mollie rolled her eyes and shook her head.

'If not money, then what can I offer you in return?'

Esmae thought for a minute. 'Nothing, really. We have everything we want right here.'

'But we *saved* your lives,' Balad argued. 'Those bandits could have cut you to shreds!'

'How could they kill what they can't see?' asked Esmae. She looked to her daughter and cast an invisibility spell on them both. They disappeared in an instant.

'Where did you go?' asked Pip.

'Still here,' answered Esmae as she let the spell fall off.

Mollie looked at Pip's wide eyes and smiled at him. 'We were never in any real danger, Prince. But it was fun watching you shoot your bow. You shot the mace right out of Cudgel's grasp. How did you do it?'

'Practise,' answered Pip, blushing again.

'If the Honoured One wants to hit it, he hits it,' said Balad.

'It's more than practise,' said Mollie. 'Mother, did you notice how he did it?'

'Unfortunately,' answered Esmae with a sniff.

'Notice what?' asked Pip. 'I just shot the arrow...'

'You're bleeding!' gasped Balad. 'Pip, your bandage! Blood is soaking through!'

Everyone looked down at Pip's left forearm. There was indeed a red patch that was spreading fast.

'I must have knocked it during the fight,' Pip said. 'Balad, can you go to the horses and get the fresh bandages from the pack? I'll take these off.'

The young Prince winced as he slowly unwound the bandages.

Unable to restrain her curiosity, Mollie came closer to inspect the injury. She hissed through her teeth when she saw his bare arm.

'What on earth did that?' she asked. 'It looks burnt, but there is no fire element. Mother, look!'

Esmae drew nearer and bent down to get a better view.

'Dark magic,' she said, mostly to herself. 'The elements *are* there, but slightly different. See?'

Mollie squinted her eyes. 'Yes, I do.' She looked up at Pip. 'What did this to you, young Prince?'

At first Pip couldn't answer. He was looking at Mollie's mouth and thinking that she had the softest lips he'd ever seen. 'Hmmm? The dragon. Sorry. Shadowclaw. Yes, I fought it. Shot it with an arrow and it sort of pinned me down.'

'Extraordinary,' said Mollie. She met the Prince's gaze and the two just looked at each other silently for a while. Esmae sniffed loudly and pinched the bridge of her nose.

'Are you going to do something about the blood, Mollie? Or do you think red is a good colour for the floor of our cottage?'

Mollie looked down and saw a small pool of blood starting to form on the wooden floor. She shook her head to clear it. 'Yes, sorry. Let me just see what I can do.'

As Mollie looked closer at the wound, she could see that most of the damage done *was* caused by magic. Just like her mother said, it was as though all the elements had been tainted by some dark force. She tried to heal the skin as best she could, but it was a complicated process. The dragon didn't just burn Pip's arms with heat—it burnt him with many elements at once. She could see frost burn, wind burn and fire burn. Undoing the damage was like trying to undo a massive knot with only one hand. Eventually though, she managed to stop the bleeding and give the skin some relief.

'These burns will never fully heal, you know?' she asked Pip. 'Even with my magic, there's only so much I can do. I'm so sorry.'

'That's fine,' said Pip, beaming at her and flexing his fingers. 'It feels much better than it did. Can you do the other one too?'

'Of course,' said Mollie, returning his smile.

Balad came back with the fresh bandages. He helped his ward bind each arm when Mollie had finished her work.

'They look much better, Prince of the Sands. Thank you, Mollie Adkins.'

189

'They're still fragile,' she told them. 'The smallest bump will split the skin again. But I do have a spell for this if you want me to use it?'

'A spell?' asked Pip.

'I call it, *Shell.* I'll gather a mix of earth and fire elements and compact them around your arm to form a really hard barrier. The first time I saw it was on Whitestaff's egg.' She looked up at her mother. 'I'm assuming Merlin put it there.'

'Of course,' Esmae sighed.

'But it kept his shell safe. It was even able to withstand being hit a thousand times with a giant hammer!'

'Sounds like what I need,' said Pip. 'Though I will steer clear of any giant hammers.'

Mollie laughed at his joke and Pip felt very pleased with himself.

When Mollie had finished casting Shell over Pip's forearms, she sent the Prince and his guard outside.

'Mother and I need a minute to discuss your proposition,' she explained to them.

'Nothing to discuss!' said Esmae, but Mollie waved at her to be quiet and she saw the two out the door.

'Of course,' said Balad. 'We will wait by our horses.'

When they were far enough away, Mollie spun around to face her mother.

'What is it, Mollie? Their problem isn't our problem!'

'I know, Esmae. But there's another dragon out there! Maybe it has some answers about what happened to Whitestaff.'

'The last thing this family needs is another dragon! Besides, this one doesn't sound like Whitestaff at all. It can *gather* magic and it burns cities!'

'I think I should go and help them.'

'Why, Mollie? We've already discussed it. They don't have anything to offer us in return. They don't have anything we want!'

Mollie's played with her hair and gave her mother a coy smile.

'Esmae, I wouldn't say they don't have *anything* to offer...'

The older Adkins looked her daughter up and down. She saw the sparkle in her daughter's eyes and the rose colouring in her cheeks. She recognised that look at once; it was how she used to get when she first met Merlin.

'Oh good grief,' she said.

31

THE BUBBLE BURSTS

In the distance, Whitestaff could see the spire of the King's Court. However, it didn't look anything like it should. The massive golden head that served as an entrance was covered with swarming Nazoor. They were scratching the face of it, breaking its teeth and had managed to smash one of its emerald eyes. The top of the spire was utterly gone. The Nazoor, having learned of the location of the entire Palal from Luzahmin, had torn away all the moist dirt. They had stripped the spire back to nothing, so now the giant dragon-faced entrance looked as though it would topple at any moment. A large column of Nazoor, almost as tall as the spire itself, waited for the excavation to finish so that they could fight, and kill, the Palal dragons inside. It seemed as though something was keeping them from getting in completely. A massive bubble of energy surrounded the chambers of the Court, and Whitestaff knew that Susset and her magic was the only thing keeping the Nazoor horde at bay. The Wyvern would dig like mad and then come up against the magical barrier. They would then hiss in frustration and dig somewhere else.

As they were making their way closer, there came a sudden shout from Xenos, and Whitestaff's Nazoor army surrounded him completely. They made a bubble around his body, keeping him, Nap and Cracone inside. It was like being inside a cage with Nazoor for bars. They were so close around him that Whitestaff could barely flap his wings. His ears ached with the sound of their beating wings and hissing beaks.

'What are they doing?' Whitestaff cried in alarm. Part of the Kai'dahl feared that he was being caught in a trap!

'The strategy!' shouted Nap over the noise.

'What strategy?'

Before Nap could answer, Xenos appeared in front of Whitestaff. He twisted his snake-like body and flew backwards, keeping his face level with Whitestaff's.

'There is no way we can fight them all, Whitestaff. But young Nap here came up with a plan to keep you alive for as long as possible.' He too had to shout to be heard. 'We have made a ball around you to keep you hidden from the army. Hopefully, we can get nice and close to the Court entrance before Mezelga's servants figure out who we are and that we're not meant to be here.'

The Kai'dahl looked over at Nap. 'Excellent thinking, Re'dahl.'

Nap grinned back, clearly chuffed.

A Nazoor from above called out to Xenos, and the leader of the Party of Peace nodded in return.

'We need to speed up, Whitestaff. We're getting closer. Just keep flying and don't stop, no matter what.'

'I understand,' said Whitestaff. 'Thank you.'

Xenos shook his head. 'No, Kai'dahl, thank you.'

'What for? I doubt any of us will live through this.'

'You rescued us. You reached out the claws of friendship at a time when you had every reason to hate. That is a thing worth dying for.'

Xenos turned and surged forwards and was almost immediately lost in the pack of flying Wyvern. The wings around him sped up, and Whitestaff could feel his body being pushed along inside the ball. From between the flapping wings and whipping tales, he caught glimpses of the Court entrance ahead. He could also see the Nazoor army. Some of them had turned around to inspect the newcomers. Xenos was right: at first they didn't attack. They just hovered and stared in confusion. But when they recognised some of the Party members and caught glimpses of the coloured dragons they were hiding, Mezelga's soldiers hissed with rage and swooped in for the attack.

'Here they come!' hollered Nap. 'Just keep flying for the Court!'

The Party of Peace heard his command and sped towards their target, while thousands of Mezelga's Wyvern came in for the kill.

Xenos's ball smashed into the wave of Nazoor. The momentum took the Palal much closer to the Court spire, but not close enough. They were absolutely swarmed. Whitestaff didn't know if the dragons around him were friend or foe, so he just kept flying forward through the mass. It was only a few seconds before the ball was cracked open and the enemy came flooding in. They pounced on the King straight away, and the ferocity of their attack made Whitestaff's hearts surge with fear. Nap flew over to help his father and Whitestaff did likewise. They pulled the clawing dragons off Cracone, while at the same time fighting attackers of their own.

'Keep moving forward!' yelled Cracone. 'Forget me! You're almost there!'

Nap and Whitestaff looked at each other and shook their heads.

'Not without you, father!'

They grabbed the older dragon by his sides and Whitestaff belched forth a stream of scorching fire, burning a path for the three. Nazoor dragons that were too slow to move were instantly roasted by the blast. The cloud of Nazoor scattered for a moment, then came at them from the sides, scratching and biting at the Palal.

Seeing the sky ahead momentarily clear, they rushed forward towards the jaws of the Court, ignoring the Nazoor soldiers that were attacking their scales. Nap was the faster flyer, and he pulled both Whitestaff and Cracone through the air and into the massive jaws. The three Palal dragons were snapped up at the last instant, and their Nazoor attackers smashed into an invisible field of magic that Merlin had weaved long ago. The Palal collapsed as soon as the jaws closed behind them and were greeted with an awful sight. The Court of the

King no longer had a ceiling. The Nazoor has stripped away the dirt and the moon was visible overhead. So too were the thousands of Nazoor, who were scratching and scraping and hurling themselves at Susset's magical forcefield.

Other dragons rushed over to Whitestaff, Nap and their King. Seeing that the older Re'dahl was gravely wounded, they took Cracone straight to the infirmary. They tried to drag Whitestaff there too, but he pushed them away.

'I'm fine! Leave me be!' he thundered. He made his way to the centre of the Court where Susset stood. She had her hood on and her arms outstretched. Her face was contorted with extreme concentration, and Whitestaff could see her whole body was shaking. A thin trail of blood began leaking from her nose. She took her eyes off the Nazoor above for a moment to look at Whitestaff.

'I'm sorry, Kai'dahl,' she whispered. 'The magical barrier... I can't hold it any longer.'

And with that, she collapsed in a heap.

It was then that the shield of magic, that kept the Palal safe from the Nazoor, vanished.

32

FINALLY

The next few moments happened in slow-motion to Whitestaff. He saw Susset was about to fall and he dove over to her to try and catch her. The magical shield fell away from the Court, and the Palal dragons were exposed to the Nazoor. The Wyvern, who had been desperately trying to claw their way through Susset's magic, suddenly found their efforts met no resistance and gave a terrifying cheer of triumph. They called to the rest of the army and so thousands of Nazoor began to descend on the Palal in the Court. Whitestaff was in mid-air, his front legs outstretched as he tried to catch the sorceress, when a human—an old man—appeared out of nowhere behind Susset and caught her before Whitestaff could. The man had an enormous white beard that stretched to his knees, and he was dressed the same way as Susset: in a hooded robe. However, his robe was patched and faded and nowhere near as elegant as anything that could be found in Susset's wardrobe.

The bearded man looked calmly at the descending Nazoor overhead. He held Susset in one arm and waved the other in a wide arc. In an instant, the shield of magic was back in place. The Nazoor overhead slammed against it and hissed with wild frustration. They clawed and screamed and bit at it with their beaks, but could not get through. The Palal in the Court drew a deep sigh of relief, for they knew that they stood no chance against the sheer size of the Nazoor army. Whitestaff halted his jump to avoid colliding with the stranger and rolled his body across the floor, missing Susset and her saviour by a few centimetres.

'I'm guessing you're Merlin,' said Whitestaff as he pulled himself up and folded back his wings.

'Indeed, Whitestaff. Great to see you again.'

'Again? What do you mean *again*?'

'Wait! You don't know it's me? Is this the first time we've met?'

'Of course it is!' replied the dragon.

'I mean, is this the first time you've met *me*?' Merlin asked as he gently eased Susset down and onto the floor.

'Yes! What kind of question is that?'

'Sorry, dragon King, I've been all through time and I've known you for years. I knew it was about here that you meet me for the first time. Are you sure? Have I told you about the Chin yet? Or do you tell that to me? Is this the part where I explain the Medallion?' Merlin seemed to be talking more to himself than to the dragon.

By now the other Palal had gathered around to get a look at the newcomer.

'I think it's Merlin,' someone whispered.

'Merlin the Magician,' said another.

'Is it really him?'

'Has to be. I think I heard him say it.'

Graggy and Armay pushed through the crowd to get to Whitestaff. All the while, the deadly Wyvern were watching and pounding against Merlin's magical barrier only fifteen dragon lengths above their heads.

'Whitestaff! Thank goodness you made it back,' said Armay. She embraced the massive golden dragon and curled her tail in his. 'We didn't know where you were!'

'Glad to see your scales are all intact! Did you find Mezelga? Did you finish her?' asked Graggy.

'I'm afraid not. She has hidden herself away.'

'Well you found someone,' replied Graggy. 'Is that who I think it is?'

Whitestaff looked over to the sorcerer, who was still engaged in a conversation with himself.

'That's him, right enough. At long last I finally get to meet Merlin. And I have one or two questions for him that I need answered.'

Whitestaff let go of Armay and marched over to Merlin. He bent down low so he could look the man in the eye.

'I have some questions for you that I need answered,' he spoke into the sorcerer's mind.

'I bet you do. I get told that a lot you know.'

'Firstly, is Susset going to be all right?'

'Good question. Shows you care. That's why we're friends you know. You have a good heart. Well, hearts. They're both good.'

'Susset?'

'Oh yes. Over-gathered. It takes energy to do what we do, you know. Like sprinting. Or flying. Do it for too long and the body shuts down. She will come around in thirty-six more seconds. Thirty-five. Thirty-four. Thirty-three. Thir—'

'Yes yes, as long as she will recover. Second question. How long can you hold this shield for?'

They both looked up and watched the savage Nazoor beat against the invisible field.

'Days, I suppose. If I had to. Which I don't.'

'Why don't you?'

'Because of your solution. You've already figured a way out of this haven't you? Or haven't you done that bit yet? I'm not sure where we're up to. Nazoor. Shield. Susset. I've lost my place.'

'Speak plainly, Merlin. What "solution" are you talking about? And what do you mean by that other stuff?'

'I'm sorry. I do apologise. It's not easy keeping up you know. I have about twenty timelines on the go at once. In about two days I'll be at my daughter's side and she'll be with you. But see, I've already done it and you haven't. So I get it muddled. But on the whole I think I do rather well.'

'The solution, Merlin! Get to the point! How do we get out of this?'

'Oh,' said Merlin, taken aback by Whitestaff's anger. 'I don't think we do that bit just yet. Has the cranky red one died yet?'

'Died? Who died?'

'The red dragon that you came in with.'

'You mean Nap?'

'No, not the surly one. The cranky bigger one. Cranky? Is that his name?'

'Cracone?'

'Yes! That's him.' Merlin spun around to address the audience who had gathered. 'You have my condolences on Cracone's death,' he told them. 'He was a good red angry dragon.'

'Don't tell them that, you fool! Do you want to start a panic? Cracone isn't dead. He was just taken to the infirmary.'

But it was too late. Some of the assembled Palal wailed in grief at the death of their king, while others rushed to the infirmary to see if it was true. On the floor, Susset had started to regain consciousness. Merlin turned his back on Whitestaff and began whispering to Susset, who looked very weak, but clearly overjoyed to see the bearded magician. He helped the young woman to her feet and then guided her over to a plump dragon cushion.

Whitestaff was hesitant to leave the man who he had hoped to question for so long, but the thought of losing Cracone was too much. Whitestaff turned and followed Armay and Graggy and the rest of the crowd into the infirmary to check on the Re'dahl King.

When they pushed their way through, they found the King surrounded by his closest friends. Nap and Luzahmin were also at his side, and Nightgale was making him sip some yellow balefruit juice. Merlin was wrong. Cracone the Re'dahl King was still alive, though Whitestaff judged by the deep cuts and bites along his body that he wouldn't be for much longer.

33

THE END OF THE RED REIGN

The colour had drained from Cracone's red scales, and he looked more like an overgrown Lili'dahl than the fearsome Palal King. His wounds were deep, and although Nightgale had applied as much poultice made from yellow balefruit as she could, it was not going to be enough to save him. Cracone fixed his good eye on Whitestaff.

'Kai'dahl, come before me,' he ordered. Whitestaff was pleased to hear the King still spoke with booming command, and he did as he was bade. 'Kneel, Whitestaff. I have minutes left and I need to do this last duty.'

'Minutes? You're not dying father!' said Nap. 'There's still fight in you yet.'

'Don't bother, son. I know my time. Ah, here it is.' At that moment, Umdir the Gra'dahl entered. He was carrying the Royal Medallion. 'Bring it here, Umdir. Hurry!' Cracone gave a weak cough and motioned Umdir over. The assembled Palal made way for the green dragon.

'Father, what are you doing?' asked Nap.

'You know what I'm doing, son.'

'But father—'

'But nothing!' snapped the King. 'You've seen what I've seen Nap. You followed him and so did his worst enemy. We'd never have lasted this long if it wasn't for him. I don't want anymore of this nonsense. He's proven himself, gold or not. Whitestaff, kneel or Latos take you!'

Again, Whitestaff was too concerned to argue. He didn't like to disagree with Cracone at the best of times, and something told him, for once in his life, to do as he was told. He knelt down on three knees and bowed his head to the King.

With his last scrap of energy, Cracone stood. Luzahmin and Nap held him under his wings and guided him over to Whitestaff.

'Kai'dahl,' Cracone began. 'You have shown that you are the bravest and wisest Palal dragon to have ever soared the Sorteyan skies. It is my honour to pass onto you, the Royal Medallion. With this Medallion comes the weight of responsibility that you have shown you are fit to shoulder. I hereby name you, Whitestaff, King of the Palal, and from this moment forth, I abdicate the throne.'

The other Palal in the infirmary gasped at the proclamation and began to mutter to each other. The Re'dahl turned to face them.

'Palal, I need you to obey this Kai'dahl to the end. I have done my best as King, but now you need to follow your real leader. All hail, Whitestaff. King of the Palal.' With the assistance of his son and Luzahmin, Cracone place the medallion around Whitestaff's neck and gave an awkward bow.

Whitestaff watched as the other Palal, including Armay and Graggy, bent down low.

'All hail Whitestaff. All hail the Golden King,' they said.

Cracone was the first to rise. He gave another weak cough and asked Nap to put him back down on the cushion. Nap led his father back to his resting place and held his paw tightly.

'Father,' he said. 'Isn't there something we can do?'

Cracone shook his head slowly in response. He gave another cough and a shimmering cloud of dragon essence escaped his mouth. Whitestaff saw it and he knew Cracone was nearly at the end.

'My fellow Palal,' said Whitestaff, his voice choked. He cleared his throat. 'My fellow Palal,' he said again. 'Please, make your way back into the Court. Give Cracone some privacy.'

The other dragons understood. No one needed to see the Red King die in front of his son. Slowly, with heavy paws, they made their way back into the chamber of the Court, where the Nazoor still madly thrashed at the sky above them.

Soon, the only dragons left in the infirmary (apart from those too injured to move) were Cracone, Whitestaff, Nap, Luzahmin and old Olfar. Cracone let go of Nap's paw and looked his son in the eye.

'You need to follow Whitestaff, son. I know what we said when he was gone, but I was wrong. The Palal need him, do you understand?'

Nap looked to the Kai'dahl he had hated for so long.

'I said I'd never follow him, father. But I was wrong also. I'll serve him as I did you, to the very last.'

'That's my boy,' said Cracone. 'Best son a Re'dahl could ask for. You've made me one proud father in this life.' His one good eye then moved to the new King. 'Whitestaff,' he said. 'We have countless Wyvern chomping down on us. They have us cornered. Any other dragon would give up. But you'll get us out of this. I'm ordering you to.'

'I will, Cracone. I promise on my honour as...'

But Whitestaff never got to finish his sentence. Cracone's eye closed and and his body went limp. His shallow breathing stopped and the dragon essence that kept him alive came curling from out of his nostrils like golden smoke, only to vanish after a few moments.

Nap saw it float away and sobbed over his father's body, tears spilling out of his only eye. Luzahmin squeezed Nap close to her, and she too wailed with grief.

Olfar and Whitestaff hugged them both and then left them to grieve in peace.

'I hate to sound callous, Nephew,' Olfar said, keeping his voice hushed. 'But thou are King now. What is our next move, Your Majesty?'

'Olfar! Cracone's body is not yet cool. Please don't call me that!'

'As you wish, Nephew. But it is now thou title and responsibility.'

'I didn't want it now, Olfar! Not like this!'

'Ahh. We rarely get to choose our own fate, Whitestaff. And sometimes the things we want least are the things we need to have. Does thou have a plan to end this war?'

'Not yet, Uncle. I have a small idea. Something that might work.'

'Well, when we get back into the Court chambers, remember all of the Palal waiting there are in pain. They have lost their old King and they are scared of the Nazoor that are literally above their heads. If thou does *not* have a plan, Nephew, I suggest thou first act as King is to keep them from knowing. What they need now is hope, Whitestaff, and thou are the only dragon that can give it to them.'

'No, Olfar. What they need is victory. And what *I* need is Merlin.'

34

ASK POLITELY?

The Royal Medallion bumped into his chest with every step
Whitestaff took. He ignored his fellow Palal, who looked to him
for some guidance now that he was King.

Soon, Whitestaff thought. *I'll deal with you soon. But first,
there's something I have to know.*

He made his way over to Susset and Merlin, who sat high up
in the Bo'dahl section of the Court. No one else was near them as it
was so close to the invisible roof. But the gnashing Nazoor didn't
seem to bother the humans.

'Susset,' said Whitestaff. 'You look much better.'

'I am. Thank you, Whitestaff. It's good to have Merlin back.'
She gave the older man a brilliant smile.

'Yes. Without your magic, Merlin, we'd be finished by now,
right enough.'

Merlin gave the Nazoor above a look of disinterest. 'Oh,
that's nothing. Sorry once more about the King, Whitestaff. But I see
he passed my invention on to you,' Merlin pointed at the Medallion

around the Kai'dahl's neck. 'I could only ever manage to make one. I suppose I could make more. Very difficult though. Takes time. And that's something I have an infinite amount of, but I always seem to be rushing. Except when I'm in between time, you know. You can stay forever in there.'

'In between time?' asked Susset.

'It's the space between portals,' answered Whitestaff. 'It was you who spoke to me there, wasn't it? The time I went back to Earth?'

'That's right!' said Merlin. 'It's the space in between portals. Of course, I forget you travel between this world and Earth!'

'How could you forget a thing like that? You're the one that trapped the portal in my egg!'

'Calm down, Whitestaff,' said Susset. 'It's harder for him than you realise. *He*,' she said, laying a hand on Merlin's shoulder, 'may not have done anything yet. His timeline isn't the same as yours.'

'She's right,' agreed Merlin. 'There are some things I know about your future because you've told me about them. But you haven't lived that part of your life yet. And there are some things about your past that I may have done, but I haven't travelled there yet to do it. It's hard to keep track, you know.'

'That makes no sense to me.'

'It will one day. You'll see. That much I know. I know why you're here now too. It's about the dragons, isn't it?'

'Of course it's about dragons, Merlin! I am a dragon, I'm being attacked by dragons, and I'm the KING OF THE DRAGONS.'

Merlin looked startled at Whitestaff's outburst. The Palal who were huddled in the Court below looked up, wondering what was happening. Whitestaff wiped his brow with his tail.

'I'm sorry,' he said. 'I have no right to yell at you.'

'No, you don't,' said Susset.

'What I'd like to ask you, Merlin, is about the Chin.'

'I knew it!' said the old Sorcerer.

'Yes. I'm sure you did. I'd like to know if you can bring them here to fight by our side?'

'Not at all!' said Merlin.

'Why not? We can't win this war without allies. We need other dragons on our side.'

'I agree,' said the magician.

'Then why can't you bring them here?'

Merlin ran his fingers through his beard. 'The Chin are beyond my control, Whitestaff. They are not just dragons. They are creation and annihilation. They are powerful beyond my comprehension. I can't make them do anything. But you could.'

'I could? How?'

'Ask them politely?' suggested Merlin.

Whitestaff fought hard to control his temper. 'How might I ask them, if I can't even speak to them? They're on a different planet, as the tale goes.'

'They are,' agreed Merlin. 'But I can open a portal to it. You can go there and ask them. They will listen to you.'

'Why would they listen to me?' asked the Kai'dahl.

'They are about ready for the next phase of their existence, I think that's what you tell me. Too hard to explain. Plus, you do something there and they agree. I know about that. You were just there! Or was I?'

'What? What do I do?'

Merlin thought for a moment, then his face brightened. 'Nope. In the future you ask me not to talk too much about the Chin. Just do it though, whatever it is you do. But first, shouldn't you tell them where you're going?' He gestured to the waiting Palal below.

The dragons on the Court floor looked defeated and terrified. They were talking in hushed tones, trying to comfort one another, but mostly they were looking up to their new King, waiting for a plan or some words of hope.

'Of course,' said Whitestaff. He flew down to the throne and sat himself on it. Where Cracone had sat on the throne with enough room to lay down if he wanted, the golden dragon found it a tight fit. He picked up the Royal Rod that lay at the foot of the throne and banged it on the floor. He needn't have bothered, for he already had the assembled dragons' attention.

'Palal of every colour and age,' he began. 'As you can see, we are besieged by the Wyvern. I sought out Mezelga with the aid of Nap and Cracone, may his essence come to rest in pleasant skies. We rescued the Nazoor Party of Peace and they fought with us to get us here. Without their help, our losses would have been higher. And so now I will turn to other dragons for help. You have heard of the Chin? Massive dragons that lived with us on Earth. I will kneel before them and ask that they fight at our side.' He looked over at Merlin, who was busy conjuring a portal at the high, back section of the Bo'dahl side of the Court. 'It is my hope that they will fight with us, so that we may overthrow Mezelga's minions, and once again know peace in Sorteya. I shall leave soon, but not for long. Merlin has assured me that his magic surrounds this Court like a protective bubble, and it will stand until I return. Take care of each other and wait for me. Soon we may have to fight, so I ask you now to rest. There is nothing more to do.'

With that, Whitestaff stood and marched back up to Merlin. Many of his fellow dragons called out questions to him, but Whitestaff knew if he answered one he'd have to answer them all, and that could take time he didn't care to waste. Olfar quickly appeared at his side and had to jog to keep up with his nephew.

'Whitestaff, is it true? Will thee go and see the Chin?' he asked.

'Yes, Olfar. Merlin is making the door now. See?'

'But we don't know what kind of dragons they are, Nephew. They could be worse than the Nazoor! Legend has it that they are capable of the most destructive—'

'I shall see for myself soon enough, Uncle.' The Sorteyan sun had started to rise. Its light shone across the leathery bodies of the Wyvern overhead. 'And if they are as destructive as the legends say, than maybe that's exactly what we need!'

35

WHAT MAGIC CAN'T DO

It was the first time in Wendy's life she'd been hitched to a wagon. The horse found it cumbersome and unnatural. Having the heavy cart attached to her body made the simple act of walking feel as though she was climbing up a steep hill. She blew out of her nostrils with frustration.

'I feel sorry for Bramble; he has to do this almost every day. No wonder he is so strong,' Wendy said to Mollie.

'I know, Wendy. I think it was very noble of you to offer.'

In the back of the cart, along with Mollie's suitcase, was Whitestaff's shimmering egg. Mollie had wrapped it in an old blanket for the journey to avoid prying eyes.

She still couldn't quite believe she was going out on her own adventure. Esmae had given in to the idea easier than Mollie would've thought.

Maybe she does care about these people from across the sea, she wondered. *Or maybe she's as curious about dragons as I am. Or maybe she knew that I'm too old to hold back. Maybe, deep down, we both knew that I was always going to go, whether she said I could or not.*

After the discussion with her mother, Mollie had gone outside to give Balad and Pip the good news. Their faces looked so pleased when she told them—especially the Prince's. She asked for them to leave without her, and to wait for her at Gibbon, near the road to Lareborough.

'As long as we don't meet anywhere near the Barren Arms,' Mollie insisted. 'After what you told me, there's no knowing what I'd do if I ever clap eyes on Jake again.'

'Why can't we all leave together?' asked Balad. He didn't want to risk losing his weapon against Shadowclaw now that he'd found it.

'Because I need to pack, and I want to say goodbye to Terry before I leave. Mother and I still have one or two things to discuss too.'

'We can wait,' said Balad.

'No, Balad,' said Pip. 'Let's leave her to say her goodbyes in private. She doesn't need us hanging around.' He gave Mollie a wink. 'We will wait for you at the top of the mountain track. Going down will be easier than coming up at least. We should be at the port by dusk.'

Balad shrugged his shoulders and he and Pip went to ready the horses. Once they were mounted, Pip gave Mollie a wave and trotted back the way he had come, his Royal Guard at his side.

Mollie then packed and waited patiently for Terry and Bramble to arrive. It wasn't long before the two had returned, hot and sweaty from the sun and ready for a drink of water. Once his mouth was wet again, Terry told them how Sir Layton handed out the punishment to Cudgel there on the spot.

'He was very happy ter have the bandit leader at last,' said Terry with a chuckle. 'An' old Cudgel confessed everything to him on the spot. Whatever yer told him seemed to have stuck.' He gave his wife a peck on the cheek. 'He sentenced Cudgel to five years labour in the mines to the north. Sir Layton said he'd escort him there himself.'

'Sounds like Cudgel will finally find out what real work is,' said Esmae.

'But yer don't sound too happy about it,' said Terry.

Esmae took a deep breath. 'I don't give a fig for Cudgel, my dear. What's upsetting me is that it seems my little girl here is leaving us for a while.'

Terry looked to Mollie. 'What do yer mean? Where are yer going, Mollie?'

'I'm going to help those men who were here before, Terry. Their homeland is being terrorised by a dragon, and they think I can help.'

'Can yer?'

'I should think so. By the sounds of it, the only thing that will stop it is magic. And we all know that magic is what I do best.'

215

'True,' Terry admitted. 'How long will yer be gone? Where do they hail from?'

'They're from Nalib.'

'Never heard of it. Far?'

'About two weeks by ship.'

'Two weeks! One way!' Terry stood so fast he knocked over his chair.

'Calm down, my dear,' said Esmae. 'She will be fine.'

'But we don't know those men,' said Terry. 'They could be lying. They could be crooks! Who knows what they really want?'

Mollie stood also and gave Terry a warm hug. 'They speak the truth, Terry. I can feel it. Plus, I'll be safe. I feel like this is something that I'm meant to do.'

'Fight a dragon?' asked Terry.

Esmae laughed. 'I think this has less to do with the dragon and more to do with the young Prince. The one with the hair.'

'Mother!'

Esmae rolled her eyes. 'Deny it then.'

'I am interested in him, Esmae. I want to know if he knows the secret to his marksmanship. Anyway, Terry, I waited for you to come back so I could say goodbye.' She gave Mr Gritbole another hug, and then she embraced and kissed her mother. The three then loaded up Terry's cart with the suitcase and the precious egg. 'I have to have it with me,' said Mollie. 'If Whitestaff comes back, I want to know right away. I promised I'd look after it and it's my responsibility.'

It was then that Wendy interrupted. 'Can't you go tomorrow?' she asked. 'Bramble looks exhausted and you're going to make him pull that all the way to Lareborough and back!'

'He'll be fine,' said Mollie. 'He's a workhorse.'

'Well I think it's wrong. I'll take his place,' she concluded. 'Hitch me up, Mollie. Let's let Bramble rest.'

Bramble tried to argue, but once Wendy had her mind made up there was no point. Soon, Wendy was loaded up, and once again Terry, Esmae and Bramble stood by the little gate at the front of the cottage to wave Mollie goodbye and good luck on another adventure. Esmae cried and Terry held her hand. He whispered similar advice to what he'd given her once before. 'She ain't a little child anymore, love,' he told her. 'I know you'll miss her, but she's a grown woman now. Only she's probably the most powerful woman in the world. I pity the poor dragon that's up against that one. She won't come to no harm, you'll see.'

'Oh, Terry, I'm not worried about her safety. I know what she'd do if anyone tried to harm her.'

'What is it then?'

'I'm worried about the only thing magic can't protect, my dear. I'm worried about her heart.'

36

BACK TO THE DART

Mollie's heart thumped loudly in her chest when she counted how many men there were. It looked to be around nine, all riding at her like they were taking part in a wild charge on a battleground. She had only expected to see Balad and Pip waiting for her, but these new strangers that were galloping her way looked fearsome.

'What do we do now?' asked Wendy. 'I can't run with this thing on me.' She flicked her head to indicate Terry's cart.

'I could freeze them, or maybe put up a wall of fire?' *Maybe Terry was right after all,* Mollie thought. *Maybe Pip didn't want my help and instead this is some elaborate trap.*

At the front of the group rode the Prince. His face was no longer friendly and charming, he wore an expression of determination and anger. His eyes met Mollies as he rode at her, and he seemed to guess what she was thinking. He called out to the others to slow down.

'Whoa, men. Whoa,' he shouted as he slowed his horse. 'Sorry, Mollie,' he called out. 'Didn't mean to scare you, but there's been some news.' He alighted from his horse and walked over to her. One of the men from the group did the same. He was tall and had a mass of shaggy hair covering his face.

'I know that one!' said Wendy. 'We met him at the fair!'

'Rio!' she said. She gave the sailor a wave and turned her attention back to the Prince. 'What's all this about, Pip?'

'I'm sorry again, Mollie. We were racing to come and get you. It seems we have to leave right away.'

'Hello, Mollie,' said Rio as he joined them. 'Captain sent us up here to take you back in a hurry. We just got news from a bloke in the port. Seems this dragon is on the move again and is terrorising towns all around the Prince's city.'

'It's the Silver Scourge,' said Pip. 'The news is already over two weeks old. The dragon must have started the day we left.'

'Which is why the Captain thought you'd like to leave now.'

'And we do,' said Pip. 'Mollie, Bob's men will have to carry your load on their horses. The cart is going to be too slow going down the mountain road.'

'I understand,' said Mollie. She gave Wendy a pat and spoke into the horse mind. 'Looks like you won't have to go the whole way.'

'Thank goodness,' said the horse. 'I didn't want to tell you, but I wasn't sure I'd make it down there and back again.'

Rio helped the rest of Bob's men unload the cart. They didn't unwrap the blanket and didn't look at all curious as to what was in it.

'Will you ride with me, Mollie?' asked the Prince.

As an answer, Mollie levitated onto the back of his horse. She tentatively put her hands around his waist. 'Ready when you are,' she said.

Wendy said goodbye to Mollie and headed back to the cottage with the now empty cart.

When everything was secured onto the the other horses, Balad gave the order to head back to the Dart at a full gallop. They set off at a cracking pace, past Gibbon and down the mountain road. Bob's crew took the lead, as they had the faster horses, and Balad and Pip took the rear. The road was well worn, so the horses didn't kick up much dust. From the top of the track, Mollie could see the ocean, sparkling like a blue jewel as the sun hovered just above it, and down below her, the thick forest that covered the bottom of the mountain. And every now and then, when there was a break in the trees, she could also see Lareborough and its tiny port with a black ship in its dock. Going so fast on a horse downhill wasn't the most comfortable experience, but Mollie didn't mind the occasional jolt or sharp turn.

'You'll have to excuse this horse,' said Pip over this shoulder. 'I don't think it's been kept in the best condition.'

The wind blew Pip's golden locks into Mollie's face. She smiled to herself and drew tighter around his waist. 'It's fine,' she said. 'I think he's doing rather well, carrying the both of us and all.'

'Maybe you'll get to meet my real horse, Jasper. I've had him since I could crawl. He's so fast and very clever. He'd do anything for a lump of sugar too.'

'Remind me to tell you about how I met Wendy, one day. That's a story I think you'll like.'

The two galloped on in silence for the rest of the trip, and before too long they were at the bottom of the road that opened up into Lareborough. They pulled their horse back to a trot and headed for the Dart. When they reached the port, one of Bob's men took the horses and led them away.

'He's going to return them to the stables,' Rio told Mollie. 'We only rented them. He will sell Pip and Balad's horses too. No need for *them* on a ship. Only leave their dung on my nice clean deck.'

He ushered Mollie, Pip and Balad up the gangplank, across the deck and to the door of Blackbeard's cabin. Mollie took in the elaborate carvings of imps on the thick door and the snarling beasts that served as handles. Pip noticed Rio gave the same seven knocks he'd given the door last time, and from inside the Captain told them to enter.

Rio opened the door, allowing the trio to go inside, then he closed it firmly behind them.

'Mollie!' boomed Blackbeard from behind his desk. He stood and walked over to the young sorceress. He took her up in his arms and gave her a powerful hug. 'It's great to see you again!'

'You too, Bob,' said Mollie. 'I love your ship!'

'The Dart? Isn't she a beauty?'

Pip watched on and couldn't help but feel a twinge of jealousy. 'It's made of tyshwood,' he offered. But Mollie didn't hear him.

'How have you been, Mollie? Catching any more sneaky crooks?'

'Yes I have. Well, the same crook actually. He came with some men to finish me off, but mother and I took care of him and his thugs. With some help from that one.' She jerked her thumb at the Prince, who blushed at being included.

'You didn't really need me or Balad, remember?'

Mollie laughed and let go of Bob.

'Take a seat,' the Captain offered. 'We have a bit to discuss.' At that moment, the ship lurched underneath them. 'Looks like we're off already. The crew want to leave while there's still a bit of light left.'

Mollie looked around Bob's office and couldn't believe how neat everything was. The books on the shelves were in good order. The windows behind the Captain's desk were so clean they were almost invisible. At her feet was a soft blue rug with two darts crossing each other. There wasn't a stain to be found on it. Mollie never dreamed Bob would keep such a tidy space.

'Rio told us you have some bad news,' said Balad. 'That is why we rushed back so quickly.'

Bob cracked his knuckles and unrolled a map. It was the same one he'd shown Pip before. The Captain pointed at their location with the feathered end of his quill. 'Right now we're here:

Lareborough. It seems that about one day after we left here, Hulum, people from further up the coast, Bridler, were attacked by a silver dragon that could turn invisible. Then it moved south here. I don't know the name of this place.'

'Tallarn,' said Balad. 'He must be searching for Nalib!'

'But he knows where it is, Balad. Why doesn't he just go there?'

'He's blind, Honoured One. He navigates by sense of smell. He's trying to sniff out the... you know.' Balad didn't want to mention the royal treasure in front of Blackbeard.

'Of course,' said Pip, catching on. 'I forgot that he can't see.'

Blackbeard took their attention back to his map. 'If I draw a line from here to Nalib,' he said, 'you can see that the dragon isn't far off. If he keeps scouting around, he's sure to find it, if he hasn't already.'

'Then we must get back there quickly,' said Pip. He thought of his mother and father, the Palace and the good folk of Nalib.

'It will take another two weeks,' said Bob. 'I'm sorry, Prince, it's the best I can do.'

Pip cursed to himself in frustration and scanned the map again. 'What if we could get there quicker?' he asked. 'What if we didn't stay along the coast this time? What if we went straight through the Pohmin Sea?'

Bob shook his head. 'It would only take five days if we did that, Prince. But we'd never make it to the other side. The kraken, remember? He'd destroy us just like he did the Night Jewell. We have a tyshwood ship, but that won't stop it.'

'Yes, but there's something you and Fogharty didn't have last time.'

'And what would that be?'

The Prince looked over to Mollie and grinned. 'A sorceress.'

37

THE CROSSING

The portal looked just like the one that used to be at the centre of Susset's cozy dugout. It shimmered like a glossy rainbow—like the mist at the bottom of a huge waterfall.

Armay and Graggy stood by Whitestaff's side, ready to wish him well. They were surprised when, just before entering, the Kai'dahl turned towards the infirmary. Nap was making his way out, having said his last farewells to his late father. Whitestaff summoned him over.

'What is it, Whitestaff? What did I miss? Is this portal our way out of this war?'

'Yes and no, Nap. There are dragons on the other side of this and I'm going to ask them for help.'

'Chin?'

'Yes, but before I go, I need you to come up with two battle strategies. Are you up to it?'

'Of course I am.'

'Glad to hear it. The first is a strategy to take the Nazoor head on, with or without the help of the Chin.'

225

'I can do that. The second one?'

'Is an exit strategy.'

'Retreat? Where too?'

'I'm not sure yet. But we need to be able to mobilise the Palal at a moment's notice. We need to plan for the worst.'

Nap nodded and scratched at the ground with his tail. 'Very good, Whitestaff. Leave it to me.' Nap left the group and went to round up the Re'dahl Council. He'd need the help of every red dragon he could find.

'Just like that?' asked Graggy. 'He didn't even insult you?'

Whitestaff clapped his friend on the back. 'Much has changed, Graggy. And not just with Nap.' He turned his attention to Merlin. 'Can you mind the Medallion for me?' he asked. 'Or will the portal work if I wear it or not?'

The old wizard's brow creased for a moment. 'Oh, I see what you're asking,' he replied. 'No, you can wear it. The magic isn't *in* the portal, you know. It's around it. I'm pulling apart space. You're going through the hole. No magic in the hole. Just in-between time.'

'That makes no sense to me, but I trust you know what you're talking about. Wish me luck,' he said as he took his first step into the shimmering mist.

The in-between time that Merlin was talking about was just a black void. Nothing moved or stirred there, and no time passed at all. You could stay in there forever and not age a day. Whitestaff walked through it, feeling as though he was being watched by Merlin from the future or the past. It gave him an uneasy feeling, so he sped up towards the light ahead. As Whitestaff neared the light on the other side, he felt the ground give way little by little under his paws. It was a strange sensation, as though the ground was slowly turning into a cloud. With one last stride, Whitestaff took a breath and leapt through the light and into the Chin planet. But his paws met nothing at all! Merlin had opened a portal into the sky! The golden dragon yelped in surprise as he tumbled like a stone in the air. He no idea how high up he was, so he instinctively thrust out his wings and tried to steady himself. Somewhere in the back of his mind, he was reminded of the first time he tried to fly on Sorteya. With a bit of mad kicking and frantic wing flapping, Whitestaff managed to steady his fall and turn it into a clumsy looking glide. When he'd managed to straighten himself out, he saw that he was still very high in the atmosphere. The air rushed across his face, and he looked down and marvelled at the world of the Chin.

This wasn't the barren planet that he'd been told of; this was a sphere of paradise. Below him the land was covered in a thick carpet of jungle. Fat fruits hung heavy in the thick trees and rivers cut through the land. The ocean to his right was deep and blue, and birds swarmed around schools of silver fish, gulping them down and chirping for more. In the distance, Whitestaff could see where the jungle thinned out. Sand from the beach looked as though it had been blown ashore to smother the trees, creating a vast desert. On the horizon, Whitestaff could see a mountain range.

Maybe the Chin are in the mountains, he thought. *That's where all dragons seem to live: up off the ground.*

He adjusted his wings and headed for the range in the distance, all the while taking in the marvellous sights down below. The very air smelled of life. It felt like everything on the planet was ancient and brand new at the same time. It made him wonder if this is what Earth would be like without the humans.

As Whitestaff drew closer to the long row of mountains, his keen eyes spotted something in the sky. It was shaped like a dragon and it was about the size of a Palal, so he sped up to meet it.

The Chin! he thought. *I've found them already!*

'You there,' he called. 'Wait for me!' Faster Whitestaff flew, until he was close enough to be heard. He drew his breath to call again, but something looked odd about the dragon. He slowed his pace and narrowed his eyes on the creature. Now that he was a bit closer, he could see that it wasn't a dragon at all! It only had two legs for one thing, much like a Wyvern, but its body was covered in feathers.

It's a giant bird, Whitestaff thought. He brought his wings around to halt himself and hovered in the air, watching as the bird flew away. It was then that the most terrifying thing occurred. The mountain range below him started to crumble. It was as though the earth itself was splitting apart. He watched in horror as the mountain range heaved itself up off the ground! It sprang upwards like a coiled snake—the front of it speared towards the bird in front of him. Up the rocks soared, showering the ground below with loose boulders, rubble and dust. Whitestaff flew backwards and out of its path. Suddenly, the craggy rocks that were heading to the sky split apart to reveal a giant mouth. A massive eye opened up on the side, and Whitestaff could see the mountains for what they were: the body of a colossal dragon!

Whitestaff looked on, his eyes bulging as the dragon swallowed the giant bird in one gulp. Whitestaff got another look at the dragon. Its body looked like that of a snake, only instead of skin, it was made of rock. It didn't have any wings, but it did have two sets of short arms with five claws on each end. Whitestaff couldn't get over the sheer *size* of the thing!

I'm smaller than its eye!

Then, as if hearing his thoughts, the dragon of rocks turned to face Whitestaff. It sniffed the air with nostrils like caves in its rocky face. It got Whitestaff's scent, then sprang at *him*, its stony mouth open and ready to devour.

38

NOT FOOD

Inside the gigantic mouth that sped towards the Kai'dahl were teeth the size of Whitestaff's wings. He knew that he'd be gone in one swallow. There was no time to fly out of the way or dodge the gaping mouth of stone.

'CHIN?' Whitestaff shouted. 'STOP!'

But the dragon didn't seem to hear over the deafening noise of its own rocky body moving. It just kept coming. Then, as its mouth was about to swallow Whitestaff whole, the golden dragon spewed forth a stream of fire into the jaws of his attacker. The result was instantaneous. The giant stone dragon roared with pain and thrashed backwards, away from Whitestaff. It shook its enormous head and sank back down to the ground with the thunder of a hundred avalanches. When the dust and flying sand finally settled, the dragon looked just like a row of mountains again, except for its head. It lay with its mouth open, coughing and trying to breathe in cool air.

Whitestaff flew down to it and looked the creature in the eye.

'Are you a Chin dragon?' he asked.

The dragon's eye focused on Whitestaff. It was the colour of steel, and Whitestaff could see his entire body reflected in it.

'I am,' said the dragon. His voice made the same sound his body did when he moved: like thousands of boulders clashing into each other. 'And you are a Palal.'

'I am,' said Whitestaff.

The dragon moved his head around to face Whitestaff front on. 'The Palal King, by the look of your colour. And you're wearing the sign of Merlin.'

Whitestaff looked down at the medallion on his chest. 'I suppose so. I'm sorry about the fire, but I'll do it again if you try and eat me.'

The massive mouth opened again, only this time a rumbling chuckle came out.

'Eat you? Yes, I thought you were a krane. Not many left, so I was glad to find two in one morning. We're getting hungrier every day.'

'We?'

'The other Chin. What brings you to our world, little one? How did you get here?'

'I've come to ask for help. Merlin opened a portal for me.'

The giant dragon spoke to himself. 'A ground-walker with the sign of Merlin? It must be time. I'd better summon the others.'

'There are more like you? More dragons of stone?'

The great dragon looked towards the ocean, his eyes scanning the horizon. There was a long pause, and Whitestaff wondered if he had heard the question. He was about to ask again when the Chin spoke. 'There are four Chin. Only one Tu'dool. That is me.'

'Your name is Tu'dool? My name is Whitestaff.'

'Tu'dool is what I am, Whitestaff. As you are Kai'dahl.' He turned his face back to Whitestaff. 'Do you Palal not use the dragon tongue anymore?'

'Not so much. Some still know it. My uncle does. I mean, we still use some words, like Kai'dahl.'

'Hmmm, the dragon tongue dies in the mouths of dragons. A pity. *Dool*, means "the element of". *Tu* means "stone" or "earth" depending on how you think of it.'

'So your name means "the element of rock"?'

'More than that, Kai'dahl. I *am* rocks. I *am* the earth. Without Tu'dool, there is no land. Do you see?'

'I think I do,' said Whitestaff.

'I *don't* think you do,' said Tu'dool. 'But you will. You will. I'll show you. Brace yourself.'

The Chin dragon closed his eyes and the very earth beneath Whitestaff's paws shook. It was just a tremor at first, but it slowly grew until the ground shuddered with such fury that Whitestaff could no longer stand. He flapped his wings and hovered above the shaking earth. He held his paws to his ears so that he wouldn't go deaf. The noise was overwhelming, and just when Whitestaff thought he could no longer bear the dreadful pounding in his skull, Tu'dool opened his eyes and in a flash the ground stopped moving. The quake was over, and Whitestaff gently let himself back down.

'Now I think you understand, little dragon.'

'I do. You can control the earth.'

'I *am* the earth, Kai'dahl. I created it. It is part of me.'

'You *created* this land?'

'The land. Yes. I gave my essence so that it could come to be. The Chin are creator dragons, Kai'dahl. We give our essence so that things may live.'

'I was told this planet was barren when you came here. Is that true? Did you create everything that's here?'

'Partly true. There was no planet here when the Chin came. Merlin gave us only space. Only dust. I gave my essence for the land. Qi'dool gave his to the air, Shui'dool gave his to the ocean. Huo'dool, the Chin of fire, gave his to the sun. This planet is our essence, Palal, as are you.'

'Me? What about me?'

Tu'dool's eyes looked back out to the ocean. 'They heard my call,' he said.

Whitestaff followed the Chin's gaze and saw exactly what Tu'dool meant. Another Chin had appeared far out to sea. Even though it was far away, it was so enormous that Whitestaff could see it clearly. Tu'dool whispered to him as they watched the dragon approach.

'He felt my call from the depths of the ocean. That's Shui'dool—the element of water. He is the tides and waves. His power is unfathomable.'

Whitestaff stared in awe at Shui'dool. He was blue in colour, but his skin appeared to be travelling liquid. His body was lithe and he moved like a terrifying snake along the surface of the water. White spray burst from his sides and his movement caused massive waves to rock the ocean.

'The black one that will come from the clouds is Qi'dool—the element of air. He is the sky and the wind and the thunder. He is the very air we breathe. Without him, there is nothing.'

Whitestaff took his eyes off the water dragon and watched the dark storm clouds that were forming out to sea. It was amazing to behold! Black clouds gathered out of nowhere and a fierce gale began to blow. Rain started to pour down and lightning bolted across the darkness. The clouds spun in a circle faster and faster, until a massive funnel was formed, like a tornado! The twister moved and grew until it turned into a black dragon! The Chin of air appeared with the clash of belting thunder. His body was dark and menacing, like a hurricane ready to unleash its anger. He didn't move like the Chin of water. Instead, he seemed to roar straight ahead, bringing the clouds with him. It was hard to see where his body stopped and the storm around him began.

'Look up, Whitestaff. Huo'dool approaches us. He is the element of fire. He burns with power so great that it can consume all it touches.'

Whitestaff used a paw to shield his eyes from the glowing sun. Through his claws he could see Huo'dool, dropping towards him from the sky above. It was hard to make out his features, but Whitestaff could see that he was red in colour. His skin was like hot lava and he had fiery eyes to match. He had two silver horns growing from the back of his skull and wisps of smoke framed his face like a mane.

Whitestaff looked from one behemoth to the next. They sped towards him with a certain shine in their eyes—a shine that Whitestaff recognised at once. He'd felt it himself when he was trapped in Cudgel's cage, and he was certain that his eyes must have held the same glint. It was the look of burning hunger. Something about it made the golden dragon's scales tingle with fear.

Maybe this wasn't such a good idea, thought Whitestaff. *Maybe there was another reason Merlin sent the Chin elsewhere.*

39

THE CHIN

The four Chin dragons surrounded Whitestaff. They lowered their heads so that they could see him, and they sniffed him as though he was an unusual flower. The Kai'dahl felt as small as an ant under their gaze. They spoke to him in words that he didn't understand, and he looked to Tu'dool to make sense of it all.

'He doesn't speak the dragon tongue, brother Chin. Only the human words.'

The dragons looked to each other, then to Whitestaff.

'No dragon tongue?' asked Shui'dool, switching languages so that Whitestaff could understand him. 'Why not?'

Whitestaff shrank under the fierce dragon's attention. 'I...I don't know. Some Palal still know a few words.'

'A few words?' When Shui'dool spoke, his voice came out as a gushing waterfall. 'The dragon tongue is your birthright. No human words could match its elegance.'

'I'm sorry. I didn't grow up around other dragons. There is a lot that I don't know.' Whitestaff knew it was a silly excuse, but he felt that the language was important to the Chin, and he didn't want to get on the wrong side of them.

'Don't be sorry,' said Shui'dool. 'Be sad. Be broken. You have no idea what you have lost.'

'You're right, I don't,' agreed Whitestaff. He could see his reflection in Shui'dool's liquid scales. He wondered what it would be like to touch them, and if they were as wet as they looked. 'Maybe one day I will learn it.'

'At least he treads the ground,' said Qi'dool, the Chin of air. His voice was like a blowing gale. 'How long has it been since one has done you this honour, Tu?'

'Centuries, Qi,' answered the Chin of stone. 'He walks the ground and bears no shame.'

Whitestaff thought of the Palal and the Nazoor and their disgust at touching the ground. He looked down at his paws and remembered that what he was doing was a terrible thing to his own kind.

'I was born on the ground,' he told the Chin. 'I never understood why the others thought it shameful.'

Tu laughed through his cavernous mouth. 'Good to hear, little one. I can tell you the answer to your question, if you don't mind stories.'

'Tell him later,' the dragon of fire insisted. 'I want to know why he is here at the end of our cycle. Why is he wearing the sign of Merlin? I'm getting hungrier and I need to know!'

'Hush, Huo,' said Tu'dool. 'I sense that he is here to keep Merlin's word. There is no harm in telling him what he wants to know. My guess is it has all been hidden away from history. The meddling Gra'dahl, no doubt. The Palal have kept secrets from themselves, it seems.' Tu coughed up dust to clear his throat. 'Are you aware of the time before man, Kai'dahl? When there were only dragons?'

Whitestaff shook his head. 'Most of my life was spent separated from my own kind. I know very little about Palal past. Only about the Exodus from Earth.'

'Exodus Day is a drop in the ocean of time,' said Shui.

'It is,' agreed Tu. 'Once, Earth was like this planet, just as you see it. No humans. No towns. Only Chin.'

'Just Chin?' said Whitestaff. 'Your ancestors?'

Huo laughed, sending sparks flying from his mouth. 'Ancestors! He knows nothing!'

Tu smiled. His mouth looked like a giant crack in a cliff face. 'He has admitted as much, Huo.'

'Ancestors!' said the fire Chin again. 'No knowledge of language or of history!'

Tu shook his head slightly and continued. 'We have no ancestors, Whitestaff. The Chin are as old as the Earth itself. We are eternal.'

'Eternal? You mean, you live forever?'

'We *exist* forever, little one. Which is not the same.'

'We live in cycles,' said Huo. 'We give our essence to create, then we sleep. We lay dormant until there is enough essence to devou—'

'Enough!' Tu rumbled. He gave the other dragons a pointed stare and they shut their mouths. 'I am the one who is giving the answer.'

The other Chin looked uncomfortable and remained silent.

What was he going to say? Whitestaff thought. *Whatever it was, Tu didn't want me to hear it...*

'As I was saying,' the stone dragon went on. 'We exist now and we existed then. We are creator dragons, as I have mentioned, and some of us wondered if we could create other dragons. Some company when life was scarce. If I remember correctly, it was Qi's idea.' The other dragons looked as though they wanted to argue the point, but weren't brave enough to speak. 'Whoever it was, I didn't agree. I wanted a land of Chin, and only Chin. But I am no master of the elements, so these three gave essence and form to create another life. Another species. A type of dragon.'

'The Palal?' asked Whitestaff.

'No—the Wyvern,' said Tu. 'Or whatever they began to call themselves.'

'Nazoor,' Whitestaff offered.

'A Wyvern is always Wyvern, no matter the name. In any case, my brothers were successful. They had created life in the form of small dragons. They could soar on Qi's air, drink Shui's water, and

239

they were full of Huo's fiery spirit. But I had not offered my essence, so they could not walk on my land. To this day no Wyvern can.'

'What happens if they do?' asked Whitestaff.

'It burns them,' said Tu. 'They are allergic to the touch of my power.'

'How do they sleep then? Surely they can't fly forever. They must lay down on something solid!'

'On Earth, they used to find the highest mountain and build a nest away from the ground.'

'But mountains are still rock,' Whitestaff argued. 'It's all the same thing.'

'Yes and no,' said Tu. The higher off the ground they are, the less they feel the burn. They would sleep on beds of pure gold too, so they didn't have to touch the rock below.'

'Gold? What's so special about gold?'

'I know not. There is something about that metal that my power cannot touch. It kept them from burning while they slept, and eventually their need for it led to a war with the humans. That, in turn, led to Exodus Day. And now you know why the Wyvern won't touch the ground.'

Whitestaff thought about this. It certainly explained why the Nazoor found touching the ground so disgraceful.

'There is no gold in Sorteya though,' said Whitestaff. 'On the planet I came from, we sleep in spires that rise from the Earth. The Wyvern sleep in them up high. How can they stand it with no gold to sleep on?'

'Sorteya is none of my concern,' said Tu. 'It has none of my power. I have never been there.'

'So they are avoiding the ground of Sorteya for no reason!' Whitestaff said. 'What about the Palal? It can't be the same for us. I was born on the ground and I don't feel any pain.'

'That's because I helped create the Palal,' said Tu. 'I saw the Wyvern and decided the other Chin were right to create them. I was curious to know what a dragon would look like if I lent my essence to the mix. So we four got together and breathed our essence into something new. The result was Palal. *Your* ancestors.'

'Really?' said Whitestaff. 'So the Nazoor are our brothers and you are—'

'Your creators,' finished Huo.

Tu didn't reprimand Huo for speaking, so Qi, the air dragon, decided it was safe to talk too. 'Soon the Palal and the Wyvern became just like brothers. Just as you said. However, the Palal adopted the Wyvern ways. They chose to sleep high off the ground. Some even slept on beds of gold. The humans came along later and they too had a greed for the precious metal. As you can see, this made for conflict. Wyvern were killing humans, humans were killing in return. Unfortunately, the humans were much better at killing than Wyvern or Palal.'

'Why didn't you stop it?' Whitestaff asked. 'You're so powerful! You can control the very elements of Earth. Why didn't you make peace somehow?'

The dragons looked to Tu'dool as if seeking permission to give the answer. In the end, Tu'dool himself gave the answer.

'We made a deal with Merlin,' he said. 'The great human sorcerer offered peace to all dragons and to all humans. We accepted his peace.'

'What did you get in return?' asked Whitestaff.

Huo and Shui spoke quickly to Tu'dool in the dragon tongue. Whitestaff couldn't understand a word of it. Tu listened to his fellow Chin and nodded sagely. When they had finished talking he turned back to face the Kai'dahl.

'In return we get to cheat nature, Whitestaff. And now I think that's enough about us. It's time for you to talk, little King. What brings you here to the planet of the Chin?'

40

KAGA OMDI DRAGEEL

It didn't take long for the Chin to grasp the situation on Sorteya. Whitestaff revealed everything he knew about the history of the Nazoor and the Palal, from the first war where his father had died, to the Tournament and the ongoing surprise attack. He finished by telling them about Merlin, and how the old magician appeared when he was needed the most.

'Merlin has a habit of doing that,' said Shui. 'He foresaw that, without his intervention, the humans would kill every Palal and Wyvern in existence. Your races would be no more. No more dragon essence on Earth.'

'There would still be yours,' said Whitestaff.

'That wouldn't do us any good!' Huo said, smoke trailing from his nostrils.

'Silence,' said Tu. 'You need to cool that mouth of yours, Huo.'

The Chin of fire looked as though he wanted to explode. It was clear to Whitestaff that Huo'dool wasn't used to being told what to do. Nevertheless he closed his mouth tight, scowling as he did so.

Why wouldn't it do them any good? Whitestaff wondered. *Couldn't they just make more of us if they wanted? That's twice now that Tu'dool has kept them from speaking. What secrets do these ancient dragons keep?*

Tu'dool turned his attention back to the Kai'dahl. 'Merlin sent us here on the promise that our creations would be spared any further harm. He said that right at the end of our cycle, he would send a dragon bearing his seal. It would be then that our choice could be made.'

'What choice?' asked Whitestaff.

'Little Palal, we can choose to help you or we can stay here. Our cycle means that it is time for us to lay dormant. With no food left here to sustain us, our bodies dissolve into the elements and we lose our dragon form. For instance, instead of this dragon of rock you see before you, I will soon crumble and become stone for a few centuries. Shui there loses himself in the currents of the oceans. Qi returns to the wind and Huo becomes the rays of the sun. We become specks of unbound elements. We sleep and we rest.'

'I see,' said Whitestaff. *That's why they're so hungry. Without food, they are nothing. And food on this planet has become hard to find. Perhaps they've eaten it all.* Then he thought of something else, something Huo'dool had half said.

'What wakes you?' he asked.

'Time itself. When enough time has passed, we return to our dragon form. It takes hundreds of years, Whitestaff. But at least it's peaceful.'

No that's not the entire truth, Whitestaff thought. *Huo said you awaken when there is enough essence. You all keep saying you're hungry. Is it dragon essence you feed on? Did you make us so that one day you could eat us?* In his mind Whitestaff pictured farms back on Earth. Farmers would sow the seeds and take care of them until the seeds became healthy plants. Finally, when the crop was big enough, it was harvested and eaten. *Are the Palal and Nazoor just crops for the Chin?* A chill ran down his spine when he remembered the looks of desperate hunger that flashed in the giant Chin eyes.

'And now that your rest draws near, are you ready to lie dormant for a few hundred years?' Whitestaff asked.

Huo drew his head back and Qi let out a gale of a breath. It was enough of a reaction for Whitestaff. *They don't want to! They want to keep their dragon form!*

Tu'dool kept his cool the most. He made a show of thinking about it. He closed his eyes and gave a long sigh.

'A peaceful slumber on this planet sounds like just the thing. My body grows tired and my stomach empty. I suppose we could sleep.'

The other Chin looked horrified at the thought. Huo looked ready to pounce on Tu'dool and throttle him. But the dragon of stone spoke again.

'But then again, the Palal are in trouble. And you have come all this way and fought so hard so save your own kind. We would be terrible dragons if we forgot your problems and stayed here. How could we rest peacefully knowing our creations are battling each other in a horrible war? What do you think, my brother Chin? Should we stay here or help the Palal King?'

The other Chin could barely keep the smiles from their faces. Shui and Qi pretended to be thinking about it, but hot-headed Huo jumped at the chance to have his say.

'We help them of course. We go to this planet of Sorteya and we devour every last Wyvern!'

So you do want to eat them! Whitestaff thought. *I knew it!* But instead, he decided it was his turn to pretend. 'Devour them? You mean fight them off and help us win the war, don't you? Why would anyone want to eat a Wyvern? They are your creation, after all!'

Huo realised his mistake and was quick to explain. 'No I meant *defeat* them! I get your human words mixed around. I don't know why we can't have this discussion in natural tongue. That way I wouldn't get confused with language! Of course I wouldn't *eat* a fellow dragon!'

Whitestaff forced a laugh. 'I see, you meant *defeat*. It does sound like *devour*. It's my fault for not knowing only the human language, right enough.'

'It is!' Huo agreed. 'We will help you *defeat* the Wyvern. Don't you other Chin think it's best?' He looked to the others for their support. After more of a show of thinking, Qi and Shui finally allowed themselves to be talked into helping the Palal.

'We will lend our claws to you for this battle,' said Tu'dool. 'It is the right thing to do. Show us where you came from and we shall leave at once.'

Huo'dool could barely contain his excitement. 'Let's go my brothers!' He reared up and was about to shoot off into the sky.

'Wait!' Whitestaff said. 'You can't go yet!'

Huo halted mid-leap and swung back around to face the Palal. He could barely contain his anger.

'And why not, Palal? Do you not need our help?'

Whitestaff's mind was whirring. 'Yes, we do need you. But the portal that Merlin made is far too small to fit you. I'll have to go though first and ask him to widen it. You Chin wouldn't be able to fit one of your claws through it now.'

Huo's mood changed instantly after hearing Whitestaff's explanation. 'I see,' he said. 'Then you'd best go and do that now. The longer you're here, the more dangerous it is for the Palal on Sorteya. Fly now, King Kai'dahl. Tell your subjects to prepare the way for the Chin.'

'That I will,' said Whitestaff. 'Should I ask Merlin to keep the portal open too, so that you can come back here for your slumber when the war is won?'

Qi, Shui and Huo sniggered at the question. Tu'dool kept his face of stone composed and answered for the rest. 'That would be best, Whitestaff. We will stay on your planet until the Palal have the upper hand, then we will return here and enjoy our sleep.'

'Perfect,' said Whitestaff. 'Thank you Tu'dool. Thank you Chin. You have saved the Palal and we will be forever in your debt.'

'Think nothing of it,' said Qi.

'It is the right thing for us to do,' agreed Shui, the water Chin.

Whitestaff bowed and took his leave and flew back up and away from the desert. As he was leaving, the Chin huddled close together, noses almost touching. They spoke excitedly, not caring if Whitestaff overheard, but used the dragon tongue so that the Palal couldn't understand what they were saying. One phrase carried on the wind of Qi's howling voice: Kaga Omdi Drageel. It was uttered with such a bloodthirsty cry that it made Whitestaff flap his wings faster in order to get away from the Chin. Huo'dool echoed it with the others. Soon all the Chin were chanting it, and as he left the elemental dragons behind, he could still hear it playing in his mind. Whitestaff repeated the phrase few times until he had it locked in his memory. *Kaga Omdi Drageel,* he told himself. *I don't know what it means, but I don't think it's anything good.*

41

THE POHMIN SEA

The Black Dart was two days into its voyage across the Pohmin Sea. The sky was bleak and so overcast that the sun struggled to get through the thick layer of clouds. Midday looked like dusk. A wind blew strong and true from behind, and the tyshwood ship rolled south on the waves it made. The crew worked hard to keep the sails full and the ship upright. They weren't as relaxed as they were on Pip's first voyage, and they grew noticeably more stern the closer they drew to the middle of the Pohmin Sea. There was no gambling or friendly betting going on, and even Garth, the master of bets, kept his Captain Cards stowed in his footlocker. Pip knew that most of the sailors would object to venturing into the kraken's territory, but for some reason Blackbeard had agreed to take the shortcut, so the crew had no choice but to follow Bob's orders: Blackbeard's ship— Blackbeard's rules.

The first day of the voyage was one of excitement for Mollie. She awoke long after the sun had risen, having been tired out from her battle with Cudgel and then the ride from Danmurk to

Lareborough. After the reunion with Bob in his cabin, she retired to the small room she had been allocated and fell asleep at once. So the rest of the people aboard had been up for hours when Mollie finally made her way onto the deck the next morning. She smiled at Rio and a few other crew members she vaguely recognised from the incident at the Quilshire fair the year before. She spotted Balad and Pip towards the bow of the ship. They were looking out to sea, and she made her way over to the pair.

'Good morning,' she said.

Pip spun around so fast that his elbow struck Balad in the spine.

'Good morning, Mollie!' Pip said. 'I trust you slept well?'

'Too well,' she replied. 'It seems I'm the last one up!'

'You are,' said Balad, massaging his back where Pip's elbow had landed.

'But that's a good thing!' said Pip. 'Not everyone can sleep easily on a ship.'

'And why not?' Mollie inquired.

'Some people get sick.'

'From what?'

'I think it's all the rocking,' Pip told her. 'They're used to sleeping on beds that don't move all the time.'

'I found it peaceful,' said Mollie. 'Like being rocked to sleep by a gentle giant.'

Pip grinned at her. 'That's a nice way of seeing it.'

Mollie smiled back and then looked out to the surrounding waters. 'I've never been at sea before. Never even seen a ship, if you can believe it. I'm sure it's not the biggest ship, but I almost got lost finding my way up here.'

'I'm no expert on sailing either,' Pip confessed to her. 'My first time at sea was the journey coming to find you. But I can show you around the Dart if you like, and tell you the things I picked up from Rio and the other crew.'

'Sounds like a pleasant way to spend the morning. Perhaps you can show me where I can get some breakfast? Or is it time for lunch? Either way, I'm starving.'

Pip took her arm in his. 'I'd be delighted,' he said.

The two made their way along the deck and down below, leaving the Royal Guard behind.

Balad wondered for a moment if he should stay back or go after his ward. In the end, he turned to watch the waves in the choppy sea. *I'm not supposed to let him come to any harm. But I don't suppose I can protect him from falling in love,* he told himself.

After Mollie had eaten, Pip made good on his offer. He took her all through the Dart. He showed her the lowest level where the ballast was, the cargo hold, and the food store. He even showed her the horrible square room below the deck that served as a prison for crew that broke any of Blackbeard's fair (but strictly enforced) rules. As they journeyed through the ship, members of the crew gave Pip a friendly smile or a pat on the back as they passed.

'They sure like you,' Mollie commented as yet another sailor gave Pip a wink. 'You must have made an impression on your way to Albion.'

Pip climbed some steps and opened a hatch in the ceiling above them. He made his way through it and onto the open deck above before reaching down to help Mollie up.

'It's nothing really,' he told her as he pulled her up through the hatch. 'I just shot them a few gulls for dinner one day, that's all.'

Mollie laughed. 'A way to a man's heart is through his stomach,' she said. 'At least, that's what Esmae told me.'

Pip blushed at her comment. 'It was sort of a bet,' he said. 'They didn't think I could hit the gulls that were flying over us.'

'But you did, didn't you?'

'I sure did. It wasn't that hard.'

'Mmmmm,' said Mollie. 'I remember your guard saying that you can hit whatever you want to. And I saw you with a bow in my cottage. You shot a weapon right out of Cudgel's hand. It was remarkable.'

'Not really. I just practise a lot.'

'Is that what you think?' Mollie asked. 'Do you really, truly believe that there is no other explanation?'

Pip held Mollie's gaze for a moment, then dropped his head.

'Well, sometimes it feels like more than practise. But what more could it be? Maybe I'm just born lucky?'

'Maybe,' Mollie said. 'Tell me, how do you feel when you shoot arrows? I mean that moment just before you let go of the string. You have your target lined up and you can see what you want to hit, but there is a fraction of time before you actually let the arrow loose. Does it feel strange, or different in some way?'

Pip was silent for a while. The cold wind tussled his hair and filled his lungs. 'It does,' he said after a time. 'It does feel different.'

Mollie nodded. 'Is it as though you can actually *feel* the air between you and your target? Like you can guide your arrow to where you want it to go?'

Pip raised his head to look at the sorceress. 'How did you know?' he asked, his voice barely a whisper. 'I've never shared that with anyone!'

Mollie placed a hand on each of his shoulders. 'What you can do is a very rare gift. I don't even think you know that you're doing it most of the time, do you?'

'No. Not really. Only every now and then I notice what is going on, but mostly it's like breathing—something that just happens without me telling it to. What is it then? Do you know about it?'

'I do know about it, Prince. I know almost everything about it. Esmae calls it *gathering*. It's what I do when I want to cast a spell. I *feel* all the elements around me and I can use them this way and that. Tell me, can you *feel* the water under this ship? Close your eyes and reach out to it.'

Pip licked his lips and did as he was told. He was still for a period of time, and then he opened his eyes.

'No, I can't,' he told her. 'The air though, it keeps getting in the way. It's all around us and it's all I can touch. What does it mean?'

Mollie thought for a moment. 'It appears that you can only gather one element. Just air. It's more than most people though. I wonder why?'

'You can feel the sea?' Pip asked.

'I can feel everything. The water, the air, the heat from the sun, even the dirt on the ground. Well, when I'm near it. Not now of course. I can feel all of it the same way you can feel the air. Like they're all just tiny specks of dust that come when I call them.'

'That's incredible!'

'For you. For me it's normal. I tried not to do it for so long. Hated it, in fact. Now, I love it.'

'So would I,' said Pip. 'But why did you hate it?'

Mollie drew a breath and wandered over to the side of the ship. She watched the water spray below her as the tyshwood hull cut into the sea. Pip joined her and craned his neck to look overboard too.

'You saw where I lived, didn't you?' Mollie asked. 'That little cottage in the woods has been my home since I was born.'

Pip didn't respond. He watched the water below and let Mollie speak freely.

'Danmurk Shire. It was my whole world until last year. And in that little world there was no one else like me, except Esmae. The other children called me a witch and refused to come near me. They were scared of what I could do. While they were all playing with each other and making up games, I was alone. They ran away if I ever tried to join them. The thing that kept me apart was my magic. It made sense to me that being able to gather was what isolated me. So if I couldn't do magic I'd be normal. If I was normal I could have friends.'

'That must have been tough, living without anyone but your mother.'

'It was. But then I got so used to it *I* grew afraid. I began to avoid people, especially crowds. For some reason, if I found myself surrounded by people, I'd panic.'

'I guess because you weren't used to it?'

'I suppose,' said Mollie. The ship beneath them continued to rock on the waves and the wind carried the sea spray high in the air.

'If you were born in Nalib, we wouldn't have been afraid of you. We would have adored anyone that could stand up against Shadowclaw.'

'Like you?' Mollie looked down at the wraps around Pip's arms.

Pip blushed again and flashed her a shy smile. 'I hit it with a few arrows,' he said. 'Then it attacked me.' Pip's eyes grew wide with a sudden recollection. 'It spoke to me too! How could I forget? I could hear its voice as clear as day, but no one else could! What does that mean?'

'It's part of the gift,' Mollie told him. 'I can talk to just about any animal, and they can talk to me.'

Pip grabbed onto the side of the ship and leant back, looking at the sky. He took a deep breath and then blew it out, his lips puckered. 'Well I can't talk to animals. The Scourge has been the only thing with four legs that I've ever heard speak. But sometimes, just every now and then, I think I know what Jasper is thinking.'

'Maybe it's because the dragon is so powerful?' Mollie wondered aloud.

'So you can talk to any animal?' Pip asked. 'Horses and such?'

'Most animals, yes. Little ones are hard. Insects, not at all. I think it has something to do with their size, or something like that.'

'What about the kraken? Do you think you can communicate with it?'

Mollie sucked her bottom lip in thought. 'I guess we'll find out soon, won't we?'

42

THE WARNING

The Palal dragons, waiting beneath a sky of gnashing Nazoor, crowded Whitestaff the instant he set foot in the Court. They cheered when his golden front leg appeared through Merlin's portal. The dragons then flew up to the high section of the amphitheatre to meet their Kai'dahl as the rest of his body came through the enchanted gateway.

Graggy and Armay tried to keep the other Palal dragons from smothering him, but it was Susset that drove them all back. 'He needs space,' she shouted at the Palal. 'Look at him!'

Whitestaff's legs folded underneath him and his eyes swam in their sockets. Clearly there was something wrong with the new King.

'Whitestaff,' Susset called. 'Close your eyes for a minute. Try not to focus on anything.' She turned back to the Palal behind her. 'He will be fine in a moment. Sometimes the body doesn't like travelling through portals. Give us some space I said!'

'Olfar,' Whitestaff whispered. 'Get me Olfar.'

Merlin was the closest to Whitestaff, and he stood next to the dragon and stroked his head. 'You'll be back to normal soon,' the old magician assured him. 'Olfar, your nephew summons you.'

The old Gra'dahl stepped out of the crowd and walked over to the King.

'Are thou going to faint again, Nephew?'

Whitestaff still had his eyes shut tight. 'Not this time, Uncle. But I need your experience. You tried to warn me about the Chin before I crossed. Are you the expert on them? I need to know as much about them as I can.'

Olfar tugged at his beard. 'I suppose I'm the most knowledgable on the subject. Old Doolun knew more than me, but he passed about sixty years ago. Everything I know was from him and a few books that we managed to bring with us on Exodus Day. But as I once told thee, I was barely a hatching back then. What can I tell you?'

'Everything you can. Merlin, is that you patting my head?'

'Yes, Whitestaff.'

'You sent the Chin elsewhere during the Exodus. You must know even more. Tell me, have they an appetite for eating dragons?'

'Eating dragons?'

Whitestaff winced as he fought off the urge to pass out. 'Yes, for the sake of Latos! Do they eat other dragons?'

'I'm not supposed to answer that. You told me not to tell you anything more than I already have. I could go and ask the future you if you've changed your mind, if you like?'

'No! Who would keep the Wyvern out if you left?'

Merlin clicked his fingers and smiled brightly. 'No one. Susset is still recovering. Good thinking, Whitestaff! If I left, you'd all be killed.'

'You said you know me in the future. Why would I not let you tell me what I need to know?'

Merlin licked his lips. 'You'll work it out in about five more minutes.'

Whitestaff resisted the urge to breathe fire over the old magician. Instead, he took a deep breath and opened his eyes. He blinked a few times and looked at his uncle.

'Olfar, the Chin told me that they created all dragons. Is that true?'

'Created *us*?'

'Yes, long ago, they said. They gave their essence so that we may live.'

Olfar paused for a moment. 'There was an old tale about something like that. Superstition I thought. Something about the Chin being fathers to all dragons. But no one ever paid it any heed.'

'Merlin, can you answer this? When you sent the Chin away from Earth, you told them that I would come and offer them a way out. They knew I was coming at the end of their cycle. What is the cycle?'

'I'm not entirely sure. You're the one that told me about it.'

'How is that possible? YOU told ME before I went into the PORTAL!'

Merlin jumped and wiped his brow. 'Yes, I see this is all very confusing for you. But try to understand, I'm not living time in the one direction that you are. You live life in the order of day one, day two, day three, day four. I live life in a jumble: day two, day four, day three, day one. Tomorrow, you will tell me about what happened when you crossed the portal. And *you* explain everything to *me*. I've already lived tomorrow, but I haven't lived today yet, you know? In fact, I only just went and sent the Chin away from Earth three days from now, which was three days ago for me. Five days ago I picked up Susset and together we hid your egg on Earth at Frendrek's command. Do you see?'

'But my father died over twenty years ago!'

'Whitestaff, I know it's hard. But I can go to whatever time I want. The things that you've heard about me doing, I might not have even done yet. But the older me will, but *I* haven't. Let me give you an example—'

'No!' Whitestaff said. 'I think I understand. Then if my future is your past, you know what happens when the Chin come through the portal don't you?'

The corners of Merlin's mouth fell, and he slowly nodded his head. 'I know, but the you in the future wants me to pretend I don't.'

'What happens, Nephew?' asked Olfar.

'I'll answer you after you translate this for me: Kaga Omdi Drageel. What does it mean?'

Olfar closed his eyes and worked his lips silently. When he thought he had the answer, he spoke. 'It's all old dragon tongue.

Kaga means something akin to *on*. It's a preposition. *Omdi* is like a feast, but it also means *drink. Drageel* translates to—'

'Let me guess: dragon essence?'

Olfar's shaggy eyebrows shot up. '*Essence of dragon*! Yes, Nephew. Well done. Thou knows some tongue after all?'

'No, Olfar. I overhead the Chin say it. If your translation is accurate, they were talking about feeding on dragon essence. They mean to *feast* on the Nazoor. That is, if I agree to let them through.'

'I see,' said Olfar. He stroked his beard and looked up at the Wyvern overhead. 'What do we do with that knowledge?'

Nap, who had been standing within earshot stuck his head between Whitestaff and Olfar.

'What sort of question is that? We let them in of course. Let them eat, I say!'

'It's not that simple, Nap. What about Xenos and Cross? What about Kigg? What about the hundred Party members we rescued?'

'I'm sorry, Whitestaff, but they'd be gone by now. Just floating essence, like my father.'

'You're missing my point. What if there are more in the Nazoor ranks like them? Wyvern that are up there fighting because they're too scared of Mezelga, but would prefer a life of peace. We'd be condemning them to die. Don't you see? Letting the Chin through is a death sentence for every Nazoor on the planet, the good and the bad. I'd be responsible for wiping out an entire race of dragons. I would be just like Mezelga!'

Nap fell silent as the weight of it hit him. Not long ago, he was fighting side by side with Nazoor. If not for the sacrifice of the Party members, he'd be nothing but essence, just like his father.

'I guess that's why you're the King,' Nap said. 'I would never have seen it like that. I would have let the Chin through without hesitation.'

Whitestaff put a paw on Nap's shoulder, then turned to Merlin.

'This is what I asked you not to tell me, isn't it?'

'Correct,' said Merlin.

'Because now it's too late anyway. I don't have a choice and there is no other way. I must ask you to let the Chin through.'

Merlin gave a wan smile and turned the portal on its side, pointing straight up at the Nazoor.

'Make it big, Merlin. About five times bigger than me.'

Merlin did as he was instructed. The portal opened so wide that it replaced the ceiling of Mezelga's soldiers. Now all the Palal in the Court could see was an empty space hovering in the air above them.

'Should you go and get them?' Nap asked. 'Tell them we're ready?'

Whitestaff gave a humourless chuckle. 'No need, Nap. They will see the portal from their side, and they won't wait for a formal invitation. I bet they'll be here in any second now.'

Just as Whitestaff finished his sentence, the entire spire shook as though it were being ripped apart.

'Here they come,' said Whitestaff. 'Brace yourselves.'

43

THE CALM BEFORE
THE KRAKEN

The Black Dart was exactly halfway across the Pohmin Sea and
things were tense on deck. Blackbeard, who usually ran things
from his cabin, paced the planks and barked orders to his crew. He
checked and rechecked the riggings and inspected every sailor
aboard, making sure that they each carried a sword. The weather had
calmed early in the morning and the waters had settled. The wind
had eased and it felt as though the sea itself was holding its breath—
waiting. The anxious mood was contagious, and Pip's heart skipped
every time the ship was jolted from an unexpected wave or wind
gust. The crew went about their work in silence. They trod lightly on
the decks and winced whenever someone made a slight noise.

Blackbeard had herded them together in the mess the night
before. He told the cook to make something special for the rest of the
sailors, and when they had finished their dinner of roasted rabbit and
vegetables, he called their attention by slapping his palm on the table

three times. By the time Bob had finished his third slap, the tables were silent and all eyes were on the captain.

'Mates,' he began, 'I know you have followed me in whatever scheme dares enter the mystical vessel that is my head. You've sailed with me into the jaws of death a few times, and shared my rum when death spat us back out.' The crew smiled and waited for him to continue.

'What I'm asking you to do is dangerous, but we've all seen danger. I suppose it's more than dangerous. I don't know the right word. All I know is, the kraken is a day's voyage from here. We will enter its waters in about fifteen hours, and of all the adventures we've had, this is the one most likely to end us. I bet you're asking yourself why in Latos we're sailing though the middle of the Pohmin. Well, I'll answer you. You, me, the Prince and his guard, we're all going to kill this blasted beast that claims our sea. But we won't be alone. We will have young Mollie.' All eyes swivelled to the sorceress.

'Most of you know Mollie from her work with us in Quilshire. She helped us get back the booty that was stolen from under our very noses. She can wield magic as most of you know, and she is certain that the kraken is no match for her skills.'

Mollie raised her eyebrow at the captain. She had never made such a claim and decided to point this out. Bob saw her about to speak, so he cut her off.

'Let's give her three cheers!' he bellowed.

The crew cheered at his order, and Mollie's protest was drowned out. Blackbeard waved the crew back to silence and continued.

'But mates, we can't rely on magic alone. I want each of you armed. Sharpen your swords tonight and keep them keen. I've met this beast before and I know its tactics. The first thing it will do is nudge us. It will use its tentacles to feel us out: see if we'd fit in its belly. Next it will throw its arms on either side of the ship. At that first nudge, you all need to split up. If you're on Rio's side of the table, you go port side. The rest of you go starboard. When the kraken throws his arms over the bulwarks, you need to hack at them right away. If he gets a good grip on either side, he will tear the Dart asunder, and no magic will be enough to save us.'

Blackbeard gave them a moment to let his words sink in. 'With no grip on the ship, the kraken will be less of a threat. But he will still be deadly. He might try to capsize us, so Mollie, we need your magic to end this monster as soon as you can manage. My crew here can keep it distracted, but you need to deliver the killing blow.'

Mollie nodded at his instruction. Pip, who had seated himself next to her, gave her shoulder a squeeze. He leant towards her and whispered, 'Do you think you're up to it?'

'If I can kill a dragon that uses magic, I can kill an overgrown octopus,' she said, with more confidence than she felt.

'Fantastic!' said Pip. 'I am so glad I met you.'

Mollie felt her stomach flutter at Pip's words. *Me too*, she thought.

None of the crew slept soundly that night. Each lay awake thinking of the deadly kraken, hoping that the young woman they'd seen aboard was truly up to the task.

And so as the third day wore on, and the Dart sailed deeper and deeper into the kraken's waters, some of the crew secretly hoped that the beast would attack, just to get the waiting over with. But nothing happened.

It was late afternoon when a sailor shouted a warning from the crow's nest of a storm brewing ahead of them. Mollie looked at the sky in front and saw dark clouds coming their way. Lightning flashed every now and then, and she could see a thick haze spreading beneath the clouds. Part of her hoped that the commotion of the storm would keep the kraken from coming up to the surface.

The news of the storm didn't help the mood of the crew. They prepared the ship by tying everything down and lowering the sails. If they were tense before, now they were practically ready to burst. Some of the older sailors complained to each other in low voices.

'What if we're fighting the kraken when the storm hits?' they asked each other.

'How can we tackle the monster and a storm at the same time?'

'What rotten luck!'

Blackbeard didn't need to hear his men to know what they were thinking. His powerful voice broke the eerie silence on deck.

'Mates!' he shouted. 'It seems as though fortune favours the kraken today. That storm will be upon us in a matter of minutes now, and I think the beast will sink to the depths to avoid it.'

Yes! thought Mollie. A few other sailors smiled in relief.

Only Blackbeard seemed disappointed. His face was slack and his shoulders slumped. His disappointment didn't last long, however. For as the crew turned from him to get back to their duties, there came a slight bump from under the ship. Blackbeard's face came alive in a second.

'BATTLE STATIONS!' he cried as the dreaded kraken attacked.

44

KILL THE BEAST

Amidst the sudden clap of thunder, the shuddering of the ship and the stirring of the fresh, wild wind, Blackbeard couldn't help but admire the obedience of his crew. He stood at the helm towards the rear of the ship so he could watch the battle unfold beneath him. As soon as he called out to his crew, they unsheathed their swords and sprinted to whichever side of the ship they had been commanded to protect. Blackbeard didn't know it, but telling the story of his encounter with the kraken over and over again was the best preparation he could've given his men. They'd heard the story so often that they could imagine the whole event as it played out. So when most men would've screamed in terror as the kraken's thick, slimy arms came of the bulwarks, the crew aboard the Dart ran at them, ready to hack away with their swords.

Bob had also been correct in explaining the kraken's way of attacking. A few testing bumps came before it attacked, so the men were confident everything else would go just as their captain had predicted. Rio actually smiled when a tentacle as tall and as thick as

269

a tree burst out of the water, towered over him, then came smashing down on the deck. The wind blew the thick fringe of hair out of his face, and if anyone had looked, they would have seen an unnerving spark of joy in Rio's eyes. He gave a battlecry and brought his sword down over and over, biting the steel into the kraken's flesh.

Not used to feeling any pain, the kraken lifted its tentacle in the air and sent it smashing down again, hoping to crush whatever was attacking it. Rio was too quick, however. He rolled to one side and was up on his feet again in a flash, sword held high and ready to strike.

Four massive tentacles appeared on the other side of the ship. They rocketed up through the water below, showering the men on deck with salty spray. The crew were temporarily blinded by the water. A few slipped as the ship was buffeted by the creature's body. Down came the thick arms, crashing onto the deck. Any ordinary wood would've cracked and splintered under the force, but the tyshwood deck withstood the impact. The men that were still standing rushed over to the thick limbs and cut at them as best they could. Not everyone was as strong as Rio though, so their swords didn't go past the monster's outer skin.

Pip saw that the men on the starboard side were in trouble. He had his bow in his hands and full quiver of arrows on his back. In a second his arrows were whistling across the deck, each shot sinking deep into the kraken's tentacles. The kraken could feel the arrows as they hit. It flailed its limbs madly trying to hit what it couldn't see. Most of the men leapt out of the way of the crazed attacks, but some weren't so lucky. Garth was hit on the side of the face. The blow sent him reeling across the deck where his head hit the wood of the main mast. It didn't quite knock him out, but it left him so dazed he couldn't get up.

'KEEP IT UP, LADS,' hollered Blackbeard as he joined the fray. 'WE'RE BEATING IT!'

The captain's words spurred the crew on. They could see that he was right; the monster seemed to be struggling against their attack. They also saw the sky above the ship grow dark. The storm broke at the worst possible moment, and almost instantly it started to pour a cold and heavy rain. The wind blew faster and whipped up the waves around them, so now the Dart was being rocked by the kraken *and* the water. It became even harder for the men to keep their balance on the deck.

Over the sound of thunder, a desperate cry for help came from the bow of the ship. Pip heard it and looked over to see Drake, the ship's poet and singer, caught up in one of the kraken's tentacles. Drake was struggling in the beast's grip. He had lost his sword and was pounding the trunk-like arm with his fists. The kraken's immense strength and sticky suckers kept him from freeing himself. It began to curl Drake up, like an enormous snake, and Pip knew that Drake would soon have every bone in his body crushed. He sent a few arrows smacking into the arm, but that only made things worse for Drake as the kraken squeezed even harder. Just as Pip cried out for more help, something long and blue whizzed past his head and smashed into the kraken. It was one of Mollie's Magic Missiles. The magical energy exploded into the kraken's tentacle, taking a chunk out of the target. The kraken writhed in pain and let go of Drake. The ship's bard crashed into one of his crewmates below, and they landed in a tangle of limbs in the middle of the deck. The kraken decided it had had enough. It withdrew all of its tentacles, causing the crew to cheer. Rio looked disappointed as the thick arms sunk beneath the choppy water.

'IT AINT OVER YET!' said Blackbeard. 'BE READY.'

Once again, the captain was correct. He knew that the kraken wouldn't give up until it had killed whatever was in its waters. The kraken had decided on a new and more deadly tactic. Instead of putting its limbs in harm's way, it would just pound the ship from the bottom, over and over again until it smashed the hull.

The first crash took everyone by surprise. The ship was jolted on the spot and everyone on deck fell over. The next smash came, and then the next, so fast that no one could stand up. It was like being in the middle of an earthquake out at sea. Only Mollie could get herself upright, as she levitated off of the ship's deck.

To Blackbeard's horror, there came the awful squeal of splintering wood. The tyshwood hull was strong, but not unbreakable. Too many blows from the giant kraken had weakened it, and now it was ready to crack. He looked over at Mollie, who was hovering above.

'Kill it!,' he told her. 'Kill it or we're all doomed!'

Mollie lifted herself higher off the deck and over the side of the ship. From there she could see the kraken's arms belting at the bottom and sides of the Black Dart. She was soaked in rain. A bolt of lightning flashed near the ship and lit up the sea. For a moment, Mollie could actually see the entire kraken. It was a super-sized squid. It was upside down and under the ship. It had four tentacles on each side of the Dart, and its mouth was chewing into the bottom of the hull. It spotted Mollie with a gigantic eye, and froze for a moment as the two looked at each other.

'Stop!' Mollie commanded. She spoke into the animal's mind, hoping to get a response.

The kraken looked away from her and continued its attack on the ship. On the deck, she could see Pip trying to stand. Every time he got to his feet, the kraken belted the ship and he was knocked over again. The ship gave another squeal of breaking wood, and Mollie knew that the Dart would soon split apart. If that happened, Bob, Pip, Rio and the crew would be eaten by the kraken.

The thought of losing everyone focused Mollie's mind. She gathered the energy of the sea and she used it to create an underwater whirlpool. It spun slowly at first, but as Mollie put more magical energy into it, the vortex spun itself faster and faster. The spinning water pulled at the kraken, forcing it to release the Dart and moving it away from the ship. The kraken fought hard against the current and desperately tried to cling back onto the ship. Now that the thumping had stopped, those aboard the Dart ran over to the side of the ship to watch the action. They too could now see the kraken clearly. They watched as it was being slowly dragged away from them by the spinning pool of water. The whole creature had come up to the surface and the crew marvelled at its size. It was bigger than ten whales! It fought harder still against Mollie's magical current. The kraken's utter fury at being beaten gave it even more strength. It thrashed itself wildly and began to creep away from Mollie's whirlpool. It came closer and closer to the ship, until it reached out with one of its long tentacles and, *smuck!* It latched onto the Dart with its suckers. Mollie saw that if she kept up the whirlpool, she'd drag the kraken and the ship under. However, if she stopped the spinning current, the kraken would be free to attack the Dart again.

Mollie took a deep breath and gathered the water around the kraken. She gathered as much energy as she could from the air too, and slowly, ever so slowly, she began to lift the enormous creature from out of the sea. The water around the monster parted, and the rear of it began to lift towards the sky. It still had one tentacle attached to the ship, so Pip leaned over the side and buried a few arrows in the kraken's long limb. The sudden pain forced it to let go, and the ship rocked with the sudden loss of the monster's pull.

Mollie let go of the whirlpool spell and focused her energy on pulling the kraken out of the water. It was an incredibly heavy animal, and the sorceress had never gathered so much energy in her life. Every muscle in her body strained and her mind felt ready to snap. A thin trickle of blood ran from her nose and over her lips. But the kraken rose higher and higher.

Pip saw the toll that the battle was taking on Mollie, so he ordered the crew to sail towards the sorceress. The crew stared blankly at the Prince and it wasn't until Blackbeard yelled at them that they moved.

'Stop standing around gawking!' he bellowed. 'Do as the man says.'

Tentatively, the crew raised the sails a fraction and tried to steer the ship towards Mollie.

To the side of them, the kraken was now completely airborne. Mollie had it strung in the air, holding it up with all her might. The head of it was pointing at the clouds and its tentacles were reaching helplessly to the sea below.

'Raise it higher,' said Pip. 'Up to the clouds.'

Now that Mollie had it out of the water, she was unsure of what to do, so she followed Pip's suggestion. She gathered a fraction more energy from the air and levitated the beast higher and higher. The Dart moved directly below the sorceress, and Bob prayed that Mollie didn't let the kraken fall, as it would smash his ship to pieces.

'Higher!' called Pip over the clashing thunder. 'Just a bit more!'

Mollie did as she was told, and lifted the thrashing kraken as far as it would go.

Then, with a blinding flash, a bolt of lightning struck the kraken from out of the clouds. The lightning sizzled into the foul beast, and with a low scream, the kraken exploded into horrid chunks. Hot pieces of it burst in every direction before raining down, splashing into the ocean and onto the Dart below.

The weight was finally taken away from Mollie, and she let go of the energy she had worked so hard to gather. The sudden release made her giddy. It was as though an elastic band had been stretched as far as it would go, and then suddenly snapped. The effect was too much for the sorceress. The world around her faded, and she passed out in the air.

Pip was ready and waiting below. He held out his arms to catch her, hoping that the spell Mollie had put around his wounds earlier would save him from the pain of taking her full weight in his arms.

45

FEEDING TIME

The rumbling in the Court grew, and the Nazoor who had attached themselves to the invisible ceiling above went still. They had been pounding and scratching at Merlin's shield in frustration, and now that something appeared to be happening below them, they froze.

Whitestaff couldn't see the Nazoor though, as he was standing directly under the portal. When he felt that the last second had arrived, he ordered Merlin to take down the magical barrier that had kept the Palal safe. The Nazoor above stumbled in the air as the barrier was taken away from beneath them. Some cheered and headed down for the kill. Older, wiser Nazoor flew upwards, and away from whatever was happening in the Palal's spire. A command for the attack was given by Mezelga's officers, but still, only about half the waiting Nazoor dove down. Those obedient Wyvern were the first to die, for a moment later, Huo'dool, the fire dragon, burst through the portal and into Sorteya. From a distance, it would have looked as though the spire was a tall volcano, and Huo was the lava eruption.

He charged into the new planet with his mouth open wide, and instead of diving into the Court, about fifty Wyvern dive-bombed into Huo's burning mouth. The Chin of fire bit down on them, breaking them with his teeth and swallowing their bodies.

'Kaga Omdi Drageel!' he shouted. The air vibrated with his voice and radiated with his heat.

He flew into the flock of the thousands of Nazoor soldiers above and made way for the other Chin.

With more rumbling, Shui, Qi and Tu'dool sprang though Merlin's portal. The force of them breaking through sent shockwaves throughout the Court. The Palal reeled as the ground beneath them shook and began to break up.

'GET OUT!' Whitestaff yelled. 'IT'S COLLAPSING!'

But he needn't have bothered giving the order as he couldn't be heard over the quaking of the spire. Most of the Palal had figured out what was happening and had taken to the skies anyway. Merlin and Susset levitated out, and Whitestaff escaped with Graggy and Armay. When they were a safe distance away, they turned and watched as the once grand spire of the Court fell crashing to the ground below. The golden dragonhead that served as the entrance shattered into pieces, tumbled down the side of the spire, and disappeared beneath the fog. As the rest of the spire collapsed in an avalanche, Whitestaff thought of Cracone. His would be the only body left inside.

The three watched as the remnants of the Court sunk beneath the fog. There was a moment of shocked silence, then Whitestaff had the air knocked out of him as something crashed into his back. He spun around clumsily to see Armay and Graggy fighting off Nazoor. Three others were coming for *him*.

They're still fighting? he thought.

Without hesitation, the Kai'dahl roasted the Nazoor in front of him with a blast of fire. He then flew over to Armay and helped her fight off her attackers. Graggy beat off his own Nazoor and joined Armay and Whitestaff. Armay was handling her attackers with little difficulty, however. Even in this situation, Whitestaff couldn't help but admire her fighting style. She fought with so much grace, it was like watching a dancer. She tail-whipped one Nazoor in the face, and then, while still spinning, cut another down with the side of her wing.

With their attackers gone, the three were free to watch the war going on above them.

'I can't believe they haven't retreated,' said Whitestaff. 'How could they hope to win against dragons as mighty as the Chin?'

Graggy's mouth was agape with wonder. 'I knew they'd be big, but not the size of *spires*! But maybe size isn't everything. Look at what the Nazoor are doing. They're using their numbers.'

The Nazoor were quick to come up with a fighting strategy. They had attached themselves to the bodies of the Chin and were biting and scratching whatever they could. Whitestaff was reminded of ants swarming a large attacker. Soon the Chin were covered with Nazoor, their large bodies crawling with Wyvern.

Some of the Re'dahl, who were hovering around the massive portal that the Chin had used, saw that the Nazoor were getting the upper hand and shot upwards to help their new allies.

'BACK!' Whitestaff shouted at them. 'GET BACK!'

But his voice did not carry over the sound of the battle. In a panic, he turned to Graggy. 'Find Nap. Tell him we are going to retreat. Tell him to pull back the Re'dahl army and not to argue.'

'Why?' asked Graggy. 'We could win this war now that we have them.' He pointed up towards the Chin.

'No one will win this, Graggy. Now please, do as I say.'

The Gra'dahl had more to ask but caught something different in his friend's tone, so flew to find Nap as fast as he could.

'Armay, I need you to do something for me too.'

'What is it? Anything, my King.'

'Down there, below the fog,' he pointed a claw. 'Near Susset's spire is my portal. The Nazoor must have tossed it out of her dugout when they attacked. I need you to find it for me and wait near that Chin portal. Take Susset too, she might be strong enough now to help you lift it.'

Armay bowed in the sky and flew off to find the sorceress.

That just leaves me. What am I going to do?

Whitestaff craned his neck to watch the action above. The Re'dahl were giving no sign of retreat, and some of the Nazoor had broken off the Chin to fight the red Palal. *Looks like I'll have to give the order myself.* Whitestaff let out a roar of frustration and flew upwards to join the other dragons battling in the sky.

46

FOOD IS FOOD

It was aerial madness in the sky. The Nazoor were attacking anything that wasn't Nazoor. The commanders of the Wyvern army were pointing at Palal and Chin and ordering to attack or change targets or change formations. The soldiers didn't know whose directions to follow, so they just swarmed at whichever enemy was closest. The Palal seemed even less organised. Some Re'dahl were pulling the swarming bodies from the Chin while others were engaged in flying combat with the Wyvern. The only dragons that looked calm were the Chin. They ignored the Wyvern that covered them and concentrated on eating as many of the mini-dragons as they could swallow.

Whitestaff flew through the battle until he caught sight of Nap. The ruby patch that covered Nap's eye glinted in the sun, making him stand out amidst the tangle of dragons. The red dragon was in the middle of the fray, giving orders and fighting at the same time.

'Help the Chin first!' Nap shouted to his Re'dahl. 'The Nazoor are trying to pull them down!'

Pull them down? Whitestaff wondered. *How are the Chin even flying in the first place? They have no wings...*

He beat a path over to Nap and helped him fend off some of his attackers. Soon the two were fighting back to back, and they made a tempting target to the Nazoor. With his eye patch and red scales, the Wyvern thought that Nap was Cracone, and so attacked him in large numbers, each Wyvern hoping to be the one to kill the King. The famous fire-breathing Kai'dahl would make an excellent trophy too, so having both dragons in the one place was like a red flag to a rampaging bull.

'Nap! We need to retreat!' Whitestaff shouted over the sounds of the battle. 'You need to get the Re'dahl back to where the Court used to be.'

'Latos! Why would we do that? We're going to win this. If we don't strike now we may never get another chance!'

'I am your King, Nap. You need to follow my orders. Now signal the retreat!'

'You made me the head of the army. You *knew* I'd be the only one the Re'dahl would follow. I say we fight.'

Whitestaff noticed that the Nazoor who were attacking the Chin had spotted them. They began to detach themselves from the Chin and fly over to the two Palal, who appeared to be easier targets. In no time at all, the Nazoor had Whitestaff and Nap completely surrounded.

'Link wings with me, Nap!' Whitestaff said.

'What?'

Whitestaff pressed his back against Nap's and wrapped his tail around Nap's chest. Nap was now pinned against Whitestaff's back, unable to fly.

'What are you doing?' He struggled and tried to unwrap himself from Whitestaff's tail.

'Hold on!' Whitestaff said.

The golden dragon beat heavily with one wing and began to twist himself in the air, whirling his body around. Faster and faster he went; round and round like a cyclone. Nap yelped as he was spun, his legs and tail flailing.

'What are you doing?' he yelled again.

The Nazoor attackers descended on the spinning pair, diving in for the kill.

Suddenly, when Whitestaff guessed the Nazoor were close enough, he belched forth a stream of scorching fire. The jet of heat twirled around the two Palal as they spun, making them look like a twister made of fire. Whitestaff's powerful flame shot out in all directions and burned every Nazoor within a twenty metre radius—their roasted bodies fell beneath the fog.

Whitestaff stopped his spin and let go of Nap, whose one good eye rattled in his head. The red dragon shook himself and tried to focus.

'Great move, Whitestaff. You could've warned me though!' he said.

'I did! Listen, Nap. If you don't give the order to retreat, then I will. If you're too stubborn to come with me, then you'll die on this planet along with everything else left on it. Do you understand what I'm saying?'

'But we won't die Whitestaff. We have the Chin now. They're on our side.'

'No we don't! Before I let them in here, they told me that they were our creators. They *made* us, Nap.'

'That's a good thing, Whitestaff.'

'No it isn't. They made the Nazoor too, and now they're eating them!'

'At least it's them and not us.'

'For now. I think that they need to feed on essence so that they don't have to hibernate. When they run out of food, they sleep until whatever planet they are on is full again. Then they feed once more and the cycle continues.'

'But they're winning this war for us, Whitestaff.'

'They're feeding on essence. Dragon essence! What do you think the Chin will do when they run out of Nazoor?'

Nap opened his mouth to answer, but stopped short, for the very air around them began to shake. The fighting in the sky momentarily paused as the dragons searched for the rumbling that grew louder and louder. Soon, all eyes moved to the source of the sound: the Chin dragons. The noise was a mix of cracking thunder and stormy seas. It was coming out of their mouths and grew louder and louder still. The Chin threw their heads back and let it rip from out of their lungs. It was laughter. Horrible, horrible laughter.

Whitestaff put his mouth next to Nap's ear. 'We need to go.'

Nap stared at the Chin and nodded.

'Now!' said Whitestaff. 'To where the Court used to be.'

Nap gave the Chin one more look then swooped off to spread the word to the Re'dahl. He flew as though he had the entire Nazoor army on his tail.

Whitestaff continued to watch as the Chin laughed. The Nazoor that were attacking the bodies of the giant dragons paused as the Chin shook beneath them. They were utterly confused. Despite their repeated attacks on the Chin, the super-dragons were laughing!

'You think you can defeat us?' Boomed Huo'dool. 'You have no idea!'

Whitestaff watched as the dragon of fire clenched his entire body. The enormous dragon roared and his scales began to glow. The Nazoor that clung to him screamed in pain as his body burst with light and his scales turned into fire. Huo'dool became a dragon of pure flame!

Those that were attacking Shui'dool also cried out. For the dragon had turned his body into water, and they were being pulled into him as though he were quicksand. He devoured them without having to use his mouth.

Qi'dool's attackers felt the dragon of air evaporate beneath them, their scratching claws hitting nothing but air. A second later, the dragon re-appeared behind them, flying at them with his mouth open wide. He caused a twister to form in the air around the Wyvern and funnelled them into his waiting stomach.

Those Wyvern who had attached themselves to Tu'dool saw what was happening to the rest and quickly left the dragon of stone alone.

'Kaga Omdi Drageel!' Huo called.

The other dragons called it back to him in unison. 'Kaga Omdi Drageel!'

The elemental dragons turned their bodies back to dragon form once more and began gorging themselves on whatever was closest to them. Whitestaff gasped in horror as Huo'dool cut through a swarm of Nazoor who were fighting some Palal. Whitestaff knew one of the fighters was Ugos. He recognised his pinkish scales and knew it was the same dragon who'd helped him sneak the Palal eggs from the Hatchery earlier. The dragon of fire paused for a moment in front of them, smiled at the fighting dragons, and then swooped down, swallowing them all whole. Nazoor and Palal alike disappeared within the dragon's giant jaws.

'Stop it!' Whitestaff screamed. 'Stop it! You're killing the Palal!'

But Huo'dool ignored him, as did the other Chin. They were in such a frenzy that they didn't care what sort of dragon they ate. If it flew, it was food.

I knew it! Whitestaff told himself. *Somehow I knew they would do this. They gave their essence in hope that they could one day feed on it. And I let it happen!*

The few thousand remaining Nazoor had just witnessed the near destruction of their entire army. It didn't take long for them to figure out the outcome of the battle, and so they fled in all directions. The Chin dragons gave a cheer and took off after the retreating Nazoor, swallowing them as they flew.

Whitestaff too turned away and headed for the giant portal that still hovered over the ruins of the Court.

Thankfully he found Nap had been very efficient. The plan he had formulated for retreat was for one dragon to tell two others the meeting place before fleeing from the battle. That way, the word spread very quickly through the Palal ranks, and soon everyone that had survived both the Nazoor and the Chin was waiting for the King. Whitestaff was relieved to see Graggy and Luzahmin there, as well as Armay and Susset who had found his portal. Merlin was there too. He looked like a man who was patiently waiting for a carriage to arrive, unaware of the carnage that had taken place around him.

The assembled dragon hovered around the King, eager to hear his words.

'My fellow Palal. There will be time to explain once we leave, but right now, I need you to trust me. This planet is no longer ours. Sorteya is no longer safe for us to live on. We need to go through there,' he gestured towards the portal, 'and we need to hurry. Take someone else's tail and cross. There is plenty of room so you don't have to crowd one another. Now go.'

None of the Palal moved. They hovered in the air, staring uncertainly at the portal above them.

'I SAID MOVE!' shouted Whitestaff.

Some of his subjects trembled at his shout and began to move timidly towards the opening in the sky.

Graggy curled his tail around Armay's. 'Let's be the first,' he told her. 'For Whitestaff.'

Armay nodded. She gave the Kai'dahl a wink and flew with Graggy. She tried to act braver than she felt as she flew upwards. The other Palal watched the pair as they disappeared into the hole.

'THE REST OF YOU MOVE,' commanded Whitestaff.

He flew around behind them and ushered them through, like a dog rounding up sheep. The Palal flew though the portal, tails linked in pairs until only Whitestaff, Merlin and Susset remained.

'One moment,' he told them. Whitestaff flew over to the nearest spire and picked off some balefruit. He returned with his arms loaded. 'Can you carry these too, Susset?'

The portal that Whitestaff had used to cross into Sorteya levitated in front of Susset. Whitestaff tossed her the balefruit and Susset levitated those too.

Whitestaff offered the sorceress his tail and she took it in her hand.

'Are you coming too?' Whitestaff asked Merlin.

The old man shook his head. 'I'm already there. I told you, I've already done the future bit.'

'Where are you going then?' Whitestaff asked.

'To the future and the past,' Merlin answered. 'I have to meet my granddaughter in the future, then take her on a very important mission. One that began almost two hundred years ago. When you cross, I'll close the portal. But you'd better go now. We have company, you know.'

Behind Merlin, Whitestaff could see Huo'dool coming for them. The Chin dragon looked as though he'd figured out where all the tasty Palal had gone, and he wasn't happy.

'See you on the other side,' said Merlin.

Whitestaff and Susset sped towards the portal, eager to get through before Huo could stop them.

As soon as they had crossed, Merlin closed the doorway between the Chin planet and Sorteya. He turned around just in time to see Huo'dool's fiery jaws about to close around him.

The old man chuckled to himself, opened his own portal and disappeared into the future, causing Huo'dool to bite down on empty air.

47

ON THE TRAIL

The storm had passed quickly after the fight with the kraken, and soon the Pohmin Sea was smooth and easy to sail on. The crew aboard the Dart didn't know whether to feel jubilant that they had defeated the tyrant of the sea, or relieved that they were alive and able to tell the tale. Drake and Garth both recovered well from their injuries, but a headcount taken soon after the storm had passed revealed that one of the crew had disappeared. The missing sailor, whose name was Kent, was one of the quieter members aboard. He was well liked by the captain because he went about his work with no fuss and didn't create any arguments with the others. No one could remember seeing him after the kraken attacked, and it wasn't known whether he'd been tossed overboard by the kraken or by the storm. In any event, Bob gathered the crew together to say a few words of respect for their lost mate. It was a sombre ceremony, and Pip felt as though he didn't really deserve to be a part of it, seeing as though he wasn't officially a member of Blackbeard's crew.

After the proper respects were shown, the Captain told each sailor they'd be given a goblet of the ship's finest wine with dinner, as well as a handsome bonus in their pay. At the table in the mess that night, the crew drank their wine and ate with relish, and it wasn't long before talk turned to the fight with the kraken. Each sailor had his own version of what had happened, and soon Pip heard about the battle from every angle. He was glad that he featured in the stories once or twice, and a few remarked on his accurate and fast shots with the bow. Balad gave the best recount though. The guard seemed to have eyes in the back of his head. He could recall everyone's positions and actions, and remembered each of the kraken's fearsome attacks. The best part was *how* Balad told the story. He wasn't content with just talking it through; he jumped up on the table and acted out the whole thing. First he impersonated the Captain's holler for the attack, then he changed into Rio, making his face light up at the prospect of the battle, and charging tentacles with his sword. Next he ducked down under the table and pretended he was the kraken. He sent his arms up and over the table and smashed them down on the wood, blindly groping for the sailors on deck. His foreign accent made everything more interesting, and his acting was hilarious. The crew cheered when he pretended he was Drake caught up in the kraken's long tentacles, and they cheered louder still when he mimed the kraken's grip being blown apart by Mollie's magic. The crew were in fits of laughter as Balad transformed himself into the kraken being pulled away from the ship by Mollie's whirlpool— his arms madly grabbing for the invisible Dart. Rio got in on the action too. He got behind Balad and lifted him up in the air by the yellow sash around the guard's waist. Now, helpless and thrashing about in mid-air, Balad resembled the kraken more than ever, and the crew were in hysterics. Finally, Balad pretended to be hit by lightning and Rio let him drop to the table with a thud. They cheered and clapped Balad at the end of his performance. The crew also gave their biggest cheer for Mollie, the real hero of the day.

Unfortunately, the sorceress was still asleep in her bed. After Pip had caught her at the end of the battle, he took her straight down to her cabin and lay her down to rest. The blood had stopped trickling from her nose and Bob told everyone he was certain that there was nothing to worry about, and that the poor lass was just exhausted. He was right too, for she awoke an hour or so later, weak but otherwise in good health. Nevertheless, Pip insisted on making hourly visits to check on her recovery.

'It's my fault,' he told Balad. 'It was my idea to cut through the Pohmin and fight the kraken. If she doesn't recover, I'll never forgive myself.'

'Fear not, Honoured One. She will be fine. Besides, something tells me that Mollie wouldn't allow herself to do something she didn't want to. She *wanted* to help, remember?'

Pip sighed heavily. 'I just don't want to lose her, I suppose.'

'You like her, Prince?'

Pip smiled and nodded. 'More than I like you, Balad.'

'That much is obvious,' Balad chuckled. 'I for one am glad that we saw her in action though. I'm a lot more confident in defeating Shadowclaw now. Aren't you?'

'I am. It just feels wrong now, forcing her to fight again. Using her like a weapon.'

'I think I know what you mean, Honoured One. But ponder this—without her, Nalib will be the next Aldallah. It is worth the discomfort of asking for her help, yes?'

Pip reluctantly agreed. He knew his home was doomed without Mollie, as the Silver Scourge would stop at nothing to get its claws on the Sultan's gold. But in his heart he hated the thought of putting the black-haired sorceress in any more danger, especially if she was still weak. Luckily though, by the time they pulled into the port at Hulum, Mollie was up and about and acting like her old self. She assured Pip and Balad that she was up for another fight, especially one that wasn't at sea on a boat in the middle of a storm.

When Mollie, Pip and Balad departed the Black Dart in Hulum, Blackbeard took it upon himself to escort the three down the gangplank and off his ship. He accompanied them into the city and purchased horses for his guests to use to get them home quickly. Rio and Drake went along too. They carried Mollie's luggage and secured Whitestaff's egg to a pack on the rear of one of the horses.

'You don't have to go to all this trouble,' Pip told the captain. 'But thank you, we appreciate everything that you've done for us.'

Blackbeard chuckled. 'This is more to thank Mollie,' he said. 'But if you want to thank me, there is something you can do.'

293

'Anything within my power,' said the Prince. 'What do you need?'

'I need you to keep our voyage, and all that happened on it, a secret. Think you can manage that?'

'I can,' Pip agreed. 'But why wouldn't you want the world to know that the kraken is finally dead and that your crew was the one to pull it off?'

'Don't like to brag,' Bob replied. 'Keep it all under wraps and I'll count you as a mate for life. Aye?'

'Yes. Of course. Thank you again Bob. Pass my thanks on to the crew as well.'

Blackbeard shook the Prince's hand and left them at the stables. As he was walking away, he began to laugh. It was that same horrid laugh that Pip had heard him use before. As the laughter faded into the distance, Pip's skin crawled with goosebumps.

'I wish he wouldn't do that,' said Pip. 'That laugh. It doesn't sound happy at all. Sounds more like a man up to no good.'

'The sound of a man whose plan worked perfectly, more like,' said Balad.

'What do you mean, Balad?'

'I mean, his plan worked perfectly. He set this all up, Prince. Remember that night on his ship when he suggested that we find Mollie? He laughed like that then. He didn't want you to find Mollie for our benefit—he wanted to get Mollie on board to fight his kraken. It was just convenient that we could use her help too.'

'You think? It was my idea to cut through the Pohmin Sea though, not his.'

'It was, but why did you want to cut through?'

'Because he got word that Shadowclaw was attacking...'

'Now you see? Perhaps there was no sighting of Shadowclaw? Perhaps Bob just said that to get you to cut through the Pohmin? And with Mollie on board, he knew he would win against the kraken.'

'Maybe. But what would he stand to gain if the kraken is dead?'

Balad held up a single finger. 'He is now the only captain that knows the kraken is dead. Which means his is now the only ship that can cross the Pohmin in five days, not two weeks. His ship will be the only ship that uses the fast route, which means he can trade or smuggle goods at twice the speed of any other vessel. Think of the money he will make! In one year, he will be the richest sailor in the world!'

'Latos,' said Pip. 'We knew he was up to something, didn't we? But I never would've guess he'd planned it out so well. I never would've guessed without you saying so.'

Balad smiled. 'I've learned a lot from Pukami over the years. I've watched him give council to your father. I've learned to spot the tricks and traps people use, and Blackbeard appears to be a master of them.'

'He sure is. But for now we have to take his word for it. If he *was* telling the truth and Shadowclaw *is* on the hunt, then we'd feel very stupid for not acting.'

'You're right,' said Mollie as she mounted her horse. 'He is a rouge but best we get a move on. Just in case.'

'Are you sure you're up to it,' asked Pip.

'I'm sure, Prince Pip. From what you've told me, this Silver Scourge needs to be dealt with as soon as possible. The question is, are you two up to it?'

Balad smiled and brandished his curved sword.

'That we are, sorceress. Now let's go slay ourselves a dragon.'

48

A WHOLE NEW WORLD

Whitestaff was baffled at what he saw when he came through the
other side of the Chin portal. The land was exactly as he'd left it:
wide, beautiful and flat. What puzzled him was the congregation of
Palal flapping desperately in a circle in the sky. Some had their tails
linked, some were weeping, others were asking furious questions
about why they had to leave their wonderful planet behind. Those
that had witnessed Ugos and the other Palal getting eaten by
Huo'dool, however, were very vocal in saying they'd never return to
Sorteya if Latos froze over. Whitestaff was about to ask them what
they were doing when Cartogras and a few Bo'dahl from the Bo'dahl
Council swooped at him. They looked blurry and out of focus to
Whitestaff. He told himself that it was crossing through the portal
that was making his eyes play tricks on him.

'Ahhh, there he is!' said Cartogras. 'He's sure to know.'

'Yes,' said a Bo'dahl. 'He's been here.'

'Excuse me, Whitestaff—I mean, Your Majesty?'

'Yes?'

'We'd like to know. We're getting a bit tired waiting for you, see? So we'd all like to know.'

'Like to know what?' asked Whitestaff, narrowing his gaze on the dragons.

'We'd like to know how long until we can go back. Our wings are getting a bit sore. When do you think the Chin will be finished with the Nazoor?'

Whitestaff blinked heavily and asked Susset to fly over.

'Susset, can you make sure my voice reaches everyone's ears?'

The sorceress nodded and gathered the air elements. With her spell, everyone would hear Whitestaff, even if he whispered.

'My fellow Palal. Welcome to this new planet. I know that some of you were hoping that the Chin would be our saviours, but it turns out, there is more to the Chin than we could ever have imagined.' The Palal broke off their own conversations to listen.

'The Chin have been around for centuries. They were on the Earth even before us, before the Nazoor. For the fact is, they created us! They used their essence to create new dragons. The Wyvern and then the Palal. They revealed all this to me when I was here last.' As Whitestaff spoke, he allowed himself to sink downwards little by little. Without realising, the other Palal drifted down with him. Whitestaff could hear the rustling of the tree below him getting louder. He didn't dare look down for fear that the other dragons would look also.

'But it wasn't out of kindness that we were created. The Chin made us to be cattle. Bred and then consumed when there was enough of us. You see, the Chin follow a natural cycle. Firstly, they feed. You have seen them do this. They feed and feed until there is hardly anything left for them to eat. Then, when they feel hunger, they enter a deep slumber. Chin can sleep for centuries, until life has renewed itself. When they feel there is enough food for them, they awaken and gorge themselves. Then, when the food becomes scarce, they sleep again and wait. It's a cycle, you see? But the clever Chin found a way to never have to sleep. They invented their own supply of food: Us!'

The Palal were so intrigued by his story, that they failed to realise they had drifted down with Whitestaff, very close to the ground.

'When the humans came and we fought with them, the Chin nearly lost their valuable source of dragon essence. And so they agreed to come here while our numbers built up on Sorteya. Unfortunately for us, the Chin were the only force that could stop the Nazoor. Mezelga had built up her numbers and had planned the takeover of our planet perfectly. Without unleashing the Chin, we would have all died. And so we can never go back to Sorteya, for the Chin would surely devour our essence as they did to the Nazoor, and to Ugos. And that brings us here: our new planet. A living, vibrant place devoid of Nazoor, Chin, and spires.'

Whitestaff waited until his words were fully understood. It wasn't long until he heard a squeal.

'No spires!' said a Bo'dahl. 'Then where are we to live?'

The other dragons looked around and saw it was true: the land was very flat. They also saw how close they were to the ground, and some of them shot upwards out of sheer panic.

'GET BACK DOWN HERE!' Whitestaff ordered, his voice amplified. He waited until the dragons obeyed before he continued.

'This planet has no spires. No tall mountains. No dugouts. We must live as all creatures do: on the ground.'

'Never!' said some.

'What a disgrace!'

'How could he have brought us here?'

Whitestaff shouted over the top of them. Susset made sure his words thundered in their ears.

'Do you know why dragons avoid the ground?' he asked. 'Do you even know the reason? Answer me now if you do.'

All the dragons remained silent. Whitestaff drifted further down until his paws touched the sand on the beach below. His wings ached from flying, and he winced as he folded them in place along his back. He told himself they were just stiff because he'd been in the air for so long, but part of him knew that wasn't the whole truth. He craned his neck to look at the other dragons as he spoke.

'The only Chin that did not lend his essence to make the Wyvern was Tu'dool. He was the dragon of stone that you saw on Sorteya. As a result, the Wyvern are allergic to his essence and touching the ground burns them. But that has nothing to do with us.

It never has. Avoiding the ground is a Nazoor necessity that the Palal of the past blindly followed.'

'Not all of us followed it.' Armay drifted down too. She stood next to the King and looked up at the others.

Graggy joined them and so did Nap.

Luzahmin gave a squeal of disgust. But nevertheless, she swooped down to join her beloved Re'dahl. She closed her eyes and screwed up her face... and landed.

Olfar joined his nephew, but not many others were forthcoming.

'My subjects,' Whitestaff said in a softer tone. 'It is not our rule or our tradition. The ground is no more unclean than the sky or the oceans. Besides, I'm sorry to say, you don't really have a choice. You have to land sometime. You can't fly forever.'

The hovering Palal looked at each other, then to the ground only a few metres below them. It was true; they had no choice. With painful slowness they each descended, hoping not to be the first to make contact with the sand. In the end, they all touched at about the same time, secretly glad to rest their tired wings.

'There,' said Whitestaff. 'Now that that's out of the way, maybe we can discuss matters of a more serious nature. This planet is not Sorteya. It is not a home we are used to. But this is not the first time the Palal have had to give up our home. Earth and Sorteya have both been left behind. But this planet is ours forever. I have decided to name it Xenos, in honour of a dragon that gave his life to protect Cracone, the Red King. May the name help us to remember the cost of true peace. This beach we are gathered on, shall hereby be known as Cross's Landing. I have seen this planet before and I know it to be full of life. I brought along some balefruit to eat, but the ocean is teeming with fish. Not enough for the hungry Chin, but plenty for the Palal.'

'I am commanding the Bo'dahl to assemble their Council and begin searching for a new place for us to build our community. Make sure there is ample space for us to grow and expand. The Gra'dahl, I'm charging your Council to map this new place and learn everything you can about it. What can we eat? What is poisonous? Where will the balefruit grow? Re'dahl, your strength will be needed to build new structures. We need a hatchery, a Court, and shelter from the weather.'

'My subjects, I know I haven't been your King for long. But I see now that this is our future. It has always been our future, ever since the day we were created. We have been given this planet as a clean start. Let's fill it with peace and Palal!'

If Whitestaff was expecting a cheer from his subjects, he was disappointed. The Palal weren't happy, but at least he'd given them something to do. They branched off into their own Councils, and were soon so busy organising themselves that the sand beneath their paws was all but forgotten. Even though they weren't meeting in an official Court, the Councils ran smoothly and dragons began flying this way and that, busily carrying out tasks that they had been assigned. So engrossed in their projects and the scenery of the new planet were they, that no one noticed Whitestaff was shrinking, or that his golden colour was slowly fading into white, except Susset.

The sorceress had placed his portal upright on the sand and gave the balefruit to Graggy and Olfar. She drifted over to Whitestaff and stroked his snout. 'Time to return I see.'

Whitestaff gave a weak nod. 'I'm draining fast, it seems. Must have been all the excitement.'

'If you call saving an entire race of dragons excitement.'

'And condemning another race to extinction,' Whitestaff added.

Merlin suddenly appeared next to the pair. He looked even older to Whitestaff, though his vision was fading in and out, so he couldn't be sure.

'Looks like you've just arrived here,' said Merlin. 'The war is over, I take it? I guess I'll live to see it soon. The Chin were horrible, I expect.'

'Yes, but effective. You haven't lived it yet, have you?'

'Not that part, no. Today will be the first time we meet, won't it. Well, the first time you meet me, you know.'

'I do know. I think I'm starting to figure out how your life works.'

Merlin smiled. 'Good. Do I make a good first impression?'

Whitestaff gave a tired smile. 'Not really. There is one thing you should promise me though.'

'What is it?'

'When you first meet me, let me figure out the Chin by myself. It's my duty to make the call to unleash them on the Nazoor. No one else's.'

Merlin agreed that he would keep his mouth shut about the elemental dragons. 'But it looks like you've arrived just in time to leave. I made your portal that way, you know. Not too long here, not too long there. Just here and there enough to do what you need to do.'

'Well I've had enough of it. My place is here now with my dragons. They need a permanent king. Not one that flies in and out, right enough.'

Merlin stoked his beard in thought. 'Just keep that medallion with you, Whitestaff. It is the key to everything you want. I have to go now, but I'll see you soon.'

'I have to go too. Susset, can you tell Armay and the rest what happened? Tell them why I had to leave?'

Susset assured him that she would. 'The Palal will be very busy transforming this place into a brand new home, Whitestaff. They can do without a king for a few months.'

'Wait! On second thought, I'll tell them all myself. Summon them to me. I need to say goodbye in person. It's my duty as the King.'

49

MAGIC MEETS MAGIC

Balad, Mollie and Pip were tired and saddle-sore. Once again, Pip wished for his own horse, Jasper, and Mollie found herself missing Wendy more than ever. The horses that had been generously donated to them by Blackbeard, were taciturn beasts that were hard to handle. They often ignored their riders and required constant direction. Mollie tried speaking to them in order to get more cooperation, but they were suspicious of her ability to communicate and became even more unresponsive to commands.

It took almost three days of riding to get back to Nalib. There was no road or path that connected Hulum to the Sultan's fabulous city. Rather, a string of farmer's houses dotted the way. When dusk fell, the trio would stop in at the closest house and ask for lodging. They were made to feel welcome at each place they stopped, but Mollie wondered if she didn't have their Prince with her, would the locals be so accommodating. No one had heard of Shadowclaw reappearing, and it was beginning to look as though Balad was right about the captain—he had lied in order to get the sorceress to fight the kraken. This, in turn, put Mollie in a foul mood. Worse still was that the more they travelled, the hotter it got. The trees began to disappear and the soil beneath the horses' hooves turned to sand. The sun beat down hard on Mollie's black hair, so she was relieved when, on the third afternoon, Pip pointed to a shining dome in the distance.

'We are nearly there!' he said. 'That's the Palace roof. The dragon has left it untouched! We're not too late.'

Without warning, Mollie felt her horse speed up and race towards the city. Sand kicked up behind her and was carried away by the wind. Mollie was taken by surprise and she fell backwards. Luckily, Whitestaff's egg was lashed to the horse and it stopped the sorceress from slipping off completely.

'Whoa,' said Mollie. 'Slow down, we'll be there soon.' The horse ignored her and stretched its body with each stride. Faster and faster it bolted, heading straight for the city ahead.

Mollie looked to Pip and Balad for help. Unfortunately for her, the two were fighting their own horses.

'Slow down!' Mollie commanded, speaking directly into the horse's mind. 'You'll toss me off!'

The mad pace of the horse made it difficult for Mollie to remain upright. She was being jolted this way and that. She held onto the reins with one hand, while the other was bent behind her trying to keep Whitestaff's egg balanced.

'I do not like this, Honoured One,' shouted Balad. 'It feels like what happened when—'

FWOOSH!

Something flew low and fast over their heads.

'Shadowclaw!' Pip and Balad yelled together.

Mollie screamed as the horse bucked wildly and threw her into the air. Her feet went over her head as she hurtled towards the sand below. Luckily, the sorceress was quick-thinking and levitated herself just before she hit the ground. The horse was not so lucky. It had bucked itself over and crashed into the sand, sending Whitestaff's egg and Mollie's luggage spilling across the desert. It picked itself up off the ground and bolted, not caring in which direction it went. Seeing that the beasts had become impossible to control, Pip and Bald jumped from their horses. They hit the sand and rolled expertly, then raced over to see if Mollie was injured.

The sorceress was still hovering in the air. She used her magic to gather up all her things, and levitated Whitestaff's precious egg over to her. She checked it to make sure the dragon's portal was still there and that there was no major damage. She frowned when she saw that Merlin's protective spell was almost completely shattered. After months of being hit with a sledgehammer at Cudgel's attraction, Merlin's magic had nearly been broken. Now, after crashing to the ground and being rolled on by a horse, it was as fragile as the eggshell itself.

'Mollie, are you hurt?' Pip asked.

Mollie shook her head and gently placed the egg down.

FWOOSH!

The sound came again and Balad unsheathed his sword and held it upright. Pip unslung his bow and reached for an arrow.

'Latos,' he said under his breath. There was only one arrow left in his quiver; the rest had spilled out when he jumped off his horse. The three stood back to back, searching the sky overhead for the Scourge of Aldallah.

'Where is it?' asked Mollie.

'Turned itself invisible,' said Balad. 'The way you can.'

'Interesting,' said Mollie.

'Terrifying, more like,' said Balad.

Pip stopped looking at the sky and scanned the ground.

'There. Look!' he said. 'The shadow!'

The others looked over at the sand where Pip was pointing. They could see the vague outline of the dragon as it flew circles above them.

'You have to account for the sun,' said Pip. 'It's sinking now, so the dragon should be about...'

Mollie gazed in awe as Pip aimed his bow in the air, while still watching the dragon's shadow on the ground.

'There!' he said, and he let his arrow fly. Pip snapped his head up to watch his arrow shoot into the empty sky above. It speared upward with a whistle, then, *sssssssssump,* it sank into the soft skin beneath the dragon's jaw.

A moment later, there came a howl of pain and Shadowclaw became visible above them.

Mollie got a good look at the silver dragon and grimaced in disgust. Bloodstains splattered its scales, and Mollie knew the blood didn't belong to the dragon.

'What sort of dragon is that?' she asked. 'It looks nothing like Whitestaff.'

'It's an angry one now,' said Balad. 'Jump out of the way!'

Balad and Pip jumped to the side and rolled as Shadowclaw sent down a massive fireball. Mollie pretended to yawn as the fireball hurtled towards her. At the last possible moment she summoned a shield above the three of them. The fireball spread out and dissipated as it hit the invisible ceiling, leaving Mollie and her friends unharmed underneath.

Shadowclaw sniffed the air. He seethed with rage when he could still smell the humans.

'You again!' it said as it took another snout full of air. 'I know your scent!'

Pip looked to his comrades. 'Did you hear that! It spoke. Just like last time, Balad!'

'I heard nothing, Prince,' said Balad, not taking his eye off the beast above.

'I did,' said Mollie to the prince. 'It remembers you.'

'You can hear it talking too?' asked Balad.

'Yes,' Mollie replied. 'And now *I'm* going to talk to *it*.' She focused her mind on the silver dragon above. 'I see you know magic,' the sorceress said. 'I know a bit about it myself. Now tell me, why did you attack us?'

Even though the dragon had skin growing over the place where its eyes should have been, it still turned its head to face her.

'You can speak to me? Interesting. A pity I'll be the last thing you ever speak to.'

The dragon summoned another spell and sent is cracking down towards Mollie. The sorceress thought it was a magic missile and she summoned another shield. It was a fraction too late when she saw that it wasn't a magic missile at all. It was the wrong colour. In fact, the closer it got the more she realised it didn't look like any magic she recognised. It looked like a lightning bolt made of blue glass!

'Look out!' she called. She tackled Pip and the two of them hurled into the sand to the left. She turned to push Balad out of the way with her magic, but the wily guard had already evaded the dragon's spell by diving to the right.

Shadowclaw's bolt of dark blue magic hit Mollie's shield and smashed it apart. The deadly spell splintered on impact and shards of it rained down, digging into the sand like knives.

'What was that?' Pip asked as he got back onto his feet.

'I don't know,' said Mollie. 'His magic is different to mine somehow. I noticed it when I was healing your arms.'

Pip looked down to at his bandages and remembered how it felt when the Silver Scourge was on top of him.

'What does that mean?'

Mollie looked up at the dragon who was testing the air to see if the humans had survived his attack. 'It means we're going to need some help.'

'Fine with me,' Pip said. 'Balad, get to the palace as fast as you can. Tell father to send out his troops. We'll keep this thing occupied.'

Balad looked as though he were about to argue, but thought better of it and sprinted for the city.

Pip ran too, but only over to where his arrows lay spilled in the sand. He snatched them up and jammed them in his quiver while Mollie and Shadowclaw traded magical blows. For every spell the sorceress had for the dragon, Shadowclaw had an answer. It looked like a stalemate of magic.

Hurry, Balad, thought the prince. *I think Mollie has finally met her match.*

50

DRAGON MEETS DRAGON

Whitestaff looked at the dragons gathered around him. Tired eyes
stared out from the hungry faces that had been changed by war.
The golden Palal swallowed hard. They all seemed so much bigger
now that he had shrunk.

'My subjects,' he started. His voice was a rasp that Susset had
amplified. 'As you can see, Merlin's magic is hard at work. My
essence has drained, and I need to recharge on the other side of this
portal.' He lifted a frail paw and gestured to the glowing disc that
would take him back to his egg. 'It is the worst possible time to leave
you, right enough. Unless you want to be led by a Lili'dahl instead of
a Kai'dahl?' He took in their tired smiles and continued. 'I know that
you don't feel at home here. Well, I guess that's how the first few
years felt on Sorteya. The difference is that we will never have to
leave this planet, this Xenos, this sanctuary. Unless you count me. I
have to leave. I promise you though, somehow I will make sure this
will be the last time. When I return from this gateway, I will return
for good. Until that time, I place the Council in charge. Please carry

out my orders so that we can live comfortably on our new home. Farewell, my subjects. But not good-bye. Armay. Graggy. If you can assist?'

The two loyal Palal dragons made their way forward and eased themselves beneath Whitestaff's wings, as they had done long ago. They propped up their friend and guided him to the portal. He rubbed their backs with his tail as a way of thanking them. At the portal entrance he turned and gave the Palal one last bow, then hobbled into the blackness.

The darkness of the portal closed around him, and the sounds of the waves crashing at Cross's Landing faded into nothing. He walked forward in the dark, feeling the sand beneath his paws from the beach he'd just left and waiting for it to change to the straw of Mollie's barn. Onward he walked, into the light in front of him, yet the sand remained.

Strange, he thought. *Where is the straw?*

He stepped through the portal and collapsed onto the ground beneath him—a ground of sand. Harsh sunlight made him squint and all he could make out in front of him was his egg. It lay on its side, open and partly buried.

Where am I this time? Where is the barn? Where is Wendy?

He closed his eyes against the glare and felt the sun's heat warm his scales.

'Mollie,' he called. 'Where are you?'

'Whitestaff!' He heard Mollie's familiar voice. It sounded nearby.

The dragon opened his eyes again. The medallion that hung heavy on the chain around his neck weighed him down, but with great effort he lifted his head so he could see over the rim of his egg. There, further along the desert, he saw a young man shooting arrows and Mollie hurling balls of fire towards the sky. He craned his neck to see what they were aiming at.

'Oh no!' he said. 'What is that thing?'

But he didn't really need to ask. In his heart he knew.

It's a Palal Alpos!

'Mollie,' he spoke into her mind. 'Be on your guard. It's an Alpos and it's dangerous! It knows magic!'

Mollie jumped to the side as another of her shields was shattered by Shadowclaw's spells.

'I know! We've been fighting it for a while. Stay hidden!'

But it was too late. The desert wind had carried Whitestaff's scent to Shadowclaw.

'Who is this?' he said as he sniffed the air. 'Another dragon!' The Scourge let out a terrifying roar. 'You want to challenge me? I will tear you all APART! I will burn you all!'

Shadowclaw unleashed a torrent of spells on the three below. Shards of electric blue sizzled and sparked in every direction. Mollie shielded Pip as much as she could, but she was getting overwhelmed. Shadowclaw roared and doubled his efforts.

Mollie had never seen so much magic being wielded at once. *How is this possible?* She threw up spell after spell to combat the silver dragon's magic, but she struggled to keep up. Pip shot his last few arrows at the spells coming towards him. Each arrow exploded on impact, and in a matter of seconds, his quiver was bare. He looked over to Mollie and saw a thin line of blood leaking from her nose. He remembered the fight with the kraken and knew that Mollie was moments away from passing out.

'Oh no,' he said aloud.

'Stop!' said Whitestaff. 'I am your King. You need to stop!'

Shadowclaw seethed with rage. 'You're no King. You're nothing!' He sent a massive bolt of blue towards Whitestaff. The small white dragon saw it coming and knew that he was doomed if it hit. With his last ounce of strength, Whitestaff grabbed his egg and used it to shield him from the deadly magical blow.

The blue bolt hit the egg with a mighty blast, exploding its shell into tiny fragments. Mollie screamed when she saw the egg destroyed, but stopped short when she saw what happened next. The portal that was inside the egg turned into a swirling mist and glowed gold. It spun like a vortex and the bottom of it channeled itself into Whitestaff's stomach. At once the dragon began to grow.

'My essence!' he said. 'Nothing is holding it back!' He watched as his own body grew in size and his scales turned to gold. 'Merlin's spell is undone!'

Strength flooded back into Whitestaff's muscles and he roared to the sky.

'This is your dragon?' Pip asked Mollie. 'The little white one?'

'This is what he really looks like,' Mollie said. 'It's the first time I've seen him change.'

Shadowclaw, who could not see the transformation, sent another powerful blast at Whitestaff. 'Why don't you insects die?' he growled.

'Look out!' Mollie shouted.

Whitestaff saw the bolt coming for him and raised his paws to shield himself. But he was too big and too slow. The blast hit him front on. Blue sparks showered everywhere. But nothing happened to Whitestaff.

'What?' Mollie whispered.

Whitestaff still stood where he was. Paws raised and eyes squinted. When he realised that the spell had gone, he lowered his front legs. He looked down at his chest and laughed.

'Of course,' he said. 'The Royal Medallion. No magic can touch me.' He picked it up from his chest and kissed it. 'Thank you, Merlin!'

'Merlin? What about Merlin?' asked Mollie.

Whitestaff didn't hear her. He launched his massive body at the dragon overhead. 'Let's see how dangerous you are without your magic.'

For once in his life, Shadowclaw looked scared. He cast spell after spell at the dragon that he could smell coming, but his magic was having no effect. Whitestaff hit him at full force and sent him cartwheeling through the air. Shadowclaw thrust his wings out to stop himself. He flapped himself upright and tried to smell where his enemy was. But Whitestaff was on him before he could even get a lungful of air. He grabbed at the silver Alpos and bound him in a crushing hug.

'Stop fighting me,' said Whitestaff. 'I know what you are. I know where you came from. I can tell you everything.'

'I don't care who I am and I don't care where I came from. All I care about is seeing you die!' With that, Shadowclaw bit into Whitestaff's neck. The Kai'dahl howled in pain and kicked the dragon away from him.

Now that he was loose, Shadowclaw fired more spells at Whitestaff. Merlin's medallion absorbed all of the magic, and Whitestaff was left unharmed. Shadowclaw seethed in frustration. 'I might not be able to kill you, but I can kill *them*.' He faced the direction of Mollie and Pip and summoned another bolt of dirty blue magic. He was about to unleash it on the pair when Whitestaff belched forth a stream of fire. Shadowclaw felt the heat of it coming. He let his blue spell disappear and created a shield of his own. Whitestaff's breath spread around the Alpos's magical shield, leaving him untouched. Whitestaff saw his chance and lunged at the dragon again. He swatted Shadowclaw around the face and made him spin widdershins in the air. Whitestaff then grabbed the Alpos from behind in another bear-hug. He pinned the Scourge's wings to his side and sent them both hurtling downwards.

Shadowclaw kicked in terror as he headed towards the sand. He fired off every spell he could manage to try and get the Kai'dahl off his back, but nothing worked. 'Not the ground!' he screeched. 'Not the ground!'

However, it was too late. Whitestaff couldn't have stopped the fall even if he wanted to. The dragons hit the sand with a vibrating thud and skidded along the dunes. Shadowclaw squealed in pain and kicked as though he was on fire. It was at that moment that Whitestaff realised that an Alpos was half Nazoor, and Wyvern were allergic to the ground.

There was nothing he could do for the Alpos. Shadowclaw was covered from tail to snout in sand—the essence of Tu'dool. It burned him as though he were in the heart of the sun. He glowed red as the sand tore through his scales and wings, eating away at the silver dragon. Mollie looked away, but she could not block the sound of the dragon's painful screams. In a moment all was silent, and only Shadowclaw's ashes remained. The dragon essence of the Silver Scourge drifted away on the wind across the Nalib desert. Shadowclaw was gone.

Whitestaff remained still for a while. He was about to speak when he felt the ground shaking beneath him. An arrow whizzed through the air and buried itself in the sand right in front of his snout. He looked up and saw a hundred men on horseback thundering towards him. It was the Sultan's men. They were armed with every weapon imaginable, and unfortunately for Whitestaff, they had come to kill a dragon.

51

FRIENDLY FIRE

Pip bolted over to the Sultan's men and ordered them to cease their attack.

'It's not Shadowclaw!' he shouted while waving his arms. 'Stand down!'

Fortunately the army was being led by Jumba, Balad and the Sultan himself. At the Sultan's signal, the army stopped their charge, and the battle horses, who had caught the dragon's scent and were quivering with fear, slowed down to an uneasy walk.

Yunas leapt off his horse and drew his son into his arms, half picking him up as he did so.

'My Son!' he said, his face beaming with delight. 'How good it is to see you.' He caught sight of Whitestaff's golden scales shining in the desert sun. 'But tell me quick, if he is not Shadowclaw, then what is he?'

'Is that Mollie's dragon?' Balad asked. 'The one from the egg?'

Pip nodded and explained to his father that Whitestaff was a friend who helped kill Shadowclaw. Yunas passed the information along to his guards, who in turn, spread the word among the ranks. The soldiers, who were seconds ago running at full pace and calling out battle cries, dropped their weapons and hugged each other when they heard that Shadowclaw was dead. Some kissed the sand, others danced with joy. There would be no dragon fighting this day. There would be no death or destruction. Nalib was safe and the tragedy of Aldallah would not be repeated.

Pip led his father, Balad and Jumba over to his new friends while the army headed back to the palace to celebrate.

'Now let me do the introductions,' Pip said. 'Father, this is Mollie. She is a sorceress from Robert Dugasi's land. She agreed to help us and so far she has done a brilliant job. We owe everything to her.' Mollie blushed at Pip's words. 'Mollie, this is my father, Yunas, the Sultan of the Sands.' Yunas stepped forward and kissed the young woman's hand. Mollie could see instantly where Pip got his looks.

'Now Mollie, I think you'd better introduce us to your friend here.'

Mollie smiled and asked Whitestaff to come and join them.

'This is Whitestaff,' she told them as the dragon made his way over. 'He is my first and most special friend.'

'Pleased to meet you,' Whitestaff said. He gave them a bow. 'Thank you for telling your men not to shoot me.'

Mollie laughed at Whitestaff's words, but the rest just stared blankly at the massive dragon in front of them.

It took Mollie a second to realise what had happened. 'Oh,' she said. 'I forgot. I'm the only one that can hear him. Sorry everyone. Whitestaff says he's happy to meet you and not your swords.'

'You can *talk* to him?' asked Yunas.

'I can,' said Mollie. 'I can talk to most animals as a matter of fact.'

The Sultan's jaw dropped.

'That's not all she can do, Father. Come, let's go to the palace. I'll explain everything along the way.'

Yunas agreed. 'Jumba, can you race back to the palace and tell the servants to arrange a feast. Tell them to make plenty of food. Enough to feed an army.' He craned his neck to look at Whitestaff's face. 'And a dragon.'

That night, the feast was held in the open air at the back of the palace; there was no way Whitestaff could fit in the dining hall. It was a huge celebration for the people of Nalib. The long palace tables were full, and those that didn't have a seat were happy to stand or sit on the ground. Music played and people danced whenever the mood took them. Fires were set to give light, and every now and then Whitestaff would shoot a fireball into the sky from his mouth, much to the delight of the Sultan's subjects. Mollie sat with Yunas and his wife Zilofa on her right. Pukami stood like a post next to the royal couple. To her left sat Pip and his guards, Jumba and Balad.

There was no table big enough for Whitestaff, so he sat behind Mollie who enjoyed having him close. Although Mollie was an honoured guest, the people of Nalib were most facinated by the dragon. His golden scales shone in the flickering firelight, and his sheer size had everyone gawking. He towered above the Sultan's table, and through Mollie, explained to Yunas and Pip what Shadowclaw really was.

'So there are more dragons, you say?' Yunas asked Mollie. 'A planet full of them?'

'That's a bit of a touchy topic at the moment, Your Majesty, but there are more dragons, yes.'

'And what would we do if another Shadowclaw were to emerge?'

Whitestaff heard the question and answered in Mollie's mind.

'Tell him that there will be no more Alpos here. The portal that once sent them across the universe is gone, along with Sorteya. I will have to find another way of dealing with Alpos eggs when I get home.'

Mollie relayed the dragon's message to the others.

Pip looked up at the dragon and then turned to Mollie. 'Why is it that I cannot hear Whitestaff, yet I could hear Shadowclaw? They're both dragons.'

Mollie shrugged. 'There is a lot about Shadowclaw that we may never understand. His magic was different to any that I've seen! He was so powerful too. Maybe that's why? And you do have a bit of sorcerer blood in you somewhere. You must have, otherwise you wouldn't be able to hear any animal or control any element. So that might explain it?'

'I guess so,' Pip replied. 'But what about—'

The young prince was cut short as a shimmering light appeared in front of the royal table.

'What is that?' he asked, jumping back from the table. 'Mollie, did you make that?'

The sorceress shook her head.

The musicians, who were playing nearby, saw it too. They yelped and let their instruments fall with a clatter. The assembled guests turned to see what the fuss was, and they too gasped in shock at the misty rainbow. It hovered ominously in front of the Sultan. Soon everyone was watching it, asking each other in whispers what is was and where it came from. Yunas eased himself up and drew his sword. The guards followed suit and moved Zilofa and Mollie out of the way. Whitestaff's eyes narrowed on the strange light, and he drew a deep breath, ready to breathe fire.

Suddenly three strange figures emerged from the light. They walked right out of the shimmering hole and looked around at the celebration.

Mollie's eyes went wide with shock.

'Esmea? Terry? Is that... What are you doing here?'

Merlin smiled and gave a chuckle.

'Why my dear, we're here for your wedding of course! Wouldn't miss it for anything, you know.'

'What? What wedding? Mum, what is he talking about?'

Merlin gave an uncertain smile and stroked his beard. 'Your wedding? The one with the...' he looked around at the stunned guests and the guards that had their swords drawn. 'Oh my. Sorry everyone. It appears that hasn't happened yet.'

52

MERLIN'S SIDE

The fires continued to burn bright at the back of the palace in Nalib.

However, many of the Sultan's people decided that after the death of Shadowclaw and having a fire-breathing dragon and sorceress at the royal table, seeing three mysterious people appearing out of thin air was too much excitement for one day, and so made their way back to their homes for a good lie down. The tension in the air between Mollie and Merlin also hurried their step. In the end, Yunas too retired with his wife, son and guards and left Mollie alone with her dragon and her family. The young Adkins was torn between hugging the great bearded man with all her might or blasting him out of the desert with a Magic Missile. Finally, when they had enough privacy, Mollie rounded on her father.

'What in the world are you doing here? How dare you show up now in the middle of the Sultan's yard! Where in Latos have you been for the last seventeen years?' Mollie tried to keep her voice down, but to no avail. 'And Mother, why are you smiling? Shouldn't you be hitting him or something? Terry? Why are you here too? What's going on?'

Merlin cleared his voice and gave his daughter a trembling smile, but it was Esmae who spoke.

'Mollie, my dear. Please don't shout. Everything is fine, I promise. Your father and I have had a good chat and I can explain everything to you.' She held her hand out for Mollie to take. 'Sit down with me.'

Mollie took her mother's hand in hers, and then drew herself into Esmae's arms. Hot tears spread against her cheeks. 'Why is he here?'

'Shhh,' Esmae whispered. 'It's fine. I'm fine. You'll see.'

Mollie nodded and then sat down with her mother at the empty royal table.

'Do you remember right before you left, before Pip came barging in, I was telling you I thought I saw your father through Terry's window?'

'Yes, how could I forget?'

'Good, now remember when I said he hadn't aged a day?'

Mollie looked to her father, who had sat down at the other end of the table and was staring into space.

'I remember.'

'Well, the truth is, he hadn't aged a day.'

Mollie screwed up her face.

'He looks old now.'

'Now, yes. But your father doesn't live his life in a straight line. Merlin? Perhaps you'd better explain.'

Merlin looked over at the mention of his name. He nodded and eased himself off of his seat and joined Esmae and his daughter.

'I don't know how to say it all.'

'Just tell it like you told me, Merlin.'

Merlin wiped his eyes and stared at his lap and spoke.

'First off, I want to say that I'm sorry for not being there for you, Mollie. I know it doesn't mean much to you now, but I make it up to you in the future. I promise. I've seen it. But the night your mother was talking about, the night I saw her and Terry through the window, that was the day after I said goodbye to Esmae.'

'The first day? It was seventeen years later, Merlin,' Mollie said. 'She needed you all that time!'

'I know that now,' Merlin said. 'But I said goodbye to Esmae and then I thought I'd check on her in the future, to see if she was doing well, you know? Well I searched through time and I found her. She had moved on. Found another man.' He looked over at Terry, who was warming himself by one of the fires further down the yard.

'She only found *him* because she didn't have *you*!'

'I know that now, Mollie. But then, I was young and foolish. I saw her future and I wasn't in it. Worse still, she looked happy. Happier than I ever made her. At first I wanted to go back in time and make sure that she never met Terry and that I was her husband for good. No more time travelling. But her face, Mollie. Her face was full of happiness and love. And I wanted her to have that, to have him, you know? If I went back in time, she'd never have found what she has now.'

Mollie considered this and shook her head.

'What about me though. What about your daughter. Don't you think I needed a father?'

Merlin looked up from his lap and into his daughter's eyes.

'Well at first I didn't know about you. But after I saw Esmae with Terry and went further forward and then I saw you for the first time. You had married a Prince of the Sands.' He looked around him and smiled. 'Right here, you know. This is where you have the wedding. I got my times wrong, but this is the place. I bring Terry and Esmae too. Not long from now, I think I just got muddled up in the excitement.'

Mollie started to speak then stopped herself. She rubbed her forehead in frustration.

'So I marry Pip? That's what stopped you from being a father to me?'

Merlin sighed and his gaze fell back down. 'It sounds stupid when you say it like that. But again, if I was there, if I was being your father, you'd never have met Pip. You'd never become Queen of the Sands and you'd never have a daughter of your own. I thought that all in all, your life would be a better one if I stayed out of it for the first few years.'

'Seventeen years!' Mollie said. She fell silent for a while. The fires crackled as they began to die down and Esmae patted her daughter's leg. 'Pip asks me to marry him?' she asked. 'And I have a daughter?'

Merlin looked back up, his face wet with tears. 'You do,' he said. 'A wonderful daughter. And I actually get to be the world's best grandfather, I'll have you know.' He timidly put an arm around Mollie's shoulder. 'I make it up to you, Mollie. I promise I make everything up to you. And you and me and Whitestaff up there all become the best of friends. All of us. Terry too. Our future gets very good from this point on. You'll see.'

At the mention of his name, the dragon cleared his throat.

'Does that mean I never get back to my own kind, Merlin? The egg is broken, so does that mean I'm stuck here?'

Merlin smiled at his daughter. 'What do you think, Mollie? Is the dragon stuck here?'

Mollie's face was blank for a moment, then suddenly it broke into a smile.

'No, Whitestaff,' she answered. 'From this day on, you can move from here to there whenever you like.'

Merlin grinned at his daughter's answer.

'How so? My egg...'

'Your egg contained a portal, Whitestaff. A portal like the one Merlin just made in front of me to bring Esmae and Terry here.'

'So?'

'So now that I've seen it done, I'm pretty sure I could make one myself, if I tried.'

Merlin laughed and clapped his hands. 'That's my daughter, you know. Show her once and she's better at it than you.'

Whitestaff shot a blast of fire into the air and roared with joy. 'I'm going home!' He leapt into the air and flew circles around the palace.

Merlin cheered him from below and clapped his hands. 'Home for you, Kai'dahl,' he said. 'Your new throne awaits! You have a glorious future, Whitestaff. And you deserve it.'

'So you know him too?' Mollie asked. 'In the future, I mean?'

'Know him? I'm the one who set all this up. This whole adventure! Without me, there would be no Whitestaff! His egg would have been smashed by the Wyvern long ago if I didn't send it here! And right now the Wyvern would reign supreme on Sorteya, the Chin would have starved to death centuries ago, and the Palal would be an extinct race. Nothing but bones.' He looked down at his daughter, his eyes sparkling like jewels. 'And you, my dear daughter, would never have met your first true friend. Oh yes, I knew you two would find each other, you the dragon, and the unicorn. I made sure of it, popping in and out of time here and there. I changed something here, added something there, all through your history. I single-handedly saved the dragons too. Well, with a bit of help. But this now, this ending, all of us together, the Palal surviving with their rightful King of gold, you on your way to be a queen, your mother, finally happy with mister Terry—this is my life's work: my masterpiece.'

'You did all of this?'

'Ninety-eight percent of it, yes.'

Mollie looked back up to Whitestaff, who was at last running out of energy. She realised that without Merlin, she would never have met Whitestaff. Her life would have been such an empty one without her dragon. 'That's amazing.' She drew closer to Merlin and hugged him around the waist. She lay her head against his beard. 'I think I can see what you've done. Thank you, Merlin. Thank you, Dad.'

Merlin smiled and kissed the top of her head. He placed his arms around his daughter and held her. Esmae saw them embrace, and she too wound her arms around them both. Terry, who left the fire saw the three hugging each other as a family. Merlin beckoned him over with his head. Terry left the fire and came closer. When he was close enough, Merlin opened his arms and pulled Mr Gritbole into the hug. Terry gave a soft laugh and hugged them all back.

At last, Whitestaff landed next to them, huffing and puffing from his flight.

'Not that I want to rush your reunion,' he said after he'd calmed down, 'but do you think you could make me that portal now?'

53

ALL IS WELL

For the first time in her life, Mollie Adkins gathered her magic into a portal. Merlin had to show her the trick of making it lead to wherever she wanted, and she knew that the other side would take Whitestaff back to his new planet. A part of her was disappointed she never got to see Sorteya, but Whitestaff assured her that Xenos would be a much better home-world for the Palal when he was through.

'Come with me,' he said to her. 'You can just have a peek to see what it's like.'

Mollie gave him a tired grin. 'Another day. Whitestaff. I'm exhausted beyond belief.' She looked over at the royal table where her parents and Terry sat. 'Besides, I'm afraid if I take my eyes off of Merlin for a second, he'll disappear and this will have all been a dream.'

Whitestaff snorted. 'I understand. He's slippery, right enough. You have to nail him down when you've got the chance. Another time?'

'Definitely. You don't have to worry, Whitestaff. Now that I can do this,' she waved her hand at the shimmering hole in front of her, 'I can see you whenever I like. Tomorrow I'm going to make a portal and fetch Wendy and Bramble so they can have a visit.'

Sounds perfect. I miss that crazy horse. We will all have to get together one day.'

'We will!'

Whitestaff put a paw on her shoulder. 'Friends for life, no matter how far apart.'

Mollie put her cheek to his paw. 'For life.'

'Quite a big adventure you've had, Mollie. I still remember the girl who spoke to me in my cage. It was the happiest day of my life. And then when you came back to break me free! Remember?'

'Of course I do! I was scared witless the whole time. But I knew that everything would work out, somehow.'

Whitestaff nodded in the direction of Merlin, Esmae and Terry. 'Something tells me everything will work out here too. Mollie Adkins, the Queen of the Sands.'

Mollie laughed. 'That must mean I marry Prince Pip.'

'Is that a good thing?'

Mollie's mind flashed with an image of Pip. She blushed when she pictured his smile. *And that hair!* She thought.

'Mollie?'

'Oh, ummm, yes. Yes, I think that's a very good thing.'

The dragon chuckled. 'Look at your cheeks. You've turned into a Re'dahl in front of my eyes! Just as long as I'm invited to the wedding.'

'I think everyone shows up for that, thanks to Merlin.' She sighed. 'Now I won't even be surprised when Pip proposes.'

'He does have a way of letting the future slip out, right enough. But Mollie, I get the feeling that our adventures are done, even if our friendship isn't. Xenos will be a planet of peace for me, and for you, there are no more dragons to save. I'm the last one here, now that Shadowclaw is gone.'

'You're wrong. I still have one more adventure!'

'What?'

'A daughter, Whitestaff. And if she's anything like me, I'm going to have my hands full.'

'Well now, that's an adventure I can't help you with.'

Mollie winked at him. 'I wouldn't be so sure. Go now, Kai'dahl. Off to your new world. The Palal need you. I'll be fine here.'

'You mean it?'

'I do. This is the best ending I could have hoped for. I have everything I ever wanted and more. Merlin was right after all.'

Whitestaff brought his tail around and encircled the young sorceress in a hug before letting go.

'Goodbye for now, Mollie Adkins.'

Goodbye for now, Whitestaff.'

The golden dragon turned and walked into the blackness of the portal. Mollie stared into it for a moment or two, then let the spell fall. She took a deep breath of sandy desert air and thought of everything she'd been through and everyone she'd met: Whitestaff, Wendy, Cudgel, Quilshire, Blackbeard, the kraken, Shadowclaw, and Pip. She wandered back to the royal table, her head full of the past and eager for the future. She took a seat next to her father and listened to him tell stories to Terry and Esmae until the sun came up. When the first gentle rays of dawn slipped over the horizon and shone on the domed roof of the Nalib palace, Mollie Adkins was tired, but happier than she'd ever been.

54

THE LAST DRAGON HOME

Armay was the first to greet him in the early morning light. She told him later that she could *feel* him close, sensed his presence in her heart, and so rose early to find him. The Kai'dahl stood on the beach at Cross's Landing. He was watching the tiny waves lick the shore, his mind spinning with everything that had occurred since the day he met Mollie. Sometimes it seemed impossible that all the things that had happened, had happened to *him*.

He turned around when he heard a dragon land on the sand behind him.

'Armay!' he said. 'I'm back!'

The blue dragon took his tail in hers. 'I can see that, my King. Why so soon? Is all well on Earth?'

Whitestaff gave her a brilliant smile. 'Everything is perfect. What about here? How is everyone taking to Xenos?'

'As well as can be expected.' She shrugged. 'Some of the old ones are complaining, but most of us are just happy to be alive.'

'I see,' he said. 'Wake everyone for me, Armay. I have a few things that the Palal need to hear.'

Armay pressed her cheek on Whitestaff's chest. 'Really? Can't we just have a few moments together? Alone? No one to rescue, no one to fight? It's so peaceful here.'

The Kai'dahl put a wing around her and drew her close. 'Sure, Armay. Maybe that's a better idea. Let them find us one by one. Until then, we can enjoy the view. Besides, I can just get Susset to use her magic and give a speech from here. She can carry my voice to their ears.'

'Sounds perfect.'

The two dragons turned back to face the sea and let the breeze caress their scales. They remained silent for a long time, happy to be in each other's company at last.

As the sun rose higher and the day wore on, some of the Palal spotted Whitestaff's golden glint from the air and shouted.

'He's back!' they called. 'The King has returned!'

Whitestaff waved back at them, happy to be welcomed, but also disappointed that his time with Armay was interrupted. Within minutes of being discovered on the beach, the Palal had crowded around the dragon, eager to talk to their King. He spoke to each of them and listened to their concerns and hopes for the new planet. Olfar and Graggy soon joined in the throng, and he gave them each a powerful hug. He even had one for Nap too, and the two joked about the first time Whitestaff held the Re'dahl in his strong grip.

'By Latos, you choked the breath right out of me!' said Nap.

'And you stabbed me with that tail of yours!'

'You deserved it. Well, I thought you did at the time. Anyway, I'm glad we got a fight in before you became the King.'

Whitestaff laughed. 'Well, maybe one day we can have a rematch. For old time's sake.'

Nap nodded so eagerly that Whitestaff was unsure if the Re'dahl knew that he was only joking.

Susset appeared at the dragon's side and he was overjoyed to see her face.

'I thought you'd be gone longer, Whitestaff. What about charging your essence?'

'That's over, Susset. In fact, it looks like everyone is here. Can you make my voice carry to their ears?'

The sorceress nodded and gathered her magic, and the dragon cleared his voice and raised himself up on his hind legs.

'My fellow Palal,' he began. 'I know that it was only a short while ago that I left you. Last time, I was gone for many months. As you might remember, Merlin created a portal in my egg that trapped my essence on two worlds. From the day I learned of this, I questioned it. Why? Why would the great magician have me live on Earth and Sorteya, but never one for long? I discovered the answer, right enough. Both planets needed me. I was needed to live among you so that one day I may lead you here. I was needed on Earth so that one day I'd fight a Palal Alpos and save Mollie's future husband.' He gave Susset a long stare. The sorceress turned red and pulled her hood over her head.

'But all that is done,' he continued. 'Earth needs me no more and I'm free to stay here and be your King. The portal that trapped my essence has been destroyed, and my paws will always tread the soil and sand of Xenos. There is much to be done here, my dragons, but this planet—this new world—will be ours forever. This, I promise you, will be the last dragon home!'

The Palal cheered his speech and shouted for joy. He waited a while and then waved them silent.

'But of course,' he said, 'what is a King without a Queen?' He turned his head to look at Armay and beamed. 'Armay, what do you say? Will you take me as your husband? Would you like to be the first Queen of Xenos?'

Armay blushed under the stares of the other dragons. She took his tail in hers and nodded. Her cheeks were wet with tears.

If the Palal cheered loudly before, this time their cheering nearly shattered Whitestaff's ears! The younger dragons celebrated by hugging each other and taking to the sky to fly loops. Nap, Luzahmin and Graggy came over to congratulate the couple. Olfar declared that he'd get the Bo'dahl and the Gra'dahl to organise a feast. Whitestaff wanted to say that it wasn't necessary, but once the idea was out it caught on quickly, and soon dragons were tearing off to find food or drink for the evening.

Whitestaff breathed a sigh of content and gave Armay's tail another squeeze.

'Everything is settled then, my future Queen,' he said to her.

The Bo'dahl was still choked with emotion and couldn't speak. Instead she squeezed his tail in return.

'However, there is still one little mystery. Susset!' he called. 'A moment?'

The sorceress was busy talking to one of the Bo'dahl dragons about the perfect place for the feast. She caught his eye, removed her hood and floated over to face the Kai'dahl.

'Whitestaff?' she said. 'Something the matter?'

'The matter? No. Just a question. You heard my speech before about Merlin. For years I questioned his actions, wondered why he'd trapped me like he did.'

'Yes. And now you know why. He saw the future of both planets and knew he had to somehow split you in half.'

'I know that now of course. But there's one mystery left.' The breeze blew gently between them, and Whitestaff peered hard at the sorceresses face. 'I always wondered how you got to be so beautiful, Susset. Since the first day we met, back in your dugout, I wondered. Was it magic? A trick with light? Were you really an old hag that was fooling everyone?' he laughed.

'But no, it wasn't any of those things. You never told me why you lived among the Palal or where you came from. You never told me about your part in any of this—why you'd travel with Merlin and live among the dragons. And yet, the answer was in front of me the whole time. The answer has been on your face, ever since we met. I think I've finally figured out who you really are.'

Susset smoothed her robe and took the dragon's massive head in her hands. She met his gaze with her own and smiled.

'I think you have too,' she said.

The End

EPILOGUE

Say what you will about Merlin, Mollie thought, *but the man keeps his word.*

It had been eighteen years since the magician had first walked into her life at the Sultan's Palace. He had Terry and Esmae with him, and he'd promised her that night that he would be the best father and grandfather ever. Mollie watched him as he told tales to the group sitting around the table. His teeth glittered through his beard and his arms waved this way and that as he spoke.

Merlin's audience consisted of Terry and Esmae and Pip, and one other young woman. Mollie's daughter, the one Merlin had promised would be born, was the most enchanted by the old man's stories. She watched him with eyes like two full moons. It was like this every time he visited. The girl was seventeen now, and had grown to idolise her grandfather. Of course, she loved Yunas too, but her connection with Merlin was special.

Mollie continued to watch them all from the tiny kitchen. She waited for water to boil so she could pour tea for everyone.

Coming back to Esmae's cottage always made Mollie feel like a giant. *How did we both ever fit in here?* She wondered. After almost twenty years of living in the palace in Nalib, she'd grown accustomed to space. *This whole cottage is the size of my dressing room.*

She'd told Esmae about this on one of their visits a while back.

'Why don't you and Terry come and live with us?' Mollie had asked. 'You could have one of the guest rooms all to yourself. One of those rooms could fit in the entire Leech family. You'd love it!'

Esmae laughed and shook her head. 'I must admit, I wouldn't mind living in a palace. But what about poor Terry? He loves it here, and a big bedroom would be wasted on him. He spends so much time in the forest hunting, he has all the space he needs. Besides, do you really think he'd be comfortable living as royalty?'

Mollie couldn't remember how she'd answered, but Esmae was right. Looking at him now, Mollie could see that Terry was an outdoors man, more at home in nature than in any house. The years had been kind to him. Being active kept him fit, and he didn't look his age at all, and nor did his wife.

Esmae remained almost untouched by time. The lines around her eyes were deeper and she didn't move as fast as she used to. Her hair, which she still kept up in a bun, had lost its dark lustre as was now grey. Rather than make her look old though, the colour gave her an air of sophistication.

She'd watched them both change over the years. Since she learned the secret of making portals, she could pop in whenever she liked. At first, there was a lot of travelling back and forth between Nalib and Danmurk. She visited almost every day to see Wendy too.

She also managed to see Whitestaff whenever she could. His new realm had come along nicely, and the Palal had made the perfect home for themselves. But then when she fell pregnant, she didn't have the energy to go wandering from place to place. After the baby was born, her duties as a queen and a mother took priority, and she made a portal only twice per year to check on the dragon. She cut family visits back to once a month, and she insisted that Pip and their little girl accompany her every time.

The water had boiled beside her on the little stove. She carefully poured the tea, placed the cups on a tray, and carried it to the others. She took her place around the wooden table, the sides of her legs pressed by those on either side of her. Merlin had almost finished his story. She'd heard this one before and knew how it ended. Her daughter had heard it before too, but looking at her it was obvious she could've heard her grandfather's tale a hundred times and not be bored. She gazed at her daughter's face. It was the perfect blend between her and Pip. Though she sometimes thought that the prince would make beautiful children with anyone, she knew that her best features were what made her daughter's looks so breathtaking.

Merlin's audience clapped their hands together, and the old magician gave a raucous laugh that echoed through the cottage. Mollie realised her daydreaming meant she'd missed the best part of the story, but she clapped and smiled too.

In the quiet moment that followed, Merlin met Mollie's eyes with his own.

'It's time for me to go now, you know. Important work coming up that can't be missed.'

His granddaughter groaned.

'Now don't be like that, sweetheart,' Merlin said. 'Today is a very special day. Isn't that right, Mollie?'

'It is?' Mollie asked.

Merlin gave her a very slow and deliberate wink. 'It is *that* day, Mollie.'

'What's he talking about mum? Dad?'

Mollie gestured for her daughter to be quiet. '*That* day, Merlin? Are you sure?'

'Sure as eggs, you know. I've seen it yesterday. Which is your tomorrow. It *is* that day today.'

'What happens on today, Granddad?'

'Can I tell her?'

Mollie shook her head. 'No, let me.' She took a long sip of her tea and pursed her lips wondering how to begin.

'Well, you remember I told you that when I was about your age, I went on a big magical adventure?'

'And you found dad!'

Mollie leant over and gave Pip a soft kiss on his cheek.

'Yes, I found your father. But I also found a dragon.'

'Whitestaff!'

'Of course, Whitestaff. I've kept you away from him for a very long time.'

'You say he's always busy.'

345

'And he is. He's the king of the dragons now and his time is precious. But that's another story. Today, you get to meet all the dragons.'

'I do? Today? I meet Whitestaff? You're going to take me to see him after all this time? I can't wait!'

Mollie swallowed hard. 'Not exactly. See the history of the dragon doesn't begin with Whitestaff. It begins when they leave Earth.'

Merlin interrupted. 'You see, sweetie, the dragon problem is a complex timeline. I can fix it, in fact I do fix it, but I need another pair of magical arms. There is so much to do, you know. First I have to go back in time and get them off the planet, then I have to make a deal with the Chin. Then I have to keep the Wyvern from tearing the Palal apart, then I have to make a magical egg for Frendrek's son, then I have to have someone there on Sorteya to keep all the dragons safe for when I get back—'

'And that someone is me!'

Mollie held her daughter's hands in her own. 'Yes, that someone is you. Merlin is going to need you, my dear. And one day, so will Whitestaff. I've arranged for you to go back in time with your grandfather and make sure everything works out for the best. It will be tough. There will be times when your strength is tested and your mind aches. But it will be worth it. You'll be alone for a while, but living with the dragons for a time is your destiny, and your big adventure.'

Merlin gave his granddaughter a wink. He stood and offered her his hand. 'So what do you think, Susset? Does this interest you at all? Are you up for your own big adventure?'

www.ingramcontent.com/pod-product-compliance
Lightning Source LLC
Chambersburg PA
CBHW072316020726
47501CB00002B/536